BETRAYED HEARTS

CHESTER'S RUN SERIES - BOOK ONE

CHERYL ROSARIO

Title: Betrayed Hearts - Chester's Run Series - Book One

Copyright © 2020 Cheryl Rosario

BETRAYED

LINDY

$\mathcal{W}$ith a smile on her face and adrenaline still pumping, Lindy sunk deep into her leather chair.

Another successful mentoring session. She appreciated when her clients followed her advice without bias or preconceived fear. Referring to her to-do-list, Lindy continued where she stopped before the meeting, analysing responses from a questionnaire of another new client. The slow slog began, but a short time later someone tapped on her door.

"Hey Zave, what's up?" she asked, abandoning the keyboard. "Not enough out there to keep you busy?"

His laugh echoed around the sizeable room.

"Plenty. Just bringing in the mail. This one's marked *'Private'*," he shook a large envelope in her direction, "I told Amelia I'd drop it off for you."

"Thanks for that," Lindy took the offering and watched as he retraced his steps. She glanced at the clock. Oh, hell. Is it that time already? There was so much to do this morning. Swinging her chair back to the desk, she picked up her pen.

Something about the envelope begged for her attention. But before she managed to attend to it, her computer chimed with an incoming email. A message from her husband's assistant Flo, informing her he had a meeting which wouldn't see him free until about nine o'clock this evening.

Lindy sighed. Just typical. Yet again Ralph would not be home for dinner. Not surprising, this was becoming an all too common occurrence. She wished because their three children were all independent, they'd make time for each other. If the truth be told, Ralph never made her his priority, and she was kidding herself if she believed he'd start now. Well, he did at the start of their marriage, but when she was pregnant with Cameron something in Ralph snapped.

His unexplained rejection of their second son was cruel, but for the sake of the family, Lindy remained true to her husband and tolerated his mood swings and new remoteness. An image of them together with Liam, their eldest, as a baby often pulled at her heartstrings. Ralph was such a loving husband and father, always home before dinner. He'd eat with one hand while holding their son with the other, loving his family life. And then date night once a week so her parents got to babysit. Those were some special nights for them early in their marriage.

After Liam turned two, everything changed. Ralph headed an architectural team to Singapore. With the huge success he'd obtained from the contract, he received a promotion. Things at work became hectic. He no longer rushed home for dinner with his family, always claiming work demands were increasing. A couple of months after settling into the new family home, he made an announcement. Ralph decided to go out on his own. Somehow, he found the money to invest in his vision. Lindy noticed the strain on him, believing business expectations were unyielding and arduous.

Shaking off the sour taste of the email, Lindy reached for the envelope and ripped it open. She pulled out a shiny green presentation folder, beautifully patterned with swirls. This wasn't unusual. She often received such documentation from potential clients with requests she become their business mentor. Opening the front cover, she picked up a letter addressed to her.

She read:

Dear Lindy,

You don't know me, but I believe I will prove to be an asset to your future. I have met with your husband.

The hairs on the back of Lindy's neck rose. She immediately scanned the bottom of the typed letter for an owner, but it was unsigned. Tendrils of chills invaded her torso, but she forced herself to read on.

I have enclosed some information which I believe will prove invaluable.

Wishing you all the best for the future.

Lindy decided to throw the presentation folder, letter, and all in the bin, but a photo partially slipped out which piqued her curiosity.

Without hesitation, Lindy turned the page. It only took a moment for the images to register. Her mouth fell open as she stared. Photos of her husband, in bed with other women, so many, as the collage before her proved. How could he do this to her? After twenty-six years? Not that she hadn't suspected things in the past. She looked down at the undeniable proof. This was beyond horrid. Just picking up the piece of paper appeared sordid.

A gut-wrenching sob wracked through her, followed by a shuddering full body tremble invading her entire being. A vile taste dislodged itself from the pit of her stomach, finally ending with her rushing for the bin.

Not sure how long she'd been hunched over when a gentle touch rested on her back. Amelia always proved a loyal member of staff and today was no exception. She held the bin giving Lindy the opportunity to gather herself. When she finally glanced up, she noticed her assistant's blushed cheeks, which told Lindy Amelia had the misfortune of viewing the X-rated images. The sound of others approaching sent a wave of heat and nausea spiralling. Breathing through the unsettling feelings, Lindy wished she'd had the presence of mind to thank Amelia for closing the folder over.

"What's wrong?" Zave asked rushing into the room.

Lindy turned pleading eyes to Amelia when she heard other voices outside her office.

"Ask someone to get a damp cloth then close the door. Let's give Lindy a moment to herself." Amelia told Zave.

After a few minutes Lindy settled down and rinsed out her mouth with some water. Amelia handed Zave the bin to remove the foul stench. An uneasy hush descended on the room while Lindy cleaned her face and gathered her composure, Amelia never left her boss's side.

When Zave returned, he leant across the desk and took Lindy's hand in his. The pleading in his eyes evoked an explanation.

"Twenty-six years of marriage," Lindy let out an agonising moan. "Over. How could I have been so foolish? How could he have been so...so deceitful?" She thrust her head back on another moan, "Oh God, what a fool!"

"What's going on? What happened?" Zave's voice penetrated her thoughts. "How did you find out?"

"That envelope marked *Private*, can you believe it, photos of him with other women. Not just one… WOMEN!" Lindy rested her head on the back of her chair again and closed her eyes, trying to make sense of the last few minutes. But the images again filled her mind, as if they were on a gigantic screen with flashing neon lights enticing her attention.

Zave frowned. "What do you need?"

Forcing back threatening tears, Lindy drew in a deep breath.

Glancing at the large framed family photo on the wall opposite, taken ten years earlier. Lindy could see the joy in the eyes of her and the children. But for the first time it occurred to her that Ralph expressed no delight at being there. In fact, thinking back to the day, she remembered they'd fought, in whispers, she'd not wanted to upset the children. Lindy remembered the severe comments Ralph made. She considered his harsh words were out of spite because he would miss a golf tournament, but in hindsight, she wasn't so sure. Pulling her eyes away from the canvas, Lindy forced herself to look at Zave.

"Other than end my marriage, I can't begin to imagine."

Amelia remained her usual anchor. "Can I get you a tea?"

Lindy fought her body's wish to remain in the chair. Instead she pushed herself up and stood before them. Forcing her shoulders back and posture to remain strong.

"No, thank you, I've got a marriage to end and a life to sort out." Her normally gentle, caring nature fell away, her muscles tightened. Protecting herself became a priority.

She grabbed her bag and the offending pages, walked to the photocopier calling over her shoulder, "Amelia can you get me another envelope please?"

After resealing the original damming material, she walked back to her ever-reliable assistant.

"Lock this in the safe for the time being. Thanks."

Both Zave and Amelia followed Lindy as she continued to the lift. Reaching the foyer, she turned to look at them, Zave shuffled from one foot to the other, while Amelia watched her closely.

"Zave, you hold down the fort till I return. Amelia will give you all the support you need. I just need to sort myself out."

Amelia held open her arms and Lindy sought the embrace. These two were part of her family and she didn't know what she'd do without them. Zave wrapped an arm around her as she walked to the lift.

"Where do you need to go? I'll drive you."

She turned to face him, reached up and patted his cheek gently. "Thank you, but I need to do this myself. I'm not looking forward to it. Petrified in fact." Lindy drew in a deep breath. "But I refuse to show him a weak woman," a rush of air escaped her lips, "Not with something as important as my sanity."

Lindy waited as the lift opened, she stepped in, turning back towards the man she saw as her third son, she added, "Wish me luck, I'll need it."

He reached out and pulled her into a hug. "Call me. I need to know you're okay." He leant back to look at her.

"Promise?"

Being so choked up, Lindy could only manage a nod. As the doors closed, she mouthed, "Thanks."

Staring at the stark, stainless steel doors and her reflection, Lindy realised she was all alone.

LINDY

Her first stop, Ralph's office. Years of marriage were over. A confrontation with the bastard became unavoidable. She poured years into their union, something Ralph took for granted. The heels of her boots tapped on the concrete as she walked towards his building. With shaking hands and churning stomach, she sucked in deeply. Her determination growing, overpowering the voice in her head pleading with her to flee. Glancing up, she searched the front windows expecting to see Ralph gazing out, a ritual he engaged in when ruling over his domain. Not today, his blinds were closed.

Straightening her spine, she headed inside. Change was eminent, a doormat she was not. This confrontation would cause excruciating pain. All these years she'd pandered to his self-fascination and perfectionism, ironing creases in his trousers or laughing at all his jokes. Well, no more. He'd abused her trust. Questioning his unfaithfulness before led to nothing without evidence. So, she'd let it pass. To her, family was everything. She backtracked to protect her children. Believing his tales. What a fool!

Not much appeared familiar. Some of Ralph's employees greeted her, others she didn't recognise. Lindy couldn't remember the last time she'd stepped foot in here.

"Morning Flo," Lindy remained calm, maintained a smile of sorts. "Is he in?" Her head tilting towards Ralph's office.

"Morning Lindy, yep," Flo gave her a warm smile and reached for the handset to inform him of his visitor.

"Please don't announce me, I wanted to surprise him," Lindy relaxed when Flo waved her on.

The narrow hallway continued endlessly. Or was that her anticipation? The echoing of her heartbeat rang in her ears. Approaching his office door, Lindy's body ached with a tension she'd never known. One hand reached out to knock while she gripped the envelope tighter in the other. After a quick tap, she entered.

Ralph sat on his chair with an exquisite, young blonde straddling him.

For a split second she contemplated fleeing, but heat flashed through her as images of the mail she'd received filled her head.

"You bastard!"

Ralph pushed the woman off his lap and stood to face his wife.

"What the hell are you doing here?"

"That's it? Nothing else to say?" Lindy's heart pounded. She needed to rub the dull pain in her chest. She drew in slow, shallow breaths, determined not to clench her fists.

The door clicked behind her. The red-faced blonde must have escaped the room. For the next few minutes Ralph copped her wrath. "All these years and I have to discover your betrayal by mail, then lucky for me here you are putting on a free show! How many women have there been? Or have you lost count?" Lindy drew in an audible breath after her unsuppressed tirade exploded from deep within.

"Mail. What mail?" Ralph rubbed his jaw, eyeing his wife closely.

Lindy held out the envelope, but changed her mind as Ralph grabbed for it.

"On second thoughts—allow me." Lindy never took her eyes from Ralph as she opened the envelope and fished out all the offending evidence. Dropping the paperwork on his desk Lindy watched as he snatched up the photos for a closer look.

The colour drained from his ruddy complexion. He cursed aloud, "Where'd you get these?" he shook the paper at her as his voice boomed.

"They arrived by mail at my office this morning." Her voice trembled then croaked, but he didn't seem to notice, too lost in the damning evidence.

"Who from?" he yelled.

Lindy noticed his loss of control.

Hell, why hadn't she told her family of her intentions. Wait, Flo saw her enter, Ralph wouldn't be stupid. A rush of breath escaped.

"That's a copy of the letter and photos I received. So how about you tell me?"

Ralph cursed again and sank down into his chair.

"Who was it? Who sent the photos? Maybe the blonde, or was it someone else?" He grunted something but Lindy continued, "Remember our prenuptial agreement, on your insistence. How fortunate my father put in a clause about remaining faithful. We are through! Get your things out of my house. We're finished."

"Don't you dare go acting high and mighty," Ralph hissed, "I have juicy gossip father dearest would love to hear concerning his precious daughter."

"What the hell are you talking about? I don't care about your accusations! Unlike yours, my conscience is clear!" She couldn't hold back a snarl, "That girl," Lindy spat out as she pointed towards the door, "How old is she? Sophie's age, or maybe younger?"

Lindy forced herself to keep moving. She wouldn't crumble, at least not in front of him. Taking a step towards the door, Ralph blocked her exit in two large strides. His hand clasped her left arm trying to pull her back. Even with the power of his unwanted attention, Lindy opened the door with her free hand. She looked out, grateful to see a crowd of onlookers gathering outside his office.

Ralph glanced from the onlookers to Lindy. His hand clenched tighter, all but cutting off the circulation.

"You're hurting me," she hissed.

He dropped his hand before stepping back, his cheeks turned an ominous shade of red. Looking around, Lindy requested a male employee escort her out. With her wits on high alert, she stopped at Flo's desk on the way.

"Could you check if Liam's here please?" Lindy's voice wobbled.

Flo dialled his extension. Lindy could hear the conversation, "Oh hi Mike, is Liam in?"

"Nope not here," the phone line went dead.

"Sorry." Flo glared at the phone and then back to Lindy. "Will you be okay? Could I get someone to drive you home?" Flo's eyes tracked from Lindy to her seething boss up the hall.

"No, thanks. I'm fine," Lindy struggled to keep her tone even.

Fleeing was her aim. Following Flo's glare, Lindy turned back to Ralph. He watched her every move, his hands balled into fists while his shoulders rose and fell with each breath.

Eager to leave, Lindy made her way to the car park with her escort in tow.

ABANDONED

JACK

Things at home weren't projecting a perfect family life. Jack's wife, Elsa, refused to take the kids to school. Jack couldn't remember the last time they attended. Her temper when he came in from the farm became intolerable. Cooking meals and her housekeeping skills were non-existent. Nate, their twelve-year-old son, took it upon himself to occupy and protect his siblings when his mother insisted she 'rest', which was often. Jack's vivid memories of Nate in the kitchen trying to scrounge up a decent meal for the family saddened him.

Though Jack and Elsa no longer shared a bed, they still shared the honour of parenting their five young children. Jack wished and prayed Elsa would make the decision to leave the children with him and return to her family in Ballarat. But the only inducement keeping them tethered as a couple, boiled down to the fact she wanted his money to support her. Last night, lying in bed in the bungalow, just beyond the main house, Jack couldn't understand why life for his family had got this bad.

Enough was enough. Jack needed to step up and confront Elsa about her addiction. His kids were miserable. Hell, so was he. Growing up, he'd been easy-going and happy.

With time against him, Jack found it difficult to focus on preparing the soil for this season's crop while doing his best to keep the kids happy and safe. He wished he could ask his mum or sister for help, but Elsa put her foot down. No longer allowing his family anywhere near the kids or the farm. His parents were only trying to help, but everything backfired with a disastrous outcome for him, the children, and his family.

After that Elsa threatened to leave and take the kids to her mother's house. Taking them away where he wouldn't easily see them. Ballarat was nearly four hour's drive from Chester's Run. To avoid such a scenario Jack convinced his family to pull back, refrain from interfering in case she followed through on her threat. When she initially warned him of her leaving, Jack didn't believe she'd want that responsibility. But he couldn't be one hundred percent certain she wouldn't shoot through with his children, which wasn't a risk he would take.

He reflected on nights Elsa left to have an evening in town and how his parents would arrive to be with the children until Jack got back. Those nights gave him the opportunity to work late knowing his children were safe. He remembered, with pain, the night Elsa put a stop to those arrangements. Banishing his parents from their own property upset him more than anything, because they weren't able to see their grandchildren anymore.

Dealing with a wife on drugs while working the farm got tough. When the last of the hired help quit, Jack didn't bother getting anyone else, they wouldn't last long, anyway. Elsa seemed to push away everyone around him, severing any chance for support.

A call to his father the other night ended in an argument. It wasn't hard to see his parent's point of view. He understood how upset they were. But as things currently stood, Elsa hadn't really done anything at this stage to give him full custody if he ended their marriage. Oh, there were the drugs, the threats and her not looking after the children, but none of this would prove her inadequacies and mental instabilities enough to give him permanent custody.

One thing was clear, at the moment the children were safe. Elsa never harmed them. In fact, with the elder four staying home from school, it meant little Bradley enjoyed the support of his older siblings, which he otherwise would have lacked. Elsa wasn't stupid to harm the children. Besides, in her own way he could see she adored them. She wasn't clever at putting their needs before hers. He'd pick up the slack amid the turmoil, somehow helping her get better at it. Though he'd been working on it with her for years. Would she ever improve?

JACK

Sitting on the tractor this chilly spring morning, Jack rubbed both hands down his face.

"Shit," he whispered to himself. This entire thing was so bloody complicated. His children were his priority.

Last night before heading to the bungalow, Jack walked into the lounge. Elsa sat watching some reality show. Finding the courage to face a tough situation, he began, "What's wrong? We can't keep living like this. The children aren't at school and there's no food in the house."

But as always, she just yelled, "When are you going to give me money for ME? I get nothing."

"Because what you get you waste on your addiction. That money I give you is for food for our children." Jack didn't want things to spiral out of control, like other tough conversations. He was aware sometimes he had to make a stand. "Not for those drugs you depend on. I've told you I'll support you to kick this addiction."

"Maybe I don't want to kick it."

That was the first time she'd admitted to her condition as an addiction.

Jack held his breath when she dropped her eyes from his. Was she reassessing the drugs she consumed and how her body demanded its daily fix? But something passed over her. A look Jack had seen many times before.

"I don't need your bloody money to get my fix."

"Oh, don't worry," Jack spat back, losing any semblance of control. His hands balled into fists as he raised his chin. There was no stepping back, he snarled, "Me and the rest of the bloody town know exactly how you get your fix. It'll only be a matter of time before our children find out what it is you do to get the drugs your body craves so desperately."

Replaying last night's argument unsettled him, he worried for his children's safety. The memory of Elsa throwing the old cast iron door stop at him sent yet another shiver down his spine. Fortunately, Jack jumped out of the way in time, but the sound of the old telly smashing into splinted fragments roused their already unsettled children. Again. It was Jack who consoled the children while Elsa stormed out of the house, taking off in his Ute.

He never considered himself a fool, but hell, she had the better of him at the moment.

The unyielding pain and spiralling dread had him abandoning another day's work. The kids' safety was his priority. He released a groan. Heading out of the paddocks in desperate need of a crop, he began the trek back to the sheds. The vision of his eldest son interrupted the ten-minute drive, which barely begun. Through his windscreen, he saw Nate running down the road towards him.

As Jack got closer to Nate, he could see tears running freely. Cutting the engine, he jumped off the tractor. Nate's face was snotty and wet. Whatever happened couldn't be good. An icy shard penetrated his heart. Jack pulled out his hanky and cleaned Nate up.

The boy's utterances were incoherent.

"Slow down buddy, what's happened?"

"It's Mum, she's gone mad and hit Bradley." Nate drew in a ragged breath or two. "Bradley's screaming and his arm's all bent." The boy's chin wobbled. He tugged his arm across his elongated face attempting to remove the combination of moisture and snot. "She packed some stuff and left. She took your ute."

"Caleb and the girls? And you? Is anyone else hurt?"

"They're crying, but fine. But Bradley's so bad!"

Pulling his son into a hug, Jack tried piecing it together. He cursed under his breath. Without another word he picked up his crying son, lifted him into the cabin and climbed up behind him.

Pressing down on the accelerator, he made the one call he should have made long before this.

"Tessa, I need your help." After explaining the situation, he hung up and he and Nate drove home in near-silence, except for the ragged breaths Nate was so desperate for and Jack's attempts at consoling words. His head swam with his son's tale. Not only had Elsa packed up and shot through, she'd assaulted Bradley.

JACK

The moment Jack turned off the tractor, Bradley's high-pitched screams made him run for the door, leaving Nate to follow. In the lounge he found his eldest daughter, Evie, leaning over her baby brother, caressing his brow while tears flowed down her face.

Jack couldn't miss Evie's love for her sibling. Neither did he miss the sight of Caleb and Joanna huddled beside her. Jack gasped for breath at the sight of Bradley's arm. He covered the distance between himself and his youngest son in a split second, wanting desperately to cradle his little tyke in his arms and make all his pain go away. Tears threatened to fall from his own eyes, but he needed to be strong. Pulling himself together, he unlocked his phone and dialled triple zero.

"Ambulance please," Jack told the operator. He answered questions as an inconsolable Bradley lay screaming hysterically on the floor of the lounge room. The shapes in the tattered carpet exposed the small body as if pinpointing the scene of a crime. Actually, that's exactly what Jack looked at. The pressure of teeth grinding teeth sent a stabbing pain through Jack's jaw. He almost choked on a rush of air.

Kneeling beside Bradley he tried to comfort him, but it amounted to nothing. Bradley's screams pierced his heart. Seeing his little boy in such pain and knowing he could do nothing made him judge himself.

In his own eyes he came up short. A weak man too useless to have predicted something like this could have happened. How was he going to fix this?

Jack looked around at the other children and cursed his wife for the pain they were all suffering. He wanted to keep them occupied, so he gave them insignificant jobs to do, allowing them a reason to escape the room for a while. He stroked Bradley's forehead and tried to keep him still while he coaxed the older children into action.

"Caleb, buddy, get me a glass of water, please. Evie, can you get some tissues from the bathroom? That's my girl. Joanna find Bradley's teddy, that might make him feel better," Jack's eyes never left Bradley as the children ran off with purpose.

"What can I do?" Jack could see Nate struggled with the events just as much as he did.

"Go wash your face and get yourself a drink. After that wait outside for Aunty Tessa. That's my boy." Then Jack called him back, "Hang on," Jack finally drew his eyes from Bradley so he could look directly at Nate. "I'm so proud of what you did. Thank you, buddy."

Nate nodded at his father's words but seemed to dismiss them almost immediately. Jack groaned, he could tell Nate blamed himself for Elsa's mess. He was desperate to curse and roar, but that would not help the current situation.

From the front veranda Nate yelled, "Ambulance is coming down the drive!"

Jack glanced at his watch for the third time in what seemed an eternity, but it had only been five minutes. Having help was music to Jack's ears, but it didn't ease his baby's pain. Nothing would ever erase the pinched face and ear-piercing screams from his mind.

The officers rushed in and got to work on Bradley, asking questions and soothing the little fellow as they worked. Jack stood, his feet glued to the floor. Bradley's high-pitched wails only letting Jack know how he served absolutely no purpose. He was a father in words but did he have the actions to make things right for his son?

Of course not. The veins in his neck pulsed. Jack rubbed his face, forcing himself to stop the persistent grinding of teeth. Joanna and

Caleb returned and huddled closer to Jack, keeping their eyes on Bradley.

Nate ran in a few minutes later with Tessa, her hair wet and T-shirt on backwards. Not that Jack would mention it.

"Thanks for coming," Jack said as she squeezed his shoulder. His eyes focused again on his son.

Another holler came from outside. "It's Uncle Harry, Dad!" Evie yelled.

Harry's presence filled the room. Jack watched as his brother-in-law surveyed the scene. Right at this moment, he was the local sergeant. Not Bradley's uncle. Jack was being judged for the current situation and if the children were anywhere else but here, Jack would make his feelings known on that score. But Harry focused on the job at hand. Still the weight of the probing sat painfully on Jack's shoulders.

Not wasting any time, Harry questioned Jack and after listening to his tale, stepped away and made a call, putting out a trace on Jack's Ute. Elsa inflicted this pain on little Bradley. Harry would find her. Jack's eyes met Tessa's. Her head shook from side to side as she bit her bottom lip.

Fortunately for Jack, Tessa occupied the other children while he swallowed threatening tears. His children should never have witnessed such events in their own home. Nate stood beside his father, watching on with eyes wide and hands clenched.

"You go with Bradley, I'll take these guys home. But first, I'll sort out his nappy bag."

Tessa was always the mother hen in situations like this. Jack gave her a weak smile and drew in a slow breath. His chest expanded as it registered he could rely on Tessa to keep his children safe. With everything awkward between Elsa and Tessa, he would have understood if his sister refused to come, but that wasn't her way.

Jack swallowed down the lump in his throat again.

"Tessa's right mate, here are your parents," Harry pointed out the lounge room window. "You go with Bradley and they can follow, Tessa's got this lot."

As Jack walked outside following the trolley holding his son, Harry called to him, "Mate, we'll talk more later about all this," his hand gesturing to Bradley and the other children. "You just look after your little man."

Other than a vague nod of acknowledgement to his parents, he stayed fully focused on Bradley and the ambulance officers. The pain wrenching his heart battled with his attempt of control yet again. Nothing distracted his focus.

The sound of Tessa's voice as she tried to comfort her nieces and nephews gave Jack something to focus on. He couldn't help but hear the explanation to their parents. Listening to Harry describe the situation was surreal. But what he heard next made him want to cry.

"W…when's m…m…mummy coming back?" Joanna's words came out in a stutter. Jack spun around and saw Nate's glare. Darla and Tony both gasped and looked to Jack, then back to Joanna. Jack's heart stopped. How do you explain this to a seven-year-old girl? No matter what, Elsa would always be their mother. Their biological mother. Mothering in her unique way. Navigating his way through this resembled a nightmare.

Jack looked on as his father took in Bradley's pain from the back of the ambulance and then focused on his distressed children.

"One of us needs to help Tessa," Tony said aloud.

Darla followed her husband's anxious glare. "I'll stay with Tessa, and help with the children, you go with Jack. Look after them both." Darla placed her hand on her husband's arm as his eyebrows drew closer. "Don't worry, Bradley is in the best hands."

Bending down, he kissed his wife, "Okay love, we'll do that."

The wails from Bradley which had echoed through the house had cut deep. Jack knelt by his son, who was lying on the stretcher, and touched his wet cheek. The moisture on Bradley's face caused Jack's own tears to fall. Who would be capable of doing this to their own flesh and blood, and a toddler no less?

As the ambulance officer closed the first door, Tessa ran out with Bradley's nappy bag. "Sorry, there weren't any nappies left. Not much in the way of clean clothes either. I'll sort it out and get something to you." Her voice faltered as she cast a glance at her nephew, "Take care of him."

Jack's moist eyes clashed with her red ones. Nothing could hide the emotion she'd held back. He could only nod. The ache deep in his chest, which began the moment he made out Nate's lanky figure running towards him, worsened tenfold.

MOVING ON

LINDY

*P*ulling into her driveway, Lindy saw the opened front door with the locksmith already at work. Yet again her father's skills in overseeing an operation proved advantageous.

Lindy swallowed a couple of times, letting a few tears fall as she freed herself from the car. Walking up the front path, her mind automatically revisited so many treasured memories. Most of them were wonderful, like the time Liam learnt to balance himself on his skateboard or when Cameron kicked the football to his brother, but ended up smashing a glass panel in the front door. And not to be left out, Sophie playing hopscotch in the driveway with her friends. Her mind worked overtime revisiting those memories.

Standing on the top step, one memory came flooding back; her, Liam and Ralph here in this very spot, admiring their home. Those were wonderful memories. Shaking herself free of these distractions, she could do without them right now.

As always, especially in a crisis, Lindy was organised enough to keep her momentum going. She drew in another deep breath and walked into the kitchen. The sight of her mother, dressed immaculately in pressed navy pants and a bright floral top, with her shoulders back and arms open wide, told Lindy what she lacked her mother would provide. Tears began again before she settled into a chair. The sound of her mother's gentle, loving words stripped away the last of her bravado, and hot tears escaped down her cheeks.

"Oh, darling." Charlotte caressed Lindy's shoulder length hair, the same shade of brown as her mother's, minus the scattering of greys.

The touch of her father's hand on her shoulder sent her into over-drive. Lindy lent into her dad's embrace and although it comforted her, the pain of this morning's reality took over.

"Hey sweetheart, we'll get you through this. The kids, your broth-ers, Mum, and I. We're all here for you," Duncan caressed up and down her spine. Lindy could only respond with heart wrenching sobs.

A short time later her brothers arrived. She expected a heap of questions and maybe even *how did you not see this*. But no, not her brothers.

"Come here, Shadow," Mal pulled her in close, giving her his shoulder to rest on. He was six-foot tall, about six inches taller than his baby sister. "He never deserved you or what you did for him and his family."

Lindy released a weak chuckle through her tears, at hearing the nickname her two older brothers had given her many years ago.

"Thank you. You both really are the best brothers a Shadow could have." With that one word, Mal had eased the tension just a little.

"Hey," Danny took his turn hugging her. "How you holding up?" When she didn't reply he continued, "He's not worth it, you deserved so much better in a husband than that bastard."

"Danny. Language!" Duncan admonished.

"Sorry Dad," Danny replied out of habit, but his tone didn't alter. He embraced his sister and she sagged against him on wobbly legs. "Tell me what brain stuff you need me to do, I'll leave the brawn to Mal." That brought a strained smile to her face.

Her oldest brother, Malcolm, was a member of the police force and you only messed with him if you were foolish. When Lindy calmed down, with some coaxing from her father, they made a list of what needed attention.

"I should probably get you to change the codes on the alarm system," Lindy told him, finally focusing. His electronic genius made him the go-to guy for everything technology. Well, that was until Cameron followed in his uncle's footsteps.

Swallowing the last mouthful of his tea, Danny stood up, "Leave it to me. How about I Ralph-proof your computer and accounts too?"

Lindy struggled to keep up with the conversation.

"Thanks son, great idea," Duncan answered on her behalf. Then he turned back to Lindy, "Well love, let's ring Anthony," referring to the family lawyer. "We shouldn't put it off."

Lindy nodded. She sat at the dining table, her head down and shoulders hunched as her father made the call. A sigh reverberated around the room. Lindy willed the emotion back—causing her parents such pain was the last thing she'd wanted to do.

Mal sat at the breakfast bar watching his father and Lindy. Turning to his mother he spoke, "If I had my way, I'd like to make that sod regret his actions."

"You and I both know that won't help the situation," Charlotte admonished. "How about we pack up his things? Looks like she'll be busy with Dad for a while," Charlotte nodded at the dining table scattered with used tissues, a notepad and a couple of pens.

Lindy gave her mother and brother a weak smile as Charlotte grabbed some large garbage bags from the kitchen and led the way down the hall.

Nearly half an hour later, Lindy stood outside her bedroom. A room she'd shared with Ralph for twenty-four years. She married at nineteen, their union lasted twenty-six years and at forty-five she found herself single again.

"I'll forever applaud your father's interference with her prenup. Lindy at least has a roof over her head."

"Yeah, but her heart's in tatters," Mal pointed out. "I never understood why he changed so drastically after Lindy found out she was expecting Cameron. Somehow that bit of news flicked a switch and he couldn't cope. He should have just left. We would have supported her," Mal growled as he shoved Ralph's expensive suits, shirts and shoes all into the same plastic rubbish bag.

That sight made Lindy grin. How Ralph would hate to have his clothes treated in this manner.

"But then we'd never have Sophie," Charlotte reminded him, bringing Lindy's attention back to her messed up life.

Talk of Sophie and her brothers brought tears to Lindy's eyes again. Her girl, her children, at least Ralph did one thing right.

Mal nodded, "I know. You're right. But seeing her go through this," he shook his head, "Just doesn't sit well."

"Don't do anything. Lindy needs to work this out for herself." Charlotte's firm voice demanded, "Promise me. The best we can do is to be here for her and the children."

"Mum's right, I need to sort this out myself."

At hearing her voice, they both glanced up with coloured cheeks and their eyes failed to fully connect with hers. Mal just nodded and Lindy gave him a small smile, letting this go wouldn't sit well with him at all. But he'd do it for her.

LINDY

With the home phone in her hand, Lindy plonked herself down at the end of the large wooden table again, this time to call her children. Well, they weren't children any longer. Liam turned twenty-five this year, Cameron, a most introverted man at twenty-three and Sophie celebrated her twenty-first birthday only three weeks ago.

A piece of her heart broke as each call went unanswered.

With no other plan in place, Lindy tried again, this time leaving messages expressing a desire to talk, but nothing too drastic as to scare them.

"I don't get it," she talked to the phone. Shaking off more threatening tears, Lindy shifted tact. "If that's the way they feel, I'll wait till they get in touch with me."

Charlotte placed a hand on Lindy's shoulder and gave a tender squeeze, "Here you go," she set a second cup of tea in front of her daughter.

"Thanks," Lindy tried to smile, but the look was a cross between a grimace and a snarl. Oh well, she tried. Without thinking, Lindy reached out to pick up the cup of solace with her left hand. Piercing pain shot up her arm and she winced.

"What's the matter?" Charlotte looked on as Mal took Lindy's arm and carefully rolled up her sleeve. A bright red welt formed where Ralph grabbed her earlier.

"Who did this to you?" Mal snapped.

Lindy sighed, knowing Mal wouldn't let it go. "Ralph, as I tried to leave his office this morning. Please Mal, just leave it."

"No. You need to press charges!" Mal's voice rose, his breathing became forced.

"You're a cop. That will be enough security. He won't try anything else."

Lindy couldn't take it. Tears streaked down her face again. "Sorry, but I can't do this anymore." It was the closest thing to a scream Lindy could muster.

"Hey, I'm sorry. But I can't handle what he's done to you," she looked up as he added, "It'll be okay, I promise."

After a brief silence which gave Lindy time to think, she explained, "I don't think I can stay here tonight. Maybe I should get away for a while," she accepted yet another tissue from her mother.

"Where would you go?" Duncan rubbed at the back of his neck.

Lindy closed her eyes, drew in a breath, and voiced her plans, "How about Chester's Run, give myself a chance to make some decisions. A change of scenery might do me good," Raising her head, she finally opened her eyes, "I'll head out once all Ralph's things have gone. He'll have no need to return to the house, so he'll not realise I'm not here."

If only the children surrounded her. Agreeing with her decision to move on. But failing those plans, a change of scenery may work. Finding meaning and purpose in life would be ideal, whatever that looked like. But most important of all was loyalty, Lindy lived by such a motto and expected to receive some from her children. Hopefully it would come. Sitting here waiting wouldn't help her. An unfamiliar environment might take her mind off the abandoned feeling deep inside.

"I'll drop his things at the office. That way he'll have no reason to come by at all," Duncan said.

Everyone agreed.

An hour and a half later everything Ralph owned took up all of Duncan and Mal's cars. They were an eclectic display of bags and suit-cases. Lindy and Duncan also boxed a few of Ralph's things from the study. Anthony, her lawyer, recommended she keep all paperwork at this stage, at least until he'd studied the prenuptial agreement thoroughly.

With that done, there were decisions to make. Getting away and regrouping seemed a wonderful idea. Chester's Run would provide peace and give her a chance to find a new direction. Duncan and Charlotte always visited the same country town every year for a few weeks over Christmas where his cousin owned a farm. Lindy's memories of the small town were wonderful, and besides Chester's Run happened during her childhood before Ralph. A calm settled over her. She'd be safe there.

FOR HIS CHILDREN

JACK

*A*fter hours of waiting with Bradley in the hospital, Jack hid a long yawn behind his hand and glanced over at his father, hoping like hell the man he'd always looked up to would manage to find answers to some questions tossing around in his head. But no luck there, neither of them were any closer to understanding how Elsa could have done this. She'd broken Bradley's arm in two places. The force she'd used must have been significant.

Jack shifted his gaze when shuffling footsteps approached. A short man with a friendly smile walked up to Bradley's cot.

"You must be Bradley's father?" Jack shook the offered hand. "I'm Dave, the anaesthetist. He seems settled," Dave offered, and Jack didn't blame him for stating the obvious. He wouldn't know what to say to a family of a child in Bradley's predicament either.

As Jack went to agree, his stomach let out a resounding growl, "Excuse me," Jack rubbed his stomach, feeling both exhausted and starving. "Yes, I'm his father, Jack Saunders," Jack forced his tired body to stand so he could talk to Dave, feeling every muscle as he did so. "He's been asleep for about an hour."

"Good," Dave launched into his spiel about Bradley being in excellent hands. "The orderly will be in shortly to take your son through to theatre. Do you have questions for me?"

Jack sighed, "No, all good, I think, thanks."

He'd never experienced anything as traumatic as this. At some point the police would be in to talk to him about the incident. Would they believe him when he explained he really didn't know what happened? Oh, he could describe the demise of his marriage, the way Elsa used him and the children. How he settled into the bungalow, and the way she played the kids off against him, determined to get her own way. Cold aching fear invaded his torso when he recalled what she'd put their children through.

Even though they hadn't slept together for over a year, Jack couldn't shake off a heaviness settling in his chest. What else could be done to prevent this dreadful situation for Bradley? He continuously questioned his actions.

Protecting his family became his new priority. The further Elsa stayed away, the better. But only a miracle would ensure he could look after his kids and get the crop in the ground. Shaking his head for the umpteenth time that afternoon, Jack cursed. How did everything spiral so rapidly?

The smell of coffee got Jack's attention. "Thanks," He reached up and accepted the takeaway cup from his father. Only now realising he hadn't even seen him leave the room, too lost in his painful thoughts.

"How you holding up?" Tony lowered himself down onto the next seat.

"None of this makes sense. Who would do that to their own child, their own flesh and blood, and then disappear?" Jack ran his free hand through his hair and down his face. He stared off into the distance. The pale lemon of the hospital walls held no answers for him.

"Shit," he hissed, leaning forward and resting his elbows on his knees. Where'd all this gone so wrong?

JACK

Gentle footsteps and a mumble of voices caused Jack to stir, even in his sleepy state he recognised his sister's tread. He wasn't sure how long he'd been asleep but he relaxed at the soft, small warm hand resting in his. Opening his eyes, he saw Harry and Tessa. Harry clutched Bradley's nappy bag which bulged at the seams. Reluctant to move, Jack closed his eyes for another minute and listened.

Tessa's hushed voice asked, "You okay Dad?"

"I'm fine. How are the others?"

"Mum's got them all settled, and she hasn't stopped feeding them."

"That doesn't surprise me," Tony chuckled, but it held no humour. "She's not overdoing it, is she?"

"No, Nate's been by her side the whole time."

"How they holding up?" Harry pointed to the bed.

Jack's moment of peace ended, time to face reality.

"Not good. He needs some answers," Tony watched as Jack sat up.

His father's face grimaced, "We all need answers. I just can't fathom any of this."

Jack hated seeing his father's pain, it must have mirrored his own.

Tessa turned her gaze from her Dad to Harry and finally Jack. "Hi love, how are you doing?" She walked around the bed and gave him a kiss. "Harry has some news."

"Good, I hope," Tony sat forward in his chair, resting his elbows on his knees and shaking his head.

Harry gave Tony a nod as Tessa walked around the bed and kissed her nephew on the forehead, gently brushing his overgrown fringe from his eyes.

Jack sat up tall. The earlier memories came flooding back, he swallowed hard. The pain of each tortuous memory replaying all over again. His son slept soundly, the only evidence of his injury was a cast which extended the full length of his little arm.

"Poor tyke, he looks exhausted." Tessa sighed.

For a minute, strained silence filled the room. Harry pulled up a seat for Tessa next to her Dad, found another for himself and positioned it beside Jack. He wasn't ready for news but he had to cope with whatever Harry told him.

After a while Harry eased into the conversation, "We have some news about Elsa." Jack heard the long pause but made no response. He cringed at hearing her name. Harry continued, "She was picked up halfway to Melbourne. She's tested positive for drugs. From the information she gave, I think she's been taking ice, which explains a hell of a lot."

Jack's head rested in his free hand. How could she do this? Putting her addiction before her children?

Neither of them really loved each other when they married. Jack was determined to protect his unborn baby, which maybe wasn't the best reason for getting married, but looking back at his life, something good came out of their union. His five beautiful children, what he treasured most in the world. Any father would be proud of them.

Jack vowed, "Never again, little man. She'll never hurt you, ever again."

He couldn't face looking at anyone, so closed his eyes tight.

Eventually he spoke, "Where is she?"

"In the lockup in Seymour, but she'll be transferred back here to face charges." Harry explained.

"If you don't want her back, we'll support you all the way." His sister stated in her usual no nonsense tone. Tessa saw the aftermath of his misery and his darkest moments. Jack's chest tightened as beads of sweat covered his torso. Once crossed, Jack never went back. Tessa was more in tune than anyone on how he operated. There wasn't any need to announce the lack of room in his life for Elsa. The last few months of family separation proved that, and what she'd done to Bradley cemented his deepest feelings. His family's protection and safety were paramount. Jack promised himself, he'd leave nothing to chance when it came to his children ever again.

SELF-DISCOVERY

LINDY

A cool spring morning greeted her just after six o'clock, Lindy coaxed herself out of bed. The first day of the rest of her life arrived and she refused to waste any more time on the husband she supported and loved, not to mention given everything to.

"You and I are through, Ralph," she looked into the bathroom mirror, focusing more closely at herself. What did she lack that the young woman in Ralph's lap possessed? Lindy was taller than the girl. At five-foot eight inches, Lindy could never be considered short. Her shoulder-length brown hair was only one colour, unlike the other girl's streaks, she wasn't immune to ageing, but she took care of herself and considered it a graceful process on her part. Lindy respected her body and carefully chose what she put into it. Her skin remained unblem-ished. Yes, there were signs of ageing, but nothing as devastating as spots or sagging. She was only in her mid-forties for goodness sakes. Well, one thing the young thing probably boasted were pert breasts and smooth skin. But no, she missed something. Considering the photos, the women were all shapes and sizes. She groaned at the images, her blood boiling once again at Ralph's deceit.

The partnership with her husband ended yesterday and her children still failed to return her calls. Lindy wished she could at least understand what they were thinking, she didn't comprehend why they refused to talk to her. Swallowing hard she looked into the mirror again as she bit down on her bottom lip. Hopefully they'd contact her, their grandparents, or uncles soon. Deciding to wait on that front, she could enjoy peace and tranquillity of this small country town before the unavoidable and difficult conversations.

Her life and choices for once became purely hers. As much as her marriage to Ralph being over devastated her, a cleansing buzz permeated. Life began again and she would become the focal point. A realisation struck her, being able to dedicate more time to herself and her interests registered as foreign. Where would she start?

Drawing back the curtains, Lindy noticed the large scattering of trees with new forming leaves, she couldn't help but assimilate the new beginning for the deciduous trees with the fresh start she sought in her own life. Even though the morning was frigid, Lindy opened the window just a crack to breathe in the clean mountain air. A trickle of water sounded somewhere in the distance. A vague memory of crossing a small bridge on walks with her family surfaced. Lindy decided after breakfast she would take a stroll and rediscover the river.

Entering the sleepy town of Chester's Run last night, Lindy remembered the times she'd spent here. The population all those years ago was a mere five or six hundred. Last night as she drove in, the sign stated two thousand, nine hundred and sixty-five locals were in residence.

She remembered Chester's Run boasted a strong horse connection. Men and women owned and ran the high country. Some of the best horses were born and raised in and around this thriving little community. Lindy recalled time here as a child, reminiscing about the fun times they'd spent here. During the day all the children would enjoy the great outdoors and by night they played board games with the family. Pulling herself out of the memories Lindy got dressed and started her day.

Walking down Park Road, Lindy's acute sense of smell sniffed out a bakery. The fresh aroma wafting through town reminded her of Wednesday morning breakfasts with Zave. The local bakery turned into their favourite meeting place where they indulged in their mutual obsession.

Stop! Her mind barrelled off in the wrong direction. She needed to let all those memories go. Scolding herself, Lindy hunted out the bakery and stepped inside to order breakfast. As the man ahead of her ordered an egg and bacon roll, her mouth watered. Perfect. Greasy and delightful. After placing her order of an egg and bacon roll with a cappuccino, Lindy sat at a table in the front window. Observing the comings and goings of the locals, she enjoyed the closeness of the small community.

While waiting for her breakfast, a man in uniform walked in.

"Morning Harry," a young woman behind the counter greeted him

"Morning." Harry eyed the occupied tables.

"You're looking tired," the same woman said. "How are they all?"

"Struggling," he leant onto the counter, "Have you been in to see them?" he asked before placing his order.

"I popped into the hospital last night, but both Jack and Bradley were asleep. Didn't have the heart to wake them."

"Jack will bring the poor thing home today," Harry ran a firm calloused hand over the stubble of his face.

Listening in on this conversation, these two seemed stressed about something. But her focus wavered as she sat daydreaming for a while, she pulled herself back to reality as someone set her breakfast down on the table.

"Thanks, that looks wonderful."

The waitress, a woman in her early thirties, Lindy guessed, with a long brown ponytail gave an enormous smile, "My pleasure. Enjoy." Still juggling plates, the waitress walked on to the next table.

Lindy took a sip of her cappuccino, appreciating the rich aroma. The first bite of the bacon and egg roll was delicious, but the second went unnoticed as Lindy lost herself again in her past and deliberating her future. Sensible was her safe place. Would she venture there again? Go home, live in the house where she raised her children and return to her business. In truth that option no longer appealed. The other options were, well, endless she supposed, but it would mean some huge life-changing decisions.

I'm capable of radical adjustments.

She conceded Chester's Run was exactly what she needed at the moment. A change of scenery and focus. Lindy reached for her cappuccino, and sighed when her hand touched the cold mug. She pushed it away, becoming lost in the darkness again until a friendly voice invaded her thoughts.

"Hey, everything okay? I see you didn't finish your coffee."

"Sorry, I zoned out and it went cold. I won't repeat such foolishness again." Lindy smiled at the open, friendly face.

"Susie, can you make a cappuccino, please? Table seven." The woman bearing the nametag Ivy called out without hesitation.

"Sure boss, coming right up." The waitress turned towards the coffee machine.

"Oh no, please, I don't mean to put you out," the burn in Lindy's cheeks highlighted her discomfort.

"You're not putting me out, I like my customers to walk out happy with my service and my food." Ivy grinned and Lindy sensed an instant connection with the young woman.

"You enjoy what you do?" Reactions like these encouraged Lindy to reach out to strangers. It intrigued her to learn and understand what drove business owners. Mentoring people and helping them to extend themselves drove her.

"Uh huh," Ivy's head bobbed, "My grandmother left me this place," she waved at the interior of the shop, "A wonderful legacy and the best thing she could have done for me. Originally this place housed my grandmother's craft shop, now it's my bakery and I'm loving it."

"You're a qualified baker? My daughter just completed her apprenticeship a few months ago," Lindy smiled at the shop owner and they settled in for a chat. Her first genuine smile and her insides warmed at the realisation.

"Yes, I moved to the city to get my qualifications, worked there for a few years. When my grandmother passed away, I longed for the only family I have left and returned home. I just wish I'd taken a course in business management, this place is a struggle." Ivy shifted the weight of the dirty dishes bucket from one hip to the other. "My grandmother encouraged me to leave Chester's Run and do my apprenticeship. I regret not coming back sooner to spend time with her before she died."

Lindy didn't miss the distant look in Ivy's eyes.

Susie delivered the cup of cappuccino. Accepting the cup, Lindy asked, "Do you have a minute to join me?"

Ivy scanned the shop, nodded to herself.

"Susie, could you make me a short black please?" Dropping the half full bucket on the counter, Ivy returned to the table and introduced herself, "Ivy Masters."

"Lindy Kemp." The two women shook hands. "Tell me more about yourself."

It didn't take long for Ivy to open up about her life and the shop. Lindy listened with a business mind as always.

"In short, the business side of things is where I struggle. I'm busy, but the money doesn't really match my efforts. Thank goodness I own the premises, that's my saving grace."

"Okay," Lindy held out her hand again, "Let's start over, Lindy Kemp, mentor for business owners."

"Really? You're not from here, obviously?" Ivy studied Lindy.

"No. Melbourne, actually. Just having a few weeks R and R. Ivy, would you accept my help while I'm here?"

Without hesitation Ivy explained, "I don't have the money to pay a mentor?"

"Let me clarify, I didn't offer my services. I offered my help, no charge. Anyway, you'd be doing me a favour, a distraction from my own busy mind." Lindy gauged the younger woman's interest in the offer.

"I hope you're serious because that'd be awesome." Ivy's friendly smile broadened as her eyes took in her premises. Lindy couldn't mistake her pride for the place.

Over coffee, Lindy and Ivy chatted about the bakery's goals and achievements. The shop filled with customers and Ivy checked the floral clock on the wall.

"Susie's going to need help."

They agreed to meet later in the day, when the bakery wasn't so busy.

Ivy pushed to her feet, "I look forward to seeing you this afternoon," she gathered the empty cups from the table.

"Definitely, see you then."

Lindy waved to Susie as she served a customer, and walked out into the warm morning sunshine.

She decided to investigate the town. It took a moment to get her bearings. She'd seen the statues in Memorial Park as she walked into town this morning, they were still much the same as she remembered. But the town itself changed a great deal. Shop fronts housed different stores than those of the past. Not to mention the new shops and businesses which expanded the town from what she'd known. The town centre doubled in size. The childhood memories of a small lolly shop, which they often frequented, had been swallowed up by the adjacent store and housed part of a classy women's clothing boutique.

Looking up and down Park Road, Lindy noticed the town's information centre on the opposite side and headed over.

All the latest tourist brochures took up lots of wall space. Lindy picked up a copy of Chester's Run Monthly among other brochures. A short time later Lindy waved to the attendant behind the counter, "Thanks for all these, I won't get bored."

"If you need anything else just pop back in," the friendly lady, probably in her mid-sixties, called. "We're happy to help."

Making her way back to the motel, Lindy couldn't help but smile. Walking through this town brought back wonderful childhood memories. Lindy admitted feeling comfortable in this quaint little place.

LINDY

Settling into a chair at Ivy's kitchen table later that afternoon, Lindy focused on the task at hand, keeping herself busy. The two women put their heads together. Lindy asked questions and took notes as Ivy answered.

Half an hour later, Lindy had introduced so many fresh ideas. She watched Ivy as she rubbed her temples and closed her eyes.

"You honestly believe I can really make a success of this place?"

"Absolutely, this place is a gold mine," Lindy gestured with arms opened wide. 'I've tasted your food. With just a few changes to improve the current system, you'll be fine." Lindy enjoyed the hope in the other woman's eyes. Right there was the reason she gave her time to small business owners, the look from despair to hope made it all worthwhile.

Next Lindy scrutinised the bookkeeping, "Correcting these common pitfalls," she tapped one column of the ledger, "You'll find putting smart practises in place will significantly impact your returns."

"I'm all ears. What else?"

"Let's inspect stock and purchasing," Lindy suggested as they addressed the bakery side of the business. Conversation flowed as ideas continued to surface.

Ivy looked exhausted, she told Lindy her days were taxing mentally and physically. "For a gold mine, I'm sitting on a lot of problems here."

"Not problems, just challenges. Ones you're more than capable of handling."

"Thanks, I'll give it a go if you think it will help. Half this stuff never entered my head. This is amazing. You don't understand how grateful I am." Ivy pulled out her hair tie and ran her fingers through her long sandy blonde hair before pulling it back into a ponytail again.

"Well, I should get going. I'll pop in and see you for breakfast tomorrow."

"Hang on. Why don't you join me for dinner?" Ivy asked.

A slight smile crossed Lindy's lips, though she said nothing.

CHERYL ROSARIO

"You look like you could use some company, and I was only going to settle down to my boring evening in front of the telly." The offer tempted Lindy. "Go on, chicken stir-fry is on the menu," Ivy raised a coaxing brow.

The only thing Lindy looked forward to, well, was nothing, which twenty-four hours ago sounded inviting. But in hindsight, it was more solitude than she could handle at the moment. "If you don't mind? That's just what I need. A home-cooked meal and some company. Thanks."

Ivy set to work in the compact kitchen of her flat while Lindy surveyed the decor of the place. She turned in a small circle, "Wow, this is lovely. Did you decorate it yourself?"

"Yep. Some knick-knacks came from Grandma's shop. Decorating was her passion. Simple but stylish, if you know what I mean."

"Yes, definitely." The country theme was apparent, but simple. "Do you ride?" Lindy pointed to stirrups hanging on display.

"I used to. Those are rather special. They belonged to my grandfather. He was an amazing horseman and a wonderful man," Ivy let out a sigh.

"You must have some fond memories."

"Yes, but I haven't gone riding in a while. It all conjures up memories of the times we spent together. Here, come and look at these." The navy and gold theme in her bedroom looked crisp and just as tastefully set out. Ivy pointed to a collage of photos of her with both her grandmother and grandfather over the years. "That's Duke, my grandfather's horse. He died about ten days after my Grandpa. It shattered me." Ivy shook her head as if attempting to dislodge a memory, "It's been nine years, I haven't ridden since."

Without thinking, Lindy lifted her arms to give Ivy a hug. Obviously, the memories saddened her. Lindy blamed herself for the tears in Ivy's eyes. Stepping in closer, the pain in her sore arm halted her. Lindy winced.

"Oh my God, what have you done? That's the second time you've winced." Lindy slowly lifted the sleeve of her pale blue knitted jumper to reveal a bruise which Ralph inflicted on her the previous day. "Oh hell. Who did that to you? Is that why you're here?"

"Yes, that's why." Lindy nodded, "I'm running away from a marriage that fell apart yesterday." She explained how the previous day unfolded as Ivy whipped up the meal. Ivy opened her mouth but closed it again.

"Thinking things through, I put up with his ways for the sake of the children. A broken marriage has a stigma I didn't want to subject them to. Maybe I just allowed his life to continue with no demands, because I never remember questioning much at all. As for my future, I have a second chance and I'm determined to decide how best to use it."

Over dinner, Lindy asked lots of questions about Chester's Run. They discussed the surrounding towns and Lindy introduced the idea of wholesaling Ivy's freshly baked goods to other cafes. The talk was casual, but hopeful.

"I've always wanted someone to show me another way with business," Ivy told Lindy, "My cousin Jack's a born businessman, but…" Ivy paused. "Let's just say he's got his own troubles." Changing the topic, she added, "I really am impressed with your knowledge and guidance."

Rising to her feet, Lindy started clearing the table.

"No leave that. I'll do them later. Would you like a cuppa?"

"No thanks, time to head back to the motel, but I'll see you tomorrow. Have a think about everything we discussed and let me know what you think. Thanks for dinner and the chat, I needed that."

Ivy got up and hugged Lindy carefully, "Thank you for everything and I'll definitely look over your suggestions before breakfast.

STEP BY TINY STEP

JACK

"Thanks for the offer," Jack sat around his parents dining table that evening. "But the farm is the children's home. For now. They need to get used to life without Elsa."

"It will be hard on everyone. You know we want to help," his mother's pleading voice offered.

"I appreciate that, but you're recovering from your operation and the doctor wants you to take it easy. Tessa's been amazing and Ivy's promised to send stuff home. The rest I'll work out. You guys are welcome anytime, even come for dinner every night. The kids and I would love that. But you also have to promise to take it easy."

"How about we agree to doing what we can without going overboard?" Darla's smile warmed Jack's icy heart.

"What do you think the future holds?" Tony asked.

"Change. Lots of change," Jack dropped his head to the table.

"I think it's time to sell the farm. As you said, the children are your priority. Speak to Ray and the boys. I know they're looking to expand."

Jack nodded, Tony wasn't sentimental or possessive. The farm served a purpose, which no longer suited his family, so making changes was a decision not a hardship.

"Let me see what happens with Elsa. Together we can form a plan. Thanks guys," Jack gathered up the empty cups and walked them over to the sink. "I'll round the rugrats up and head home."

JACK

Jack smiled at the clean house and food in the fridge. He'd have to do a proper shop in the next few days, but for now they'd get by.

After putting Bradley to bed, he walked into the girls' room to tuck them in. "You both okay?" The girls bunked in together just for tonight.

"Yes Dad," they chorused.

"Good. Get some sleep and I'll see you in the morning."

"Dad," Joanna called when he got to the doorway.

"Yes, love?"

"Where's Mum?"

Logically he expected one of them to ask, eventually. But so soon. The words sucked all the air from his lungs. He walked back into the room and sat beside Joanna, "You know your mother's not well, don't you?"

"Yes, but I miss her," the tremble of her lip tore at his heart.

Taking her hand in his, Jack scrambled for a response. Considering how they lived and what Elsa inflicted on Bradley, it stunned Jack to hear Joanna still wanted her mother.

"Sweetheart, I promise to let you know how she is." He wasn't mentioning jail. "But at the moment the doctors say she can't see us just yet."

"But will we see her soon?"

"When she's better," he gave her a nod.

"Okay," Joanna snuggled down beside her sister once again.

"Goodnight."

Jack was stopped again, this time by Evie, "Will you be sleeping in the bungalow?"

"No darling. I'm in my old room. If you need me just call out, okay?"

"Yep, night." The girls settled after a second goodnight kiss.

He crossed the hall to the boys' room. "All good in here?"

"Yep," they answered.

"I'm next door with Bradley, if you need anything."

"Okay," Nate said.

Jack lingered with a hug for Caleb and looked over at Nate. "I can't tell you how important your help was, buddy. Even Grandma and Grandpa are so proud of you. I know how much you helped at Aunty Tessa's yesterday. Thanks for that," Jack walked to the door.

"Dad," Nate began, "I don't want Mum to come back. I don't want to see her, ever again." He paused briefly, then added, "Does that make me a terrible person?"

Unclenching his fists, Jack turned and walked back into the room. He settled onto the end of Nate's bed.

"Buddy, your Mum will always be your Mum. Just because she and I aren't together anymore doesn't mean we won't see her sometimes." Jack studied the faded pattern on Nate's doona cover, searching for what else to say.

"She doesn't love us, Dad. If she did, she wouldn't have hurt Bradley." The pain in Nate's eyes made Jack want to scream. How could a mother do this?

"Your mother isn't in a good place. Let's hope she gets help. Don't go worrying about any of this. Okay?"

"Yeah," Nate adjusted his covers and rolled onto his side facing the wall.

Jack wasn't a fool. Nate took no solace in his words, but at the moment, nothing else would ease Nate's fears. Tomorrow would be another day and they'd try again.

"Night." Caleb called.

"Night," Jack closed his eyes and shook his head when Nate said no more.

He walked back into the kitchen and chuckled, compared to how they lived only a couple of days ago, this became his idea of bliss. A clean house, quiet kitchen and settled children. Even if the television worked it wouldn't hold his attention tonight.

Maybe one day he'd start again. Find a woman he truly wanted forever with. Though, a relationship wasn't a priority. Besides, having someone who valued and respected the children seemed a distant hope.

Creating a cheerful home for his kids became his priority.

Jack looked around the house. No, tonight wasn't a night to rush in and make rash decisions about his future. Planning would be his form of attack towards his current predicament. He pulled out the laptop he'd hidden away in the bungalow, opened up an Excel spreadsheet and a Word document. He listed things he'd need to achieve and then listed pros and cons for each option, calculating the financials involved. Switching between spreadsheet and document, he assessed and reassessed, lingered on options and ordered the non-negotiables. Looking down his list, each one of the non-negotiables were for his children. Right there was his proof, he was moving, or at least thinking in the right direction. The children were his life and their safety and happiness were paramount.

His phone buzzed in his pocket. Jack pulled it out and saw Harry's name.

"Hey," he greeted his long-time friend, as he walked into the lounge to settle down for a chat.

"Mate, are the kids settled?"

"Is that my sister asking?" Jack laughed.

"No, that one was me. Your sister is lying here on the couch with me waiting for her turn to talk." Harry's amused tone rang out but Jack sensed something was weighing on him.

"Fair enough. The kids are wonderful. Bradley will be out till morning, hopefully. The girls are sharing a bed. And the boys seem to be okay. So, I'm hoping for a decent night's sleep."

"Excellent. Listen mate, I've spent an hour with Elsa tonight. She intends on pleading guilty to all charges and has asked for help. She keeps talking about coming home again."

A knife twisted in Jack's gut. Like the previous day when one thing after another tried to take him down, here it was again.

"Never, ever going to happen. The children are my one and only concern. Elsa and I have no future except for the kids."

"I get that." Harry replied.

"I've got some serious decisions to make—the farm, my livelihood, they're all at a crossroads."

"I'm here if you want to talk things out. Anytime."

"I appreciate the offer. Is my sister there?" Jack didn't mean to dismiss Harry, but he was desperate for an early night.

"Hey," Tessa said.

"I can't thank you enough for what you've done around here." Jack blurted.

"Anything for family." Tessa's voice sounded strained. He could imagine tears in her eyes.

Jack couldn't go there, so instead he pushed on, "I've spoken to Mum and Dad about the farm. I don't have a choice, the best thing we can do is put the farm up for sale. How do you feel about that?"

"The farm has always been your thing. If selling and moving on is the best you can do, then sell it."

"But you know we both get money if we sell," Jack rubbed his hand down his face. Making life-changing decisions like this clutched at his heart.

"Jack," he could hear her moving. She was probably sitting up to force her next point. "That money has never been part of plans for Harry and I. Whatever comes my way is a bonus and won't change anything for us, whereas for you it's helping you move on from this. Don't think you have to sell the farm for me or Mum and Dad. We're fine the way things are. This is about you."

"I can't do the farm and be a single dad. Even if I had help, and besides, no one would love the children like we do." There was a dull pain in his chest which was increasing in intensity.

"Are they going to school tomorrow?"

"Monday. Tomorrow the doctor wants to see Bradley and I want the children to just have a few days at home where they can settle."

"Shall I come by tomorrow so we can talk?"

"How about you come for lunch?"

"Sounds like a plan. Oh, how was Mum when you left?"

He didn't need to be a genius, he heard the tightness in her words. "Tired, but happier than I've seen her in months."

"Elsa really hurt them," Tessa was always the straight shooter.

"You don't have to downplay the pain she put you through either." He huffed out a breath, "Anyway, that's all behind us. I'm falling asleep here so I'd better get to bed. I'll see you tomorrow for lunch."

UNEXPECTED INTERVENTION

LINDY

*L*indy enjoyed the leisurely walk in the setting sun from her motel room to the local church. To think she'd only been here for three days. With So much happening, in some ways time flew, yet in others, time seemed to stand still.

Saturday night mass became her tradition. None of her children attended mass with her anymore, and Ralph always claimed to have better things to do with his time. She'd treasured the weekly ritual on her own. Attending mass tonight meant tomorrow would leave her free to set off early with a local walking group to visit the national park, one of the many activities she planned with Ivy's help.

Walking along Park Road, Lindy pulled her jacket tighter against the slight chill as her mind wandered to the family she'd left behind and the recent acquaintances she made in this town.

Finding a seat, Lindy settled in for a time of reflection. Getting to mass early gave her an opportunity to think things over in a peaceful environment without being by herself. The silence of the motel room and its unfamiliar surroundings made her wonder if coming to

Chester's Run achieved her goals. In church others sat talking, a couple of women smiled and nodded to her and she returned the gesture. With others came a sense of companionship, even if she didn't know any of them.

Just before mass, a familiar face settled into the seat in front of her. Jack carrying Bradley with the other four children in tow. Lindy looked up to see the toddler smiling at her. She looked down at the other children who were waving.

She remembered back to yesterday morning when Jack came into the bakery with his children for breakfast and Ivy doted on all of them. Lindy smiled at the memory of the children making their own milkshakes and eating freshly made pies and sausage rolls at Ivy's insistence and Jack's dismay.

"Hi," she mouthed and waved back to the children.

The toddler stood in his father's lap, taking in the church, he let out a whimper. His cast must have been causing him some discomfort. Taking notice of the interaction between father and son, it warmed her heart. She couldn't help but smile at the way this man cared for his little boy, actually for all his children. No one could deny his love seeing them together.

Jack turned and smiled at her when one of his son's tugged on the hem of his shirt and pointed to Lindy sitting behind them. But when the whining from Bradley continued, Jack's focus diverted again.

As mass began, Lindy tried to pay attention to the priest, but became lost in her troubles. Her children hadn't returned her calls. Looking at the situation, it seemed they'd all but disowned her. The pain and realisation of such a betrayal shot an arrow to her heart. A short time later she heard Bradley cry out.

"Mumma, Mumma, Mumma," he screamed as he squirmed in his father's arms.

"Shhh, shhh," Jack whispered, rocking his son gently.

The baby hushed briefly, but didn't hold his silence long. For a second time he locked eyes with Lindy.

"Mumma, Mumma, Mumma." His good arm stretched out as if grabbing for her.

Lindy's heart ached for both father and baby. The cries reached piercing screams but no matter what Jack tried to do, he could not comfort his son.

JACK

"Sorry," Jack mouthed to those around him.

People gave a friendly smile or a nod. He locked eyes with Lindy, her warm eyes saying so much.

He couldn't believe how quickly Bradley had taken to her. "Shhh, shhh." Jack repeated while rocking from side to side.

He looked around, why did he choose to sit here? Smack bang in the middle of the church. What was he thinking? Racking his brain, Jack tried to come up with a solution to stop Bradley screeching before he upset the entire congregation. The screaming stopped. Thank goodness.

Turning slightly, Jack looked out of the corner of his eye, Bradley was fixated on something. He turned a little further, and a smile formed. Bradley clasped Lindy's hand in his and she was whispering to him.

"Hehehe."

Jack raised a brow when he heard Bradley laughing.

He watched the interaction and only turned back around when it was time to sit. He couldn't even remember what part of the service they were up to, he was a sheep, just following the herd.

He sucked in a deep breath as Bradley began to struggle again.

LINDY

Stretching out her hand a second time, Lindy cooed when the little boy took it. He wrapped his lips around her middle finger and sucked, silencing as he did so. Definitely teething, poor little fellow. Lindy remembered the pain Cameron suffered when he was teething, but little Bradley also dealt with his arm in plaster. Finally, Lindy tapped Jack on the shoulder, "How about I take him?" she whispered.

"Would you mind?" he mouthed back.

Lindy shook her head, "No, not at all. Do you have his bottle?"

"I tried that," he stretched his free hand down for the bottle sitting on the seat next to him.

Lindy took Bradley and watched as Jack's rigid shoulders relaxed a little when the baby quietened down and sucked on his bottle.

Ivy shared a few details yesterday after Jack left the bakery about what happened to the family, part of Lindy ached for them.

The baby's free hand traced her face, pulled on her necklace, and stuck his fingers into her mouth. After Bradley finished the bottle he played for a few minutes, then snuggled into her neck. He mumbled to himself as he tugged on her thin necklace and her top before slowly dozing off to sleep.

The feel of Jack's eyes on her spoke of the devoted father she believed him to be. Lindy met his gaze with a smile, no judgement here. Jack nodded as he heard Bradley's gentle snores.

"Well done," an older woman next to her said with a broad grin, "He's such a good little boy. There you go, Jack," she spoke slightly louder this time and patted his shoulder.

"A miracle worker," Jack murmured with a slight smile.

He gripped the back of the pew in front of him and sunk down. She tried not to stare at how well he wore his faded jeans, especially with a lady from the purple rinse brigade watching closely. Bradley cuddled into her, his body relaxed, sleeping soundly in her arms.

Sensing the eyes of the congregation upon her, Lindy excused herself and stepped past the parishioners to her right and then again apologised as she gained access to the pew in front, carefully manoeuvring herself and the child. Who would be happy allowing a virtual stranger to hold their baby without being able to see them? Those watching would have seen as Lindy did, Jack's knees buckled under him when she settled in beside him, cradling Bradley.

"Thank you," he whispered as he brushed the long fringe off his son's face before kissing him gently.

Lindy gave him a smile in return. For the rest of mass, they sat in companionable silence.

JACK

"Looks like we have both sought the church as a haven this evening." Lindy conceded after the mass.

Jack could only respond with a weak smile and a small nod. He'd always been excellent at wearing a mask, there was nothing readable on his face. He swallowed hard again.

"Dad," Evie tugged on his arm, "Could we see Jemima and Rosy?"

Jack looked over to see the girls' friends beckoning them from the doorway. "Of course, but stay near the front of the church."

"Thanks," Jack watched as his four children caught up with their school friends.

With a smile on his face Jack turned back to Lindy who looked around the small ornate church.

He took in her appearance. This woman was beautiful. She radiated respect and care, which sat well on her just like her shoulder length hair and gentle smile. She was a tall woman, being just a few inches shorter than him. Her slender build, though matching Elsa's skinny one, was healthy, and this woman seemed content in her own skin. Jack held back a sudden desire to reach out and touch her, for so many reasons, but mainly the fact that his wife was in jail and his children needed a parent who would love them unconditionally. He didn't have time for anything else right now.

"This is a beautiful church. I love visiting old country churches."

"So, you're a city girl? What brings you to our neck of the woods?" Jack asked in a quiet voice.

Lindy gave him a half-hearted laugh. She stared at the traditional wooden altar, "Running away from my troubles. Trying to work out who I really am and what I want out of life."

"Spouse problems?" Jack inquired, happy to have the focus deflected from himself.

Lindy tore her eyes from the alter and stared at him.

"Sorry," Jack said, "I didn't think. Please forgive me." It was obvious they were both experiencing something similar at the moment.

How did he tell her he didn't mean anything by his question without giving away his own situation? She began to talk again.

"Yep, him and disowned, I think, by my three adult children. I've rung them and left messages, but I've heard nothing back." She glanced at Jack and he swore he could see a bruised soul staring out.

Holding out his hand to her he said, "Jack Saunders. I can't tell you how glad I was to have your help tonight," shaking her free hand and looking down at his baby in her arms.

"Lindy Kemp. Privileged to have something so gorgeous to occupy my troubled mind." Jack grinned, and he noticed the moment she'd picked up on her double entendre. Lindy fumbled to clarify it was the child she spoke of. "He's a beautiful boy." He couldn't miss her hot cheeks, and a smile for Bradley, sound asleep and looking like he didn't have a care in the world. "May I pry and ask what happened to his arm?"

He leant forward, resting his elbows on his knees, puffed out a breath and clasped his hands in front of him. The stiffness cramping his neck and shoulders got worse as he gripped his hands tighter.

Jack avoided eye contact and changed the subject, "Have you had dinner?" he wasn't ready to answer that probing question at the moment.

"No," she stared at him for a moment and then continued, "I was planning to eat at the pub attached to my motel after church."

"Would you mind if I joined you? I'm not ready to return home, maybe I can leave these rugrats with my parents for a while."

Not waiting for a reply, Jack leant over and scooped up his little man. He could see Lindy grappling uncomfortably with the dead weight in her arms.

"You know what? I'd love some company, if you don't mind? I'm not used to being so alone."

SHOW OF GRATITUDE

JACK

Jack drove to the pub after dropping the children with his parents. The noise of the engine echoed in the silence surrounding him. He pulled into a parking spot at the end of the car park and sat wondering whether he was doing the right thing.

How could it be wrong? This was only a thank you dinner. After her help this evening, how could a meal together represent as anything else? Granted, the woman was pretty, even though she was a city girl. But there wasn't time in his life for a relationship with the farm and five kids, not to mention an estranged wife in jail. Who in their right mind would even consider him romantically? Jack shook his head as his lips lifted in a slight smile.

Get a grip, Saunders. This is nothing more than dinner and a chat with a woman who assisted you this evening.

Throwing caution to the wind, Jack got out of his car and walked into the pub.

He found Lindy sitting at a table in the far corner of the bistro. For a minute he observed her as she typed into her phone. The sight took him to vivid memories of Elsa with her phone planning her hook ups. A groan left him. Why was he tarring other women with the same brush as Elsa? It could be one of her children finally contacting her. He headed over to the bar.

"Hey," the bartender greeted him, "Long time no see."

"Mick. How's things?" Jack wasn't conversing with this man other than to order a couple of drinks and their meals.

"Great mate. Hey, sorry to hear about little Bradley. How's he doing?"

Jack sighed. "We've got a long road ahead, all of us." He could feel the eyes of the pub on him. Knowing full well this town survived on gossip, Jack straightened his shoulders, what he did next would be fuel for their favourite pastime.

"Mick," Jack nodded towards Lindy sitting in the corner, "What's she drinking?"

"Nothing yet. She's waiting for someone," Mick glanced at Lindy and then continued to wipe down the bar.

Not only were Mick's eyes on him but also the rest of the patrons' as he walked over towards Lindy.

He smiled when Lindy greeted him. "Hello again," her friendly, open face was sincere and free from any pretence. He appreciated that she locked her phone and put it away, giving him her full attention.

"Hope I haven't kept you waiting too long."

"No, not at all. I've only been here about ten minutes."

"Good, what would you like to drink?" He couldn't help but notice how relaxed and at ease she was.

"White wine, please."

Jack returned to the bar again. "A light beer and a white wine, thanks Mick," He could tell the barman's interest spiked, but Jack offered nothing, "And could we have two menus as well?"

When Jack settled down at the table he began to talk, determined to answer the question Lindy had asked him after mass. Eager to clear the air between them. Why? He wasn't sure.

"Bradley's arm was broken by my wife, soon to be ex, before she took my Ute and shot through. Police found her just out of Seymour."

He drew in a raspy breath, "I don't know what happened other than what my children told me, but the doctors have lodged a report for child abuse. I have custody, but I'm still considered a suspect at this stage." Jack rambled as he leant forward on the edge of the table whilst looking off into the open fire.

"Oh, I'm so sorry. I didn't mean to pry."

"I pried first, so I probably wanted to talk about it," he reassured her. The woman sitting across from him was the most peaceful sight he'd seen in a while. Giving her a small smile, he stretched out his legs and settled back in his chair. Around her he was a different person compared to the one at home. The tension in his body seeped away and the responsibilities that filled his head since Wednesday, seemed to diminish from that of a raging beast to a frolicking lamb. "Thanks again for your help with Bradley at mass. I'm not sure what possessed me to go. I think I just want routine back in my life and taking the children to mass is one of those."

"Did you find any answers?" Lindy asked.

Shaking his head, Jack met her gaze again, "I'm not sure I sought answers. More like solace, I think. Elsa forbade us to attend church about three years ago. We only attended when the children were making their sacraments," he ran sweaty palms down the legs of his well-worn jeans. Opting for a change in topic he continued, "Enough about me. What's it about our town that brought you to Chester's Run?" he asked, straightening his cutlery.

She laughed and Jack noticed how much was conveyed in such a simple gesture, "Mum and Dad used to bring us here to visit cousins on Dad's side. You may have known them, Greg and Heather Chapman."

"The name Chapman rings a bell," Jack offered.

"They were wonderful times and amazing memories. I can still see myself following my two older brothers and cousins, uninvited might I add, down to the creek or through the bush. We had freedom here we never experienced at home. Not to mention the peace."

"Yes, I remember them, Stephen and…hell, what was the older brother's name?" Jack racked his brain.

"Patrick. Stephen, Patrick, oh and little Carmel, I'd forgotten about her, she died of an asthma attack at about twelve, I think."

"Oh yes, Carmel, I remember that. It was so sad when she died." Jack recalled. He watched as her eyes clouded over at the memory. Jack decided he needed to change the subject yet again. "Well, you'll definitely get peace here. I find that in the tractor, when you're happy, it's the best place in the world to be. But when the weight of the world is on your shoulders, well you have way too much time to think."

Lindy nodded at his observation.

"As for you, if you want something to do there's plenty, but if you'd rather remain low key, that's an option as well. I really love this place." Shaking his head, Jack finished with, "Pity Elsa didn't feel the same way about Chester's Run." He drew in a deep breath. Why had he shared that titbit of information? "What are your plans now?"

"Well, I've been mentoring Ivy at the bakery. She's your cousin, I believe?"

"Yep, that's right. Ivy, Tessa, and I go back a long way. She was *our* uninvited tag along over the years." He chuckled, at the pleasant memories flooding him.

"Yes, she idolises you and Tessa."

"Tessa's great with her," Jack crossed his arms in front of him, "I haven't had the chance to help as much as I would've liked. Not with everything on the farm. Anyway," Jack's voice trailed off. That conversation was for another time and a different pair of ears.

"I've been here three days and Ivy has been a superb source of information and a good friend."

Jack made no response.

When his focus returned to his guest across the table he saw Lindy watching him, "Sorry. I must have checked out on you."

Lindy took a sip of her wine before answering. "Please. I totally get it. You were questioning yourself, weren't you?" The crackling of the open fire drew his gaze once again, and he stared as flames danced and hypnotised him.

"Yep." The word came out rough, he cleared his throat with a coarse cough before continuing. He'd spent hours upon hours trying to justify his decisions and actions. Still he didn't accept his actions. His chest tightened as he fought the urge to apologise for his failures. It wasn't Lindy he should be apologising too. Jack swallowed a few times. "Every time I rehash it, I come up with the same answer. I let my children down, especially Bradley."

"Jack," Lindy reached out and touched his hand, "Just remember most kids are resilient. I'm not downplaying what happened to Bradley, but he's young enough not to remember any of this. As for your other children, time and love will heal those memories and besides, I bet they remember it differently to you."

LINDY

When Jack finally spoke again Lindy noticed the emotion of the situation masked his otherwise attractive features. His hair looked too long and the scruff on his face, though it suited him, made him look older than he probably was. At a guess she'd say he was at least four or five years younger than him. In the silence settling around them she pictured his children—they weren't shabbily kept, but looked like life had dealt them a harsh blow. She couldn't help but wonder if her face revealed the conflict of the last few days as his did.

"How will you cope with the children?"

"I truly don't know." Jack shook his head as if unable to believe the fact, "Father of five. I'm not sure what's next, that's probably what scares me more than anything. I can't see how to keep the farm going and look after the kids. I can't remember the last time they attended school. Elsa just stopped taking them."

He ran his finger down the side of his glass, wiping away the condensation as he went. "No matter what I tried to do, if Elsa was against it, it wouldn't happen. I can't tell you how many times she threatened to leave and take the kids." Jack closed his eyes. Was he trying to hide the pain from the world? Torment like that reflected out to anyone who payed attention. "Elsa spent Wednesday and Saturday nights in town with whoever and doing whatever, but the rest of the week she'd be at home. But it got worse a little while ago. I'd finish late on the farm and when I got home, the kids would be starving. It happened every night. No food in the cupboards and Elsa missing." Jack sat back and crossed his arms over his broad chest. Lindy's eyes followed the movement. She swallowed hard.

"The relationship side of our marriage ended a while ago, a mutual agreement, but she still wanted me to support her financially and I still wanted to be with the kids." Jack's head dropped and Lindy could see he wanted to elaborate, but something stopped him. He wrestled with his inner demons. Conflict written all over his face.

Jack's focus shifted, he glanced around the pub.

Lindy spoke into the silence. "I remember coming here for meals when I was little. Once every holidays Dad would pay for all of us to come for dinner."

"Yep, it's true what they say about the local being the centre of town. Shooting pool with my mates, dinner out with friends. I often wonder where that life has gone."

"Kids change everything, especially if you put their needs before your own."

"Is that what happened to you? You put the children before yourself?"

Lindy's chuckle sounded more like a cat's cry for help. She could hear it ringing in her own ears. "Apparently I put everyone's needs ahead of my own. It feels like I've got nothing to show for it," she added with a shrug of her shoulders.

"I understand that. I'd love for my family to be a part of town life again. What makes it hard is...see those three at the bar?" Jack pointed to where one of a trio had eyes on their table at all times.

"Had crossed my mind that you might be acquainted."

"Old friends, and from all reports probably the ones who supplied Elsa with the drugs, and gave her a way to fund them. Do you think they see a gutless wonder or a father trying to protect his children?"

"Does it matter? And besides do they ever contemplate their role in destroying families, good decent families?" Lindy questioned glancing over at the three men who were now openly staring at her and Jack.

"Those people are in it for the money. They have no consideration for who they hurt."

"Are these folks judging us for being together here?" The realisation of backlash and how it would affect Jack and his family registered.

"Hell yes," he smirked.

"And you're laughing?" She couldn't hold back her own chuckle.

"Just days after Bradley's arm's broken and Elsa's arrested, here I am in town with another woman. And now you're thinking, 'How could he be so bloody stupid?'"

Lindy sat quietly watching him, she shrugged her right shoulder before agreeing, "Maybe."

"Well, we're out to dinner so I can have a break from the crap that's going on, and as for you, I'm saying thank you for your help with my son in church this evening. They need not know anything other than we are two friends giving each other moral support."

"If you're sure? Truth be told, we probably won't see each other after tonight anyway," Lindy reasoned.

"Exactly. Let's forget those watching us and just enjoy a meal together. Okay?" Jack's voice was more confident now, and it was obvious he had justified his decision to be there.

Her smile grew. Picking up her glass she raised it and said, "To friends."

"To friends," Jack echoed as he clinked his bottle with her glass.

But Lindy wasn't watching the toast, she'd spotted a woman making a beeline for their table. The glare she gave Lindy was unsettling.

"Evening Jack," the woman greeted. Lindy turned back to him, watching the carefree expression transform as his posture slumped slightly. Whoever this woman was, Lindy was sure there was no delight in seeing her.

JACK

Holy cow! What were Tessa and Harry doing here? Jack swallowed hard, forcing a semblance of calm.

"Tessa, hi. Lindy, this is my sister Tessa and her husband Harry, otherwise known as the local sergeant. Guys, this is Lindy Kemp from Melbourne."

"Pleased to meet you," Lindy smiled.

Tessa's brow raised as her gaze swept from her brother to the stranger. Jack could only imagine what scenario she'd already concocted in her evil little head. The conversation paused only for an instant. Tessa's twenty questions began thick and fast.

"Where are the kids, Jack?" Her voice was sharp and face livid. Without drawing a breath, she continued. "How long have you two known each other? And why have I not heard about her?"

Jack attempted a stuttered reply, but she just talked over the top of him.

"So, where did you two meet?" Turning to Lindy, she asked, "How long are you here, Lindy? I haven't seen you around?" Next, Tessa turned to her husband, her look filled with scepticism, "Did you know she existed?"

Her gruff and accusing tone silenced them all.

Jack looked to Harry, begging for his brother-in-law's intervention.

"Well, we'd better find a table and order some food, lovely to meet you, Lindy." To Jack, he added in a whisper, "Thanks for blindsiding us. I suppose I'll have to deal with this one," Harry took Tessa's hand leading her from the table

"Your sister seems lovely."

Jack let out a rumble of laughter. "Do you seriously believe that? She's still checking you out. Be careful with that one."

Lindy scrunched up her face.

"You can't say that and expect me not to turn around."

"If you do, you'll see she's staring daggers at you," Jack grinned, but he kept looking in Tessa's direction.

"I take it she doesn't approve?" Lindy picked up her menu.

Jack closed his eyes and blew out a breath, "Things were difficult with Elsa. She tried to cause a rift between me and my family. I suppose you can say Elsa succeeded and Tessa's the over protective big sister. Yet again."

"Should I tell her that you're safe with me?"

"I don't think so, she wouldn't believe it if Mother Teresa herself was sitting there," Jack pointed to Lindy's side of the table.

Lindy laughed at his mock seriousness. "Surely not."

"Just give her time, once you're ready to head back to Melbourne she'll have exonerated you of any or all of the accusations she's charged you with."

"But I haven't done anything," Lindy stressed every word.

"In her mind you're having dinner with her brother, whose wife was arrested just a few short days ago. It's obvious you'll have your way with me and leave me shattered," he shrugged his shoulders. "Makes perfect sense, you're a city girl."

Lindy's mouth dropped open but nothing ventured forth. She turned around to see Tessa staring back at her. "You're serious, aren't you?"

"Don't take it personally. She'd be the same with any city girl," Jack laughed as Lindy's eyes widened. "She's not bad. In all serious-ness, she'll be my knight in shining armour. It'll be her mission to run the two households and look after us all."

"Will she cope with that?"

"Not even close," he chuckled again, "She's amazing, but no one will cope with such a load. I need to work out an alternative, and soon."

Determining his next step kept him up half the night, his main concern was his children. "Anyway, enough pondering. Let's order. I'm hungry."

OFFER OF SUPPORT

LINDY

𝒲hile waiting for their meals, conversation continued, "What are your plans for the children and the farm."

Jack opened his hands wide and shrugged, "No clue. The only thing I'm certain about is it's all about the children."

They talked, laughed, and both were emotional when they spoke about their families, hers and his. Sharing such intimate topics with a stranger shouldn't have been so comforting. They sat in comfortable silence listening to Cold Chisel's *'Flame Tree'* as it engulfed the room.

"Jack, I have a proposition for you," Lindy ventured once the song finished.

Jack's head tipped to one side, as his lips curled at the edges. "Right?" he stuttered.

"Sorry, that didn't come out properly." Lindy sensed her ears turning the darkest shade of red. She looked down trying to hide her face.

Jack couldn't help laughing, "I'm sure it's not going anywhere it shouldn't, so how about you tell me your suggestion?"

Lindy smirked at Jack's rephrasing of her words, "I need something to do and you've got your hands full with the farm." She drew in a breath, "I was thinking, I could help you out for a bit. Five kids would keep me busy and help keep my mind from spiralling out of control."

Jack raised his eyebrows. "What? Like a nanny?"

Lindy laughed. "I guess so. I'll be your very own Mary Poppins."

Jack gulped down the last of his beer as he considered her offer, "You'd be doing me a great service. I need to plant the crops. They're already late and that poses a problem for harvesting and bringing in money to feed the family. I'll pay you if you're serious."

"Bushman's pie?" the waitress asked as she looked between them.

Neither of them saw her approach.

Jack raised his hand, "Thanks."

The waitress then placed a roasted pumpkin and chicken risotto in front of Lindy. "Enjoy your meals."

"Thanks," Jack and Lindy replied simultaneously.

Lindy saw Jack watching as she forked a scoop of food into her mouth.

"Good?" he asked.

"Mmm, lovely," she smiled.

She could see Jack wanted to ask something. "What is it?" Her intuition wasn't off, hardly ever was.

"I'd like to know a bit about your children."

She crocked out the next few words, "They really are lovely young adults. Especially Cameron and Sophie. Liam has always been his father's favourite and now," she paused, swallowed hard and cleared her throat, mentally arranging her words. There was no other way of saying it, except truthfully, "I can't help but think he's very much his father's son."

"But they've deserted you?"

"I've rung and left messages and heard nothing. I have no explanation for that. My plan is to wait it out and see what happens." Lindy crossed her arms tight against her chest.

They enjoyed easy conversation once they suspended with the topic of family.

"Have you travelled?" Jack asked.

"Yes, mainly when Ralph needed a wife on his arm to close a business deal. Otherwise he'd travel alone." That got Lindy thinking. What had he got up to on those trips when she was home with the children?

Before that train of thinking could spiral, Lindy asked, "What about you? Have you travelled?"

Jack laughed, "Most of my children haven't been more than three hours from here. Occasionally we'd travel to Ballarat to catch up with Elsa's family, but that hasn't happened in the last four years." Picking up his empty bottle, Jack asked, "Would you like another drink?"

"Water would be great thanks," Lindy tracked his path to the bar. The odd person said hi or nodded. But no one attempted to draw him into a conversation. Would the treatment of the locals get to him?

"Here you go," Jack offered the glass of water, lowered his own drink onto the table as he sat down again.

"Have you ever longed to travel?" Lindy questioned.

"You know, recently I have. I'd love the children to see the world and if I don't encourage that, then who will?" The smile caressing Jack's lips was genuine.

"What are you thinking about? It must have been something good."

JACK

"My kids," Jack chuckled. "I need to change everything." Holding his finger up he revealed a little more, "In the hospital it occurred to me I probably should sell the farm to look after the children." Jack picked up his utensils and continued, "You know, although I don't want to sell, the idea doesn't scare me as much as it probably should."

"You seem at peace with your decision," Lindy offered. "What will you do for an income?"

"I'm not sure. Maybe get a job on another farm in the area." Jack couldn't remember the last time he was this relaxed. He gave Lindy a crooked smiled before taking another mouthful of beer.

"Well Jack Saunders, I wish you well with your sea change." Lindy paused for a moment, "Funny, isn't it, we are both at crossroads in our lives?"

"It's hard when those crossroads are caused by others and we're the innocent party," Jack conceded.

"At least my children don't need my support every day. You have five dependents."

"Five under the age of thirteen," Jack met her eyes, "Five of the most amazing children I've ever known. They've been through a great deal, I owe them the world." Jack forked the last bit of pie into his mouth and pushed his plate away. "Thank you, I feel like a different man returning to my kids than I was when I left my parents place a couple of hours ago. I needed this."

"My pleasure and thank you." Lindy wiped her mouth on the serviette before neatly folding it and placing it on her empty plate.

Although reluctant to leave, Jack needed to get the children home. It was getting late. "Thanks again for a lovely evening and for your help with Bradley at mass." He hesitated, was her offer to help him genuine.

"Are you serious about your offer? I'd understand if you've changed your mind."

"Oh, I am serious. I love kids, I'm sure we'll get along fine." Lindy stood. "I need to keep busy otherwise my other option was actually to return home and face the mess awaiting me there, but I'd prefer not to. Not until I clear my head, and I need time for that."

"How long do you plan on being here? Just working out how much time I have to make my next set of plans."

"Let's say three weeks, then we'll see how you're positioned. Will that work for you?"

"Perfect! You don't understand what a relief this is."

Jack guided her over towards his sister and brother-in-law. On instinct, he placed his hand in the small of her back, loving the way Lindy leaned back into his touch. He couldn't help but notice a tingle travelling along his arm. It had been a long time since these feelings invaded his body. Jack dropped his hand before they reached Tessa and Harry's table. Craving the memory of her closeness.

JACK

"Do you mind if we pull up a chair?" Jack asked as they stood beside his sister's table.

"Sure," Harry agreed. "What's up?"

"Lindy has offered to help with the children for the next three weeks," Jack ignored the raised eyebrow from Tessa.

"It means I'll be able to get the crops in and still know the children are safe and back in school."

Tessa spoke up before Harry said anything, "How long are you staying?" her neutral tone asked.

"I've taken three weeks long service leave from my business." Lindy smiled.

"When will she start?" Harry asked.

"Well, tomorrow if Tessa's available to stay with her so I can get some work done on the farm?"

"Sure," Tessa's voice slowly easing. "I'll be there about ten. Would that suit?"

"Perfect." Jack nodded.

"Bye, lovely to meet you, I'll see you in the morning." Lindy needed to work with this woman to help Jack, so she'd win her over.

Jack walked Lindy to her motel room. "You'd better get some sleep. My mob will keep you on your toes tomorrow. Thanks so much for this."

"My pleasure, I'll see you about ten," This distraction would occupy her mind and exhaust her body. More importantly, she believed she'd enjoy the opportunity.

Jack repeated the directions to the farm and said goodnight.

He walked away feeling a tad lighter about the challenge ahead.

"Jack."

He turned back to her, his face scrunched up. Had she'd changed her mind in those couple of seconds?

She held up her phone, "Maybe we should exchange numbers."

He gave her a smile and a nod.

"Good thinking." Jack read out his number, and Lindy typed it into her phone. A few seconds later she sent a message to him and heard his phone ping. "Thank you, I've got that."

"Sorry, should have thought of that earlier. I always get my clients to give me their numbers and wait to see if they receive my message. When you're mentoring people, you leave nothing to chance."

"I like your thinking. Goodnight," he gave her another wave and turned towards the pub again. Tomorrow was another day and hopefully they could provide support for each other and discover the strength required in moving on.

SHORT-TERM DIVERSION

LINDY

*L*indy stretched out her limbs after a solid night's sleep, completely at ease in Chester's Run. For the first time in a while she genuinely smiled. How would her day pan out?

Jack and Tessa explained how much work there was. Getting the children back to school was the family's highest priority.

Lindy enjoyed an early breakfast in the hotel's dining room and then made her way back to her room. Funny how expectation made her feel present in the world again. Since Wednesday she somehow become a bystander in her own life. No longer. The idea of being needed eased the tension gripping her. Hopefully, her input would make a difference to this family.

The drive to the farm was as easy as Jack had described. Lindy listened to her music, sometimes singing along to her favourite tunes. Something in the air indicated the first signs of turning things around. In truth, Lindy looked forward to this challenge, proving she could move on. With or without her children's approval.

LINDY

Once the car turned down the long driveway, an unusual sensation tingled in the pit of her stomach. Uncertain what this meant, Lindy gripped the steering wheel a little tighter and surged forward, focusing straight ahead.

Her life would progress as of now!

She would give this everything she could to help Jack's family. An image of little Bradley popped into her head and she couldn't help but smile.

As she came to a stop next to a silver SUV, Jack and Tessa walked out the front door to greet her.

"Good morning," Lindy called as she emerged from her car.

"Thanks for coming. Come on in," Jack held open the screen door for Lindy to follow Tessa inside. "Please excuse the state of the house." Jack grimaced and his nostrils flared.

In the lounge, the children slumped in seats as if waiting for something they were certain of. Lindy noticed the sullen expressions and wanted to sigh.

"Okay," Jack began, "Well this is Nate, my eldest, Evie and Joanna my two girls," he tapped their heads gently. "Then Caleb and Bradley," he pointed to the little fellow on the floor, "Guys, you remember Lindy from the bakery and church. She'll be helping us out for the next few weeks."

"Hi," were the strained responses. Lindy watched closely as the younger children edged closer to their father. Her heart tightened as wide eyes stared back at her.

"Lovely to meet you again," Lindy understood the importance of being open and calm. This was a tough time for the family and a friendly face may help ease the tension.

Next Tessa introduced her three, "These are mine. This is Ben, Lachie and Penny."

"Good morning," she noted the easy-going nature of Tessa's children compared to the nervous glances from Jack's. "Wonderful to meet you all," Lindy clasped her hands in front of her. How could she not feel for these children? The sad expression on their faces reflected the pain they'd suffered over the last little while.

Bradley lay on the floor kicking and reaching out for her with his good arm, "Mumma, Mumma, Mumma," he was determined to get her attention.

Bending down next to him, Lindy took his good hand in hers, "Hello Bradley. Did you sleep well last night?" she brushed his long fringe from his eyes.

He giggled and kicked his legs even harder.

"I think that's a yes," Lindy hedged before standing up again.

Jack smiled and nodded. "He didn't do too badly. We all managed a good night's sleep." Turning to the other children, Jack said, "Okay you guys, off you go. We'll call when lunch is ready." Once the lounge was empty apart from the three adults and Bradley, Jack stepped towards the hallway. "Well come on, let's show you the disaster that's our home."

Looking around, there was ample work here. The task assigned to her didn't include judging anyone, so instead she listened to Jack and Tessa as they recommended a starting point in all the chaos.

"Well, if you girls are okay here, I might head out and try to sow a paddock before dinner." Jack headed towards the door.

"That's fine. What about lunch?" Lindy called as an afterthought.

"I'll eat later, I know the children are fine, so the crop is my next priority. You have my number if you need me for anything, right?" She didn't get to answer before he bolted from the house.

Jack kissed each of the children as she watched him all but sprint to the shed.

They spent the next hour organising a routine for the coming week. Tessa and Lindy walked through the house looking at what needed doing.

Lindy saw emotion grip Tessa on seeing the full extent of the house and the children's belongings. Tessa struggled with the reality of Jack's situation.

How much of what happened did the children understand?

After a while Tessa led them back to the kitchen. The now speechless woman looked around for a second time, uncertain of where to begin. Eventually Tessa spoke, "Sorry, I can't believe what's happened." Tears leaked down her face. "The children's precious things," Tessa's face paled as she fumbled for her hanky. "All gone. She must have pawned the lot. How could she?"

Stepping up, Lindy wrapped Tessa in a comforting hug and let her cry it out. Trying to keep this from the children.

The most obvious and devastating thing to Lindy was these children suffered so severely at the hands of their own mother. She refused to be caught up in the middle of their nightmare, her job was to help them regain a normal life.

By the time Tessa calmed down, Lindy searched the cupboards, pantry. Yes, as predicted, all were as bare as the children's wardrobes. Appliances were obviously missing and the cutlery and crockery were a mismatched collection of essentials. Opening the fridge next, Lindy bit back a sigh and shook her head. This explained Jack's speedy departure, he didn't want to witness her reaction. Lindy gathered a notebook from her handbag, one she kept close for ideas and sudden impulses, and planned a shopping list.

Whilst she did this, she made two cups of tea and placed one in front of Tessa and kept the other with her as she worked. It was only when the boys came in asking for lunch did Tessa rally herself.

But before she could speak, Lindy responded to the boys in her usual comforting tone, "Okay, today's my treat—hamburgers, fish and chips or the bakery. What would you guys prefer?" A wide grin smeared across Nate's face. "Go on, gather everyone, we're heading into town." Lindy declared with a wave of her hands.

"You don't have to do that. I'll just get hotdogs or something." Tessa's voice sounded low and strained.

"Please let me do this. If I'm not mistaken, the kids would enjoy an outing." Lindy could see Tessa wanted to argue so she rushed on. "This has been a shock for you, I can see that. I suggest we work together to get the children ready for school tomorrow. We need to plan what to tackle next. If there's one thing I excel at, it's organisation." Lindy's brow danced whilst gathering her handbag and the shopping list, ready to tackle the essentials.

The children rushed in ready for lunch in town.

"I think you're onto something," Tessa mustered a smile, unable to deny the children this little window of pleasure amid the disappointment their lives had become. With Bradley settled on her hip, Lindy pushed on as Tessa succumbed to the outing and followed everyone out to the cars.

PLANNING AND PARTNERSHIP

LINDY

"Over there, Ben," Tessa spotted a vacant picnic table right next to the playground. Lindy settled Bradley into his pram when Tessa turned to her, "Look at the difference having lunch in town has made. The children needed this."

Jack's children weren't the only ones, Tessa suffered also.

"It's good to see them smiling even if it's still a struggle," Lindy replied.

The children were hungry. Time to order some food, "Okay, what would everyone like for lunch?" Lindy called before they took off to the playground.

The quiet mumbles were adamant they wanted food from the bakery. Lindy spoke to each child taking down their order.

"Are you happy to stay here?" she asked Tessa as the children reached the play equipment. "I'll take Nate and Ben with me."

"Thanks, I'd love to stay with them. Being their aunty from a distance has been so difficult."

"Good," Lindy said as she turned to her designated helpers. "Come on boys, let's go organise some food, I'm starving." The two boys fell in step beside Lindy. "Okay, which way to the bakery?"

JACK

The tractor kept a straight line as Jack continued up and down the rows sowing his crop. He'd picked up the hay contract with the local horse stud a while back and for the first time in a long while a glimmer of hope simmered. Maybe he'd be able to meet the terms of the contract in time. The stiffness in his body increased, the fact Elsa hurt the family hit harder and harder. Fortunately, before his mind could spiral, his phone rang.

"Hi Jack," Tessa's voice comforted him.

"Hey. Is everything okay?" He worked hard to tamp down his need to hang up and hide from any further imminent disaster.

"Everything's fine. I wanted to let you know we're in town to do the shopping and have lunch at the park." Tessa's swallowing rang out, "They're so subdued compared to the other kids here. I can't believe what Elsa's done to them." Jack's ears rang as if blocking any more unwanted words. Then Tessa added, "But, I must say, Lindy's great."

"Perfect," he gulped, "That's music to my ears." overriding the ringing only seconds earlier. He heard the unevenness in his own voice.

"Yeah, it's a relief for me too. What time will you be back?" Tessa was giving them both a chance to settle their emotions.

"Hopefully about four. Will you be back by then?"

"Yep should be. Lindy's written out a shopping list so we'll head back after that's sorted," the tight knot in the pit of his stomach was releasing ever so slightly.

"Okay, I'll see you then."

Still jarred by the conversation, Jack wiped away a stray tear, not sure why he was crying.

LINDY

Harry plonked down the heavy tray of food in front of Tessa with a groan, "Hell, this lot eat way too much," he joked as she spun away from him. Lindy saw him walk around the table to stand in front of Tessa.

"Hey Hun, why the tears?" he pulled her into a side hug and waited.

"Boys, round up the others," Lindy was giving Tessa a moment to compose herself.

"Thanks for your help, Harry," Lindy handed him his beef salad roll and a bottle of water.

"Where did you run into each other?" Tessa choked out.

Lindy presumed this was a deflection tactic.

"At Ivy's, of course," Harry laughed, "Lindy and the boys walked in and she quickly enlisted my help," Harry climbed onto the bench seat beside his wife.

Tessa only nodded as the children ran to the table, their faces rosy and eyes large.

Once Lindy and Tessa distributed the food, each child sat with their meal and a large milkshake. Silence invaded as the Saunders children's huge eyes studied their lunch before diving in. How bad had life been over the last couple of months?

Harry made the children laugh with his silly dad jokes and winked at the women when they shared a smile. The food gave the children energy they'd previously lacked.

"Thanks," Nate collected the rubbish before he ventured to the playground.

"My pleasure," Lindy focused on Caleb as he tried to gather his empty wrapper in his small hands.

"Here, give me that," Tessa said, "Go join the others."

"Nate, how did you get up there?" Caleb called out, tracking his brother on the high bars as the adults watched on.

"Hang on a minute," Nate made a quick descent and spent the next few minutes guiding Caleb safely up and down the climbing gym.

"Hey look Aunty Tessa," Caleb called from the top of the dome.

"Wow, look at you. Be careful up there," Tessa cautioned forcing a smile.

When it was only the three of them, Harry asked, "Now tell me, why the tears?"

"I didn't understand what was happening. Maybe when I tried to convince her to get help, I pushed her over the edge. How could a mother put anything ahead of her own children?" Turning to Lindy, she added, "I thought she'd listen to me back then, but…"

"What you did was with Jack and the children's best interests at heart. One thing I know about a person with an addiction…any addiction," Lindy was speaking from her own experience here, "They'll justify it to themselves, whatever it takes. They have no regard for anyone else."

Tessa nodded and looked to Harry, "You won't believe it," her previously empty stare suddenly found life. "The children's precious gifts from when they were babies have gone." Tessa's hands flew as she spoke, "And kitchen appliances and God knows what else. Gone." Her reply was a rush of words and her overly bright eyes filled with tears again.

Harry tightened his hold, "That's addiction for you, love. She would have done everything and anything to get her hands on the money to buy the drugs. But we have to move forward. Don't waste energy on what's happened." He pulled her in even closer, "Hey, they'll be okay, we're here for them. And with Lindy's help, Jack will see it through. You know as well as I do, how much he loves those kids." Looking at Lindy, he continued, "Where do we go from here?"

"Food. And the children don't seem to have much in the way of clothes, so if you don't mind Tessa, would you help me go through everything and this week we'll go shopping."

"I'm not sure how much money is available for anything. We'll talk to Jack." Tessa's now controlled voice replied.

"Okay, but I won't be compromising on the food, I'll pay for today's shop. Sustenance and stability are the most important things for these children right now."

The conversation stopped as Bradley woke up. Lindy watched as Tessa carefully picked him up and cuddled him close, trying to support his broken arm. She kept dropping juicy kisses on his forehead, making him giggle.

"You're so beautiful," she told him as a smile spread across his adorable face. Lindy found the Vegemite roll she bought for his lunch and handed it to Tessa. He devoured every piece hungrily as Tessa handed the torn bits to him, next he drank his bottle. His eyes grew wide as he sucked harder on the teat.

Tessa questioned aloud, "Why do you think he's drinking so fast?"

"Well," Lindy began, "Considering how little food there was in the house, maybe he wasn't getting formula from his mother. Maybe it was only water or watered-down milk."

"That woman has a lot to answer for. If I never see her again, it will be way too soon."

"Tessa, Elsa's their mother. We know what's good for the children, but it's not up to us. The courts will decide. It requires dire circumstances to keep a mother from her children," Harry explained, "It's possible Elsa could be back in their lives soon."

"If that's the case, the courts are wrong. No child should have to suffer like they have." She all but screeched as she ran her hand through Bradley's fringe again. Tessa finished with, "Especially this one."

Harry kissed his wife and passed an assessing glance over the children, "Well, that's all for another day. How about I meet you guys back at the farm after my shift?"

"Sounds good," Tessa kissed him again.

Harry called and waved to the children before walking back towards Park Road.

LINDY

Lost for a moment, the two women sat in silence.

Tessa looked up from the bundle in her arms, "Do you know why we were banished from the farm?"

"No." Admittedly, the question crossed Lindy's mind.

Tessa sucked in a breath. "Something was wrong. We could all see it. We called Jack and asked him to meet us at Mum and Dad's, but he couldn't get away, so instead he told us to come over Wednesday night the following week." Tessa shifted Bradley in her arms, "We got there and Elsa was nowhere to be seen." She paused and sat for a moment, "We bought fish and chips and sent the children outside to eat. Mum and Dad, Harry and I talked to Jack and he opened up and told us everything."

Tessa paused again. Lindy wasn't sure whether she was ordering her facts or struggling with the conversation.

"That's how we found out about Elsa's," Tessa lifted one hand making air quotes, "*nights off*. Together we devised a plan that would see Mum and Dad arriving after Elsa left to go into town." Tessa looked around at the children. Not that she needed to because Lindy just finished her head count.

"They would bring food and feed the kids, do the bath and bed routine. It was a win-win because Elsa wasn't around yelling at the children and everyone relaxed and enjoyed themselves. Mum found it hard not to clean or do anything else, because we didn't want Elsa to work out what we were up to." Lindy handed Tessa the cloth to mop up Bradley's face. "It all went south one-night when Elsa returned home, she'd forgotten something. Mum and Dad told us how aggressive she'd become. They were both so upset by it. She warned us all off after I tried to encourage her to get help for her addiction, that must have been the final straw."

"Don't blame yourself. What you did was admirable. And your parents too."

"You know, she threatened to take the kids away from him if he didn't tell us to stay away. Jack's never given in over anything until she made that threat. We were all walking on eggshells, hoping she didn't follow through with that scheme of hers."

They fell silent, and Lindy could see Tessa trying yet again to settle herself. Her brows furrowed and she swallowed noisily.

After a while Tessa spoke again, "I want to help you get sorted as much as possible, we'll need to talk to Jack. He'll need to understand what we have to do."

Lindy drew out her trusted notepad and flicked to the first clean page, "Tell me what you're thinking," Lindy waited.

Tessa rattled off everything she could think of, "School uniforms and clothes are a priority. Oh, and bloody haircuts, those poor kids. It's driving them nuts, especially the boys."

"Sounds like it's driving you just as nuts," Lindy teased as Tessa yet again pushed Bradley's fringe out of his eyes.

"You're not wrong," Tessa's grin finally reached her eyes.

Continuing with the list, she added, "Food shopping. Shoes, they all need decent shoes. I'd like to see the state of the bills too. Hopefully Jack's been paying them, not Elsa."

Tessa sighed and stood up. Sitting still wasn't helping her process things. "How do we help them move forward?" This must have been playing on her mind because the question came out with such force.

"Talk to them. Ask what they want. You're showing them you care and love them. Maybe and this is only my perception," Lindy reiterated, "Maybe, they're questioning why none of you were there to help."

Tessa spun around to face Lindy, "Oh shit, do you really think they believed that?" Tessa backed up as if struck, then her large strides ate up the dirt as she paced again, "What do I say? How do I approach it with them?"

"Maybe we should take our lead from Jack. He's the one in the trenches with them." Lindy gathered up the last of the lunch wrappers and threw them in the nearby bin.

"Yes, I suppose you're right. This entire thing makes me so angry," Tessa hissed through gritted teeth.

"Harry's right though, we can't change what happened. Our job is to help them move forward." Lindy tried to calm her. "It will be a rough road ahead, so how about we focus on what the children want from us."

Tessa nodded, her head bobbing as she sucked in her bottom lip.

Lindy checked her watch and scanned the children, "I think I'll head to the supermarket? You okay here?"

"Yeah fine. Sorry Lindy, I don't mean to dwell, but it all hurts so much," Tessa's face read like a ticking time bomb. She was dealing with something so foreign to her, and Lindy could see the struggle it took to process it all.

"I know. But for now, just keep them occupied and smiling, okay?"

Tessa nodded and forced herself to smile.

"I'll take the car and meet you back here as soon as I've finished," Lindy didn't wait for a reply, she walked away and then turned back, "Oh maybe we should exchange numbers," she waved her phone in the air to exaggerate her point.

Searching through her bag, Tessa sighed, "At least one of us is thinking. It's definitely not me."

"Force of habit. I always made sure my clients gave me their number so I could text them, that way they had no excuses." Lindy explained.

Over an hour later, Lindy pulled into a parking spot at the park. After collecting a few shopping bags from the back of the car, she headed for their picnic table.

"Hi Lindy," Caleb called, as he swung upside down on the monkey bars.

"There's Lindy. Can I help her?" Nate asked, his voice now sounding more confident.

"Good boy. Yes," Tessa said and the kids abandoned the playground and ran over to help.

"What's in there?" Ben asked as he took a carry bag from her overloaded hands.

"Fruit," Lindy handed out all the shopping bags to eager helpers. "I'll be back in a minute, take those to Aunty Tessa."

This time when Lindy returned, she held a slab of bottled water.

Nate ran back, "I'll take that," Lindy handed it over and walked beside him as he carried the water to the picnic table.

Tessa distributed bananas, apples, pears, and oranges to the children. While Lindy used the car key to cut into the plastic surrounding the slab of water and watched on as each child reached for a bottle.

"Thanks," they chorused.

"Oh yum," Joanna bit into a crunchy red apple, the juice running down her chin.

"Nate," Caleb asked, "When was the last time we had fruit at home?"

Such an innocent question told Lindy and Tessa more than they wanted to know. After a quick glance at each other, they shifted their focus to the food on the table.

"Ages," Nate answered. "The last time Dad bought fruit Mum yelled at him for wasting money on crap."

Hoping to change the subject, Lindy told Tessa, "I bought strawberries for Bradley. They might be easier for him to eat," Lindy handed over the punnet, intent on keeping Tessa occupied and not mulling over what Nate and Caleb let slip.

MAKING A DIFFERENCE

JACK

*E*nthusiastic smiles and rosy-cheeked children greeted their father as he came in from the farm. The sight caused tears to burn the back of his eyes.

"Guess what we had for lunch?" Caleb asked, bouncing on the balls of his feet as Jack walked out of the shed towards the house.

"What might that be?" he swallowed back his emotion, and scooped his six-year-old son in his arms.

"Lindy and Aunty Tessa took us to the park, and we had food from Ivy's bakery." Caleb wrapped his arms around his father's neck, "Could we go back to the bakery again, Dad?"

"Hahaha. One day. Where's Aunty Tessa?" Jack asked glancing in the kitchen window, seeing a silhouette of a woman working away.

"Inside somewhere," Jack put Caleb down and watched as he took off after his brother and cousins.

Jack grinned at the sight of the girls sitting under a tree chatting away. "Hey girls," he said, walking towards the backdoor.

"Hi Dad," Joanna called, "Have you finished on the tractor today?"

"Yep, sure have." He swept away her long fringe and kissed her forehead, "Did you have a good time at the park?"

"Yeah. Lindy got us lots of food and we played for ages."

He could get lost in one of her beaming smiles, and couldn't help but display one of his own. At least he and his children found something to smile about. No walking on eggshells and being careful not to annoy anyone. Relief flooded him with this realisation.

He noticed a change in his children since he left this morning. He charged Tessa and Lindy with the responsibility of five lost, sullen children who because of circumstances, youngsters their age should never hear about, let alone see. This afternoon they morphed into a semblance of their former selves.

He ventured inside to see both women locked in conversation.

Were they arguing?

He listened for a minute. No. The harsh tone referenced the situation, not each other. Jack prayed these two would see eye to eye. Would it be asking too much for at least an undercurrent of mutual respect because expecting friendship probably asked way too much? Tessa's introduction to Lindy showed a rather testy side of his sister last night at the pub. Watching them he concluded Lindy must be a forgiving soul. The consideration filled him with hope as he stepped towards the kitchen door. Jack desperately needed these two women to work in harmony for the benefit of him and his children as they moved forward.

In the kitchen Lindy and Tessa discussed the availability of school uniforms and bags.

"Hi Jack," Lindy turned towards the back bench. There was a plate of food in her hand, "Here's your salad I'll just heat up the pie Ivy sent home for you," her smile relaxed him.

"That woman has been my saviour over the last month, sneaking food to the children when she could." He walked through the kitchen towards the hallway, "I'll go wash up, thanks." Taking two steps, Jack turned and headed back to the counter, snagged a banana before retreating again, both women laughed at him.

Jack walked back into the kitchen with fresh clothes and wet hair. His two-minute shower and change did wonders for him.

"Thanks for this," Jack offered as he tucked in at the breakfast bar.

LINDY

It impressed Lindy how well she and Tessa worked together when they returned home. They began by cleaning out the fridge, freezer, and pantry before putting the shopping away. Next Lindy began organising dinner while Tessa went in search of school uniforms, bags, lunch boxes and drink bottles.

"Anything I can do?" Nate asked Lindy as the boys grabbed a piece of fruit from the overloaded basket.

"Yes, Aunty Tessa needs you to find school shoes and hats."

"I'm on it. I hid them in Dad's cupboard in the bungalow," he took off at a run, with Lachie, Ben and Caleb in tow. Lindy could see the news of going back to school boosted his spirits to no end. His normally lethargic walk became animated and purposeful.

"Oh, that reminds me," Jack said around a mouthful of food. "There's a lot of the kids keepsakes I saved when I noticed Elsa was selling off our stuff. It's all in the bungalow."

Lindy glanced to Tessa as her emotions took over again.

"I thought she'd pawned it all," Tessa swiped at a tear trickling down her face.

"Some things she did but not much, I hid most of it. The kitchen appliances and stuff I didn't worry about but the children's treasures I hid as soon as I worked out what she was up to." Jack sat back from the bench. After a moment his hands balled into fists. "After she'd sold off everything she could, well let's just say she turned to selling her soul."

No one spoke. What could you say to that?

Jack gathered his dirty dishes and moved towards the sink when he collided with Caleb, "Hey slow down there, buddy, what's the rush?"

"School Dad. We're getting ready for school," Caleb replied as he bounced off his father's legs and continued on his way.

It was enough to break the silence, giving them a reason to laugh.

The afternoon was busier than Bourke Street at rush hour. Lindy sidestepped as the children ran around in search of this and that, in preparation for school the next day.

Dinner was ready and baking done for the children's lunches tomorrow. A large plate of Anzac biscuits, seemed to be mysteriously disappearing. Lindy turned her attention to organising the pantry in a child friendly way. The children needed to help, so Lindy intended to keep what they needed in arm's reach especially for the younger ones.

Tessa found and washed the school uniforms, which swayed in the warm spring breeze on the clothesline. She'd cleaned all the school bags out, wiped them and put them out the front to air. Black school shoes were polished, even though they were on their last legs and pins and hair ties were sorted for the girls.

Lindy scrubbed and sterilised lunch boxes and drink bottles leaving them on the designated shelf in the pantry. With a smile on her face, she went in search of Tessa.

"Do you think Harry could stop at the supermarket for me on his way here?" she asked when she found Tessa and Jack organising wardrobes in the girls' bedroom.

"Sure thing, what do you need?" Tessa took her phone out of her back pocket.

"Fruit." Lindy struggled to hold back a laugh.

"No way. You bought heaps, I can vouch for that." Tessa's raised brow accompanied a grin.

Studying Tessa, Lindy could see how pretty she was once the stress eased. Much like her brother.

"All gone. Every piece."

Both women turned accusing gazes at Jack. He raised his two large calloused hands.

"Hey, I only pinched a banana. And boy, it was good. I can't recall the last time we had fruit in the house," his eyes darkened. A cloud passed over Tessa's face and Lindy recalled the conversation between Nate and Caleb at the park. Maybe Tessa thought about that too?

LINDY

By the time Tessa and Harry left, and Jack and Lindy put the children to bed, they were both exhausted. As Lindy waited for the last load of washing to finish, it occurred to her their initial agreement of this being temporary was unrealistic? Each and every one of these children had begun to trust and depend on her, even Joanna who asked about her mother at bedtime. Without question, young Bradley was her favourite. A feeling of belonging hit, not here on this farm, but with this family. From the way the children reacted to her today, an inkling of inseparability dawned.

Heavy boots on the lino drew her attention. Jack walked into the laundry. She eyed his powerful body from a distance. Was it possible to feel her pupils dilate because Lindy was sure she recognised a change?

He was a tall man and his broad shoulders made her feel, well, too much. Especially for a recently separated woman.

"What are you doing? You really need to get some sleep. You must be exhausted?" His eyes settled on her.

Admittedly, she'd worked non-stop since she arrived this morning. "I just need to hang out this load," Lindy began as the whirling noise of the spin cycle rang out, "Tomorrow I can start cleaning the rooms." Lindy folded the last of the washing, "Tessa did an amazing job today cleaning out the wardrobes. I love how you and your sister are close."

Jack smiled.

"My brothers have always been my strength, I'll never underestimate how much they protect me."

"Yep, I know what you mean. Tessa's wonderful. She flies off a bit, but she means well. She's really taken to you. You must have endeared yourself there," Jack teased.

Lindy tried to keep her eyes off his tanned, muscular body, which seemed to hug the black T-shirt he wore. He looked worthy of anyone's attention as he stood perched against the doorframe.

"After last night, I wasn't sure she'd talk to me." She failed to hide a grin. "Yes, I like your sister very much." The machine began its last cycle, Lindy crossed her arms and leant against the sink, intent on waiting it out. She let out a sigh, which had nothing to do with the washing machine and everything to do with the feelings whirring for the man across the room.

"Have you got a minute? Something I want to show you." He turned and walked towards the kitchen without waiting for her reply, so she followed.

Passing the fridge, he grabbed a set of keys from the rack on the wall and continued out through the glass doors, into the backyard.

"Tessa and I wondered if you might prefer to move into the bungalow. It will need a good clean out, but the furniture is all there. When things got tough, I slept out here and eventually moved in permanently. Some nights all five kids joined me," he led her across an expanse of weeds and dirt, scattered with some grass runners.

Jack opened the bungalow door and switched on the lights. He stepped aside and Lindy entered, walked around the small but well-furnished room. The kitchenette and bathroom were old but in working order. The bed looked purposeful, minus any delicate trimmings. The only thing she wasn't sure of was, should she be out here by herself with Jack and his family?

"The fridge and stove both work," Jack looked around the kitchen, "Maybe this is a better option than travelling to and from town every day, it could save you some money." Jack turned to Lindy. "But I'll understand if you decide against it."

Something about his face told her he was sincere in his offer to help save her some time on the road each day. Her days would be full and this would be to her advantage, especially if Jack worked till late on the farm.

"Sounds perfect. I'll check out of my motel room tomorrow, if you don't mind. I'd love to move in."

"Excellent, I'll wash the bedding and hang it out before I go to sleep."

They walked back towards the house, their arms full of washing. Jack stopped and turned to look at her.

"I really can't thank you enough for everything today."

Oh, hell, why was she drawn to that gorgeous crooked smile?

"These guys haven't been this happy for months. They couldn't stop telling me about lunch in the park. Not just them either, Tessa and Harry were also singing your praises. You have made a positive impact on my family."

Lindy noticed a buzz between them. Swallowing hard, she steadied herself before speaking, "Thanks, but your family has made an enormous impact on me as well. You're extremely blessed with such a beautiful family." Lindy tried to avoid his adorable light brown eyes, but his gaze drew her in.

Her body experienced a surge of…something. Maybe moving in wouldn't be her brightest choice. But looking at the offer logically, the use of the bungalow would save her time on the road and maybe give her an extra hour's sleep every day. Those were pros she couldn't ignore.

Lindy gulped for air when their eyes met again. Eventually, Jack turned without another word and led her into the house.

JACK

The warm sensation zipping through his body startled Jack. He stood on the front veranda waving goodbye as the taillights of Lindy's car travelled the length of his long driveway. Once she turned left onto the highway towards town, he allowed himself to think about the moment they shared outside. In her own way this woman was stunning, her appearance didn't match Elsa's. No, Lindy's beauty was more her mannerisms, gentleness, and devotion she'd shown in the last couple of days.

Sitting on the swing, he rocked back and forth, remembering the change in his children. The stranger who drove away was responsible for the smiles on their faces. Not sure how much time passed in his meditative state, Jack pushed himself to his feet, sent a silent prayer of thanks to the heavens above and walked inside.

He admired the clean, organised kitchen. Such harmony and order hadn't been in his life for so long. His mind circled back to his chance meeting with this wonderful woman. She'd only been here for a day and now that she'd left, the house lost its earlier cheer and warmth. Sighing to himself, Jack locked the doors and turned out the lights. Tomorrow was another day with so many important decisions to face and he needed a clear head to make them.

He spoke with Harry earlier regarding Elsa. Trying to process everything Harry said about the process she faced. He carefully considered the children's mother. The necessity to protect his children was paramount, but looking after Elsa was also important for him to move forward. In years to come, telling the children he'd done everything he could for their mother, in his mind proved vital. Therefore, his goal for tomorrow would be to devise a plan that meant he could live comfortably with the outcome.

Lying in bed, Jack's mind returned to the angel who graced them with her presence today. The stability she would provide over the next few weeks meant peace and serenity, which he and his family deserved. Drifting off his calm mind and exhausted body sent him into a tranquil sleep restoring his energy for another day. A smile settled on his lips, Lindy would be back to help in the morning.

ENSCONCED IN THE JOB

LINDY

*L*indy's alarm stirred her before dawn appeared. She listened to the sweet melody which woke her daily. Her Grandpa instilled in her a love of classical music from a young age. This reminder of him had her pondering what he would think of her current circumstances. Hopefully, he would have understood her decision to walk away from her marriage and get away for a while. He'd been a man of high morals and an important member of the community. To him your good name was paramount. Being a divorced woman probably wouldn't meet his superior standards. That thought saddened Lindy, none of this was her doing. Mentally shaking herself, Lindy focused more on her day ahead than on what other's opinions of her were.

Dragging herself out of bed, she finished the last bit of packing. A slight thrill passed over her thinking about the five children who kept her so busy yesterday. She needed a total shift in focus to get her through the next few weeks. Deep down she accepted the ploy, moving her attention from herself to someone else in need. She looked forward to helping Jack put some structure back into his family's lives.

Glancing around the room, Lindy ensured she packed everything. Using the bungalow at Jack's made sense. The fewer trips into town for the day, the better. And besides, this way she'd have more time to get the house back into shape.

The sun peaked over the ranges as Lindy made her way out to the farm. The chilly spring morning promised another glorious day ahead. Spring in Chester's Run was another of the warmer seasons, unlike Melbourne, renowned for its four seasons in one day.

Heading down the long drive, she could see Jack out the front having a cuppa, indulging in the blissfulness of the quiet morning. Was this his morning ritual?

Pulling the car to a stop in front of the house, their eyes met through the windscreen. His relaxed posture matched the gentle smile he gave her. Lindy pondered his face, a different person to the man she met a few days ago. Yesterday his worries eased, he was a changed man, a sight which stole the breath from her lungs. The man sitting on the weathered wooden bench was gorgeous. His messy brown hair, which like his sons', was way too long. His few day old scruff, on some would look unkempt, on Jack, it only made him look more rugged and handsome. Those piercing brown eyes were hypnotising. Swallowing hard and distracting herself, Lindy broke eye contact to collect her handbag and this morning's newspaper from the passenger seat, giving her valuable time to refocus. Drawing in deep breaths, she got out. Jack was walking down the front path to meet her. Her ten-second lecture centred around the mantra echoing in her head.

This is for the kids, don't lose sight of the end goal.

She opened the car door and called out a nervous, "Morning."

"Want a drink? Best to make the most of the calm before the storm."

"Thanks, that would be great."

Jack waved towards her car. "Have you brought all your stuff?"

"Yes, it's in the boot." Lindy could feel her tension as if it was a second skin. Even her fingers tingled for some stupid reason.

"Okay, why don't you drive around to the bungalow," Jack hitched his thumb over his shoulder, "And I'll meet you out the back."

The rising sun created amazing streaks of oranges and reds across the sky. Lindy stopped outside the bungalow taking it in. Something about this place appealed to her. Shaking herself of those deliberations, she focused on unpacking the car. Before she got to the boot for her suitcase, Jack was hauling it out.

"Where do you want it?" he was relaxed and full of smiles.

"Just on the bed, thanks," Lindy closed the boot of the car as he carried the suitcase in and settled it on the unmade bed.

"Your tea's on the table," he pointed to a black mug, "This place served me well for over a year. I hope you'll be comfortable here," Jack stood in the doorway of the familiar dwelling.

"It'll be great." She wrapped both hands around the mug for comfort, before inhaling the scent. The crisp spring morning was warming up. The early rising sun stretched its rays over the property. They took a seat outside the bungalow, drinking in the aromas and the sights of the morning.

"This is spectacular. I don't think I've seen anything as beautiful as this." She focused on the scenery.

"Not sure how much longer I'll have it. Especially when I'll probably have to sell up to take care of the kids." Jack ran his fingers through his messy brown hair.

Lindy tried to imagine Jack with close-cropped hair. Did he normally wear it short? She smiled to herself. Never had her mind raced off on such tangents.

"Do you know what you'll do?" she searched for comfortable conversation.

JACK

"I want to get the crop in, either way I'm better to have the paddocks sewn. But when I spoke with Dad the other night, we agreed we need to sell to make everything right for the children. Mum's devastated about what happened to Bradley." Jack kept his focus on the distant ranges. He could always think more clearly when they were in his sight.

"I hope you understand how appreciative I am," he took in her encouraging smile.

Everything about her spelt class, organisation, and focus. He could never use those words when describing Elsa's limited qualities.

"The children were so happy yesterday," there was a crack in his voice as he spoke, and he drew in a noisy breath, "I think they've forgotten what it's like to feel safe."

A genuine smile lit up her face and he couldn't help be drawn to that open, friendly sight. When she spoke to him, Jack's breaths grew sharp. She affected him like no one else ever had, not even Elsa.

"Don't think I'm not getting anything out of this, you must see I'm profiting from our arrangement as much as you are," her smile carried a ray of sunshine amid the dark few days he'd experienced.

"I accept that it'll help you but there's no way we're on an even keel here."

"Well, only time will tell, I suppose," she shrugged.

Their eyes met and it was the most natural thing in the world that his heart fluttered at the sight of this creature.

"Just you remember I'm super grateful. I might forget to thank you over the next few weeks, but don't think I'm taking you for granted."

"I hope by the time I leave the children will be back into a routine and you'll have done all you need to do to sort out your family's future." Lindy watched Jack, opened her mouth to continue but stopped herself.

"What do you want to say? I'm sure it'll be something useful." Jack's easy smile was a vast improvement to the one he shared with her at the pub Saturday night. He couldn't believe a stranger offering her help would have calmed him and his children so quickly.

Her nervous laugh reverberated, "Not sure about that, but here goes. I'm a business mentor, so if you wish to talk things out. I can crunch numbers and maybe give you a varying opinion on things."

"You know, that sounds fantastic. But I'll ring Ivy for a referral just in case." Lindy laughed, joining in with his easy banter. "Seriously, you might just be able to help me see things more clearly."

"Excellent."

Elsa never offered to listen to him about anything to do with the farm. Very early on he discovered her interest lay in the bottom line, how much she could spend. Downplaying his profit margin to his wife proved a smart choice. Her interest in the farm earnings were purely selfish. Now his family would enjoy the efforts of his hard work over the years. Reaching into his pocket, Jack pulled out a wad of one hundred-dollar bills.

"Here's a thousand dollars, I was thinking maybe we start a petty cash tin. Thanks for the receipts I found in the bin last night," his mock snarl made her laugh as he reached into his other pocket and pulled out another five hundred dollars. "This is the reimbursement for yesterday."

"That's way too much," Lindy admonished.

"That includes lunch. Tessa rang last night explaining you paid for everyone's lunch and asked me to apologise. She'd forgotten to settle the account before she left."

"I offered to do that. It was my treat."

"The lack of food and possessions have nothing to do with a shortage of money. We have plenty, the business is split three ways, Dad and Mum, myself then Tessa. I get a bigger cut because I work the farm, but we all benefit financially. That's the way Dad set it up." Jack focused on the stunning orange and pink in early morning across the sky. "No, the lack was my way of trying to stop Elsa from doing drugs. Not that it helped," he shook his head, "So please take the money."

Lindy took the rolled-up cash wrapped tightly in a rubber band, "Okay."

"And this," he continued, "Is for anything you need."

"Haircuts for the children?" she raised a brow and tried to hide a smirk.

"Oh hell, yes," brushing the fringe back from his own eyes Jack laughed, "I promise I'll be in town over the next few days for a haircut too. Could you also buy the children new school uniforms and shoes, hell anything they need?" He paused for a moment, "They're all in desperate need of clothes and shoes. That's the biggest priority now." Jack had a purpose. He understood the importance of giving his children a secure home and ensuring they were happy.

Now that Elsa was no longer there to use the children as pawns in her game of deception, Jack was free to provide them with the necessities and a few luxuries. Lindy began by filling the cupboards, fridge and the children's stomachs with sustenance they'd been denied by their mother and Jack was determined to sort out anything else they needed. "Oh, Tessa has offered to help on that front."

"Great. I'll speak to her this morning and we'll arrange something." Lindy's head turned towards the house when a baby's cry rang out, "Well, I think my morning has officially begun."

Together they stood and walked into the house. The morning madness was now under way.

JACK

Jack met Lindy and a dressed Bradley in the kitchen, his arms spread wide to take his son.

"I've got his bottle," he told her as she stepped around them to the bench. "Morning my little man. How's your arm this morning? You're all smiles."

A small gurgle of laughter rang out from the toddler as father and son bantered. Jack saw Lindy smile and liked the idea that at least for the next few weeks she could be a part of this morning routine. He watched as she started to prepare for the day ahead.

Organising lunches, snacks and drink bottles was her next task. Even for Bradley as they would spend a fair chunk of time in the car today. After finishing those jobs, Lindy tidied the kitchen, Jack settled Bradley in his high chair while he went down to wake the other children.

Breakfast was fun, that was the only way to describe it. The children spoke with sing song voices about being back at school with their friends and cousins. There was a buzz of delight as they dressed, checked bags, made beds, washed dishes, brushed teeth and hair. Jack and Lindy were the centre of it all.

By the time everyone was buckled into their seats with clean faces and huge smiles, Jack stood back with a mixture of pure pleasure and deep pain. How could it be that a complete stranger made his children feel both happy and safe? Something their own mother failed to do for months now.

"See you at lunchtime," he wore an enormous grin, ignoring his internal pain as he waved them off.

After a nod of understanding he watched as Lindy drove down the long driveway heading into town with everything in the world precious to him, his children.

BACK TO SCHOOL

LINDY

"*N*ext stop, Chester's Run Primary School," Lindy announced, receiving raucous cheers. Even Bradley chimed in making Lindy laugh. A short time later they turned into the car park and all piled out talking over one another as they gathered their bags. Lindy secured Bradley in his pram and walked beside her charges, each carrying their school bag and a huge smile. She didn't miss how they all huddled close to her as they entered the school yard.

Jack and Tessa gave them a pep talk last night, followed by the phone conversations with their grandparents wishing them well. Hell, these children were so loved by Jack's family.

She leant across Caleb and untangled the shoulder strap of his schoolbag.

"Thanks," he grinned up at her and took off after Nate.

Pushing the pram a tad faster, Lindy stayed close. Eager friends watched and waited, the boys doing that fist pump thing she'd never really understood, and the girls were being pulled into hugs warming her heart.

Evie and Joanna chattered away to friends but watched her continuously, still not confident of being alone. After about ten minutes someone called her name and Lindy turned to see Tessa walking towards her with a man dressed smartly in a suit.

"Morning, we made it," Lindy tried to ignore the curious glances from onlookers.

"You did well, nice and early. The kids look relaxed," Tessa focused on each and every one of her brother's children.

Lindy counted, making sure she could see each of the four siblings.

"Lindy this is George Tuttenham, the principal."

"Morning Lindy, lovely to meet you," The man held out his hand, Lindy took it in a firm handshake. She met his gaze with steady eye contact, her confidence was important for the children to see.

"Good Morning, nice to meet you too."

"The kids look great, Tessa said we'd notice an improvement, she's right. Good for them, they've been through a lot."

"Jack insists they get back into a routine," Lindy offered.

George Tuttenham squatted down before Bradley.

"Hey mate, how are you going?" Bradley hid his face into the side of his pram. He wasn't ready to meet any unfamiliar faces just yet. The fact he took to Lindy so warmly puzzled his father and aunt.

Knowing parents were watching her every move, Lindy looked to Tessa willing her to be discreet. Fortunately, George lowered his voice as he spoke to Tessa again.

"Can you bring Lindy into the office to see me when the bell goes?" To Lindy he added, "I'll see you later."

"Bye." Lindy focused once again on her charges ensuring they were coping with the pre-class stress.

With loud music echoing out over the playground, each child ventured to their lines with their classmates. Lindy and Tessa waved as the children settled in happily. Once they joined their teachers Lindy let out a long slow breath, one she didn't realise she'd been holding.

"Come on," Tessa escorted her into the office.

While they waited Tessa introduced Lindy to the office staff. "These two lovely women will be your first port of call if you have any problems. This is Poppy and Dianne. Ladies, this is Lindy Kemp, she'll be helping Jack with the children for a while." What happened to Bradley was common knowledge and required no further mention.

"Morning ladies." Lindy's mind flashed back to her time as a school parent. She was an old hand, "I hope you don't mind but would you have a copy of last week's newsletter, just in case we've missed anything important?" Lindy mentally ticked another item off her list.

Dianne came around the front counter to the newsletter holder, "Poppy, there's none left could you print another copy, please?" Turning to Lindy she asked, "Would you mind if we get your mobile number? Just in case we can't get hold of Jack."

"Of course," Lindy wrote her phone number on the piece of paper Dianne slid towards her.

"I see you've met the brains behind this operation," George stepped out of his office with another parent. Nodded a goodbye to them and said to Tessa and Lindy, "Well come on through."

"You look like you know this office too well," Lindy quipped to Tessa.

She laughed. "I've been keeping George up-to-date on the children. To us outsiders it was obvious interference by anyone would cause further problems for the children and Jack," Tessa's eyes held a depth of pain Lindy remembered at the park. "If only we understood the truth of the situation."

"Sometimes, unfortunately, things are beyond our control. I hope this doesn't sound harsh but Bradley won't remember this, it's the others I'm worried about," George revealed.

"Yes, I think you're right," Tessa agreed.

Turning to Lindy George explained, "I've known Jack since kindergarten and I could never believe he's capable of neglect or abuse. I can't imagine what I'd do in his position. Anyway," George clasped his hands in front of him, "I just wanted to let you know we're here if you need anything."

"Thanks, I won't hesitate."

The two women left only after they had purchased all the uniforms required. The children came to the office and returned to the classroom in their brand-new clothes. They were still in need of school shoes, but they'd sort that after school. Lindy and Tessa thanked Dianne and Poppy and headed out, Tessa again pushing the pram.

On the way home Lindy turned to check on Bradley as he munched away happily on a quarter of a Vegemite sandwich. Lindy planned the jobs to tackle once back at the farm. Through the rear-view mirror, she watched Bradley kicking his legs as he muttered gibberish to himself, with a huge smile.

JACK

At ten-thirty Jack opened the container Lindy packed his snack in. He chuckled, a childish feeling resurfaced as it did when he picked up the container from the bench this morning. He selected the celery and carrot sticks first knowing full well the blueberry muffin would mask the bland taste of the vegetables. He finished with the banana and pear, licking his lips and grinning to himself.

Hunger pains growled and Jack checked his watch, definitely lunchtime. He longed to see a welcoming smile, a cheerful baby and food in the fridge for him to make himself a decent meal. Pulling into the shed, Jack jumped off the tractor with the enthusiasm of a twenty-year-old, not the thirty-nine-year-old he was. Walking towards the house in search of his lunch, a voice drifted over from the bungalow. He walked over to say hello. Outside he saw the vacuum cleaner, mop and bucket and a tub of cleaning products. It had been a long time since someone other than him used those around here.

Lindy's voice rang out from the bungalow's interior, "You hungry? How about some lunch before I put you down for a sleep?" Jack stuck his head into the bungalow. Bradley lay under his play gym, kicking his legs as he repeated 'yum' as Lindy talked.

"Someone's looking rather satisfied with himself," Jack bent down to pick up his son.

"Oh, hi," Lindy was slightly startled, "I didn't hear you drive in,"

"Sorry, didn't mean to scare you," He cradled Bradley in his arms and kissed him, "How were the kids this morning?"

"Good, the girls were unsure but the boys happily went off with their friends. Oh, and I met George Tuttenham, I gave the office my mobile number in case they need anything," Lindy explained as she collected up the cleaning equipment and made her way back to the house.

"Excellent. George will keep an eye on them," Jack followed with Bradley and the play gym.

"We also fitted them out in new uniforms and this afternoon we'll get school shoes." Lindy kept him up to date with her list of things to do. "Oh, that reminds me, could the children get new runners as well? Nate asked me."

"Lindy get them whatever they need. The money's there, you don't have to ask."

In the kitchen Lindy made a cheese sandwich for Bradley, cutting it into small pieces and handing it to Jack.

"Will a ham salad sandwich be okay?" she asked, turning back towards the fridge.

"I can make it," Jack put Bradley's lunch in front of him on the tray of his high chair.

"You can make the coffee, one or two?"

"Never one to say no to food, I'll have two please," Jack beamed, "You will need to stop with this delicious food or none of us will let you go."

Her cheeks reddened slightly. He swallowed hard and changed the subject.

"Are you settled into the bungalow?" his pitch a little strained as he asked.

"Yep, all done. This afternoon I'll make a start on this place while Bradley's sleeping." Lindy met his gaze briefly. When she turned away, he continued to watch her. Closely admiring her side profile. Only drawing his gaze from the lovely vision when Bradley bellowed for more food.

Jack gulped hard. He must stop staring. Hoping to appear nonchalant, he spoke, "Don't overdo it Lindy. This place has been a mess for a long time, another couple of weeks won't hurt us. Don't run yourself into the ground on our account."

"Don't worry, I know my limits, and besides, I'll have you know I'm no timid wallflower," she let out a chuckle.

"The children and I did what we could to keep the place clean but…" Jack stopped, not finishing that sentence. The memories tore at him, Elsa never allowed noise so using the vacuum when she slept in after a big night resulted in her yelling, and her yelling upset the children. Jack did what he could to avoid the children feeling unsettled, especially in their own home.

"I hope you know how thankful I am to be here keeping busy. I could have so easily curled myself up in the foetal position by now with no plans to resurface." The dejection in her voice rang out.

Jack agreed, "Funny you say that. If you hadn't offered your help on Saturday night, I wouldn't have totally dismissed doing the same thing yesterday. It was all too overwhelming." Lindy nodded at his declaration.

Her blue eyes sparkled when she laughed.

"Tessa would never have allowed you such luxuries. Hope you understand that."

How did Lindy stay positive through her bleak moments?

"I'll put Bradley down and head back out. Thanks for lunch. I'll be home as early as I can."

"No, it's okay. Give Bradley to me," Lindy held out her hands to take the sleepy toddler. Jack kissed his son, handed him over to Lindy and stepped out the backdoor.

JACK

The sound of Jack's ringing phone stopped him just outside the backdoor.

"Jack Saunders," he put the phone on loud speaker so he could put his work boots on.

"Hi Jack, Ray here," his neighbour said.

"Hi Ray, what can I do for you?"

"Well, it's more like what we can do for you. The boys and I are finished sowing our crop. I believe you're a tad behind."

Jack heard the sarcastic tone in his laugh as it escaped. "Yeah, just a bit." It didn't surprise him that Ray was hyperaware of his lack of progress this late into the season.

"Okay, we'll head out now and meet you at the shed. You still at home?"

Jack was lost for words. He sucked air into his lungs with a sharp intake, giving him a much-needed moment to stabilise the swirling in his stomach. Finally, he replied, thankful that Ray had been patient. "Yep. Thanks, a few hours would be great if you don't mind."

"See you in ten," Ray said before hanging up.

Jack dropped his mobile into his pocket and leant back onto the wall of the house. He blew out a breath and sighed. He heard footsteps and Bradley's chatter.

"Everything okay?" Jack turned to see Bradley on Lindy's hip. He liked the sight very much.

"That was my neighbour, Ray," he sighed, "Him and his two sons are coming over to give me a hand with the crops."

"Oh, that's wonderful."

He could see she really cared. Should he feel such warmth radiating from her enthusiasm?

"They'll be here in ten, so I better get organised." Jack hesitated, then kissed Bradley again and pulled back, eyeing Lindy, "I think I'll call you my good luck charm."

He turned and walked off. Maybe it was true, Lindy was his good luck charm. He relaxed a little more and revelled in hearing his little boy's gurgled laughter as he walked away. Before entering the shed, Jack turned back to see Lindy still standing there, allowing Bradley to wave and call after him. Nothing was too insignificant for her. She took the time to see to the little details, which for him right now made a huge impact.

LINDY

"There you go little man," Lindy eased Bradley carefully into his stroller. She fumbled around in the back of the car for his food bag and jumped when Tessa arrived next to her.

"Oh hell, you scared me," Lindy's hand settled on her heart.

Tessa laughed.

"Here, you push the stroller," Lindy looked around at the throng of mothers watching her closely.

"Don't let them rattle you," Tessa whispered.

"Poor Jack, when I leave, they'll be staring down the next woman who comes to help him." She followed Tessa into the schoolyard and found a quiet spot so Tessa could feed Bradley his yogurt.

"Maybe he should get a male when you leave, that'll have tongues wagging," both Tessa and Lindy burst out laughing which drew more attention than Lindy was comfortable with. "Let them stare," Tessa eyed a handful of nosey parkers, "How's Jack?"

"Some of his neighbours came over this afternoon to help with the crop," Lindy explained.

"Who, Ray?"

"Yep, him and his two sons. Ray rang Jack just after lunch and they were at the farm ten minutes later." Lindy handed Tessa a cloth to wipe yogurt off Bradley's face.

"Bloody brilliant, I wonder if Dad rang him. That'll take a load off Jack," Tessa seemed relieved on Jack's behalf.

Lindy checked her watch for the third time in two minutes, with so much to do time was dragging. The bell rang and children began gushing out of every doorway, determined to find their family. The children's faces lit up as they spotted her, and ran towards Lindy and Tessa. In such a brief span of time Lindy was becoming their constant and security. Chills of reality hit again. This short-term deal would be more difficult than she first expected. Surrounded by content faces, Lindy drew her musings from the future to the present, dealing with the here and now.

"How was school?"

Caleb answered first, "Look," he held up his hands, "Miss Edmund gave me back my footy. She said the kids have been taking care of it for me." The ball was old and tattered, but Caleb obviously treasured it.

"Lucky you, maybe you can have a kick outside this afternoon," when his eyes widened and a grin spread across his face Lindy questioned its meaning. She didn't think it would be hard to understand how their life had been when Jack wasn't around. "How about you, Joanna?"

"Great, I got lots of homework though,"

"Me too, I'll do it as soon as I get home," Evie chimed in.

"That sounds like an excellent idea," Lindy agreed.

Nate walked over with Ben and Lachie, "Hi Lindy. Hi Aunty Tessa, how's Bradley doing?"

"Good, he slept well, and he's eating all the food out of the pantry," Lindy joked.

"Did he leave anything for us?" Nate asked, "I'm starving,"

"There might be something," Lindy replied, running her hand over his long hair. "We should get going. Haircuts and shoes to buy. Ready Tessa?"

"Sure am. If you guys are good, we might even have time for a treat at the bakery. Ivy wants to see you all."

Cheers erupted as they walked to the car park.

"Follow me. How about I do shoes and you can do haircuts?" Tessa suggested as the children tossed school bags into the boot of the car.

CREATING A NEW NORMAL

LINDY

Turning up the driveway, Lindy stopped the car by the letterbox and waited for Nate to collect the mail and the local paper. For a twelve-year-old boy he'd taken on more burden than anyone his age should.

"There you go," Nate dropped the offering into the console between them. Once the door closed Lindy took off up the drive towards the cream weatherboard house the family called home.

Bringing the car to a stop, the children piled out, grabbing school-bags and their shopping.

"Remember the new routine," Lindy called after them, "Put lunch boxes and drink bottles on the sink and get changed.

"All right," the children replied rushing into the house.

"See you at the table for homework in ten minutes," Lindy called again so everyone could hear. She pressed down on the buckle to release Bradley, "Come on little man. Don't you look handsome with your new haircut?" Bradley babbled a reply as Lindy settled him carefully on her hip.

Changed out of their uniforms, the children reluctantly descended on the kitchen table to tackle their homework.

"Can't we play?" Caleb asked as he dropped his books onto the kitchen table with a thud.

"You can," Lindy replied before adding, "After you finish your homework."

Nate shot a scared glance at his brother, releasing a heavily exaggerated warning, "Shhh." Lindy watched as his features transformed. This was the boy of earlier, not the relaxed one she was slowly getting to know.

"Nate, it's okay," Lindy told him in a soft voice which partially relaxed Nate's features. "He loves the outdoors, I don't mind him having a different opinion, but as long as he understands he needs to do his homework."

Both boys took in her nod of encouragement and the genuine smile. Putting Nate at ease was her priority. From over the top of Joanna's reader Lindy watched as the brothers open their books. One not sure what he'd done wrong and the other watching her closely. What had their home life been like?

None of the children were overly bright, but they all tried, which Lindy appreciated. Meanwhile, Bradley vied for his siblings' attention, to get out of a bit of work while Lindy was busy with someone else, one of them would lie on the floor next to him. Lindy could see this but didn't make an issue out of it.

After a gruelling hour of homework and school bags re-packed for the following morning, Lindy encouraged the children outside.

"You mean it?" Nate asked as he followed Caleb.

"Go on have a kick, I'll be watching from the window."

When the kitchen was clear, Lindy walked around the breakfast bar and picked up her phone to call Jack.

"Hi Lindy."

"I was wondering what time you'd be home?"

"I want to finish this paddock. Eat without me but make sure you save me something."

"Oh, the kids are so excited to tell you about their day, could we come down and have a picnic somewhere?"

"Oh okay," the surprise in his voice rang out, "I'll ring you back soon and tell you where to meet me. That's if it's not too much trouble."

After hanging up, Lindy walked to the door and called out to the children, "Who wants to meet Dad for a picnic?"

They stared at her with opened mouths and wide eyes. Caleb was the first to move, dropping the football before he ran towards Lindy cheering.

"Me. I want a picnic and to see Dad," He threw his arms around Lindy and clung to her. "When can we go?"

"As soon as we pack. Grab your football, you'll need it."

Caleb took off at a run, fetching the ball.

"Can we take our netball too?" Evie's voice rising above the usual whisper.

"Of course. Bring them into the house, then could you all please come and help," the four siblings ran off in search of sporting equipment.

Within the hour Lindy packed a picnic basket and gathered some rugs and even found a few dusty old camp chairs in the shed. The children were loading the last of their jackets into the back of the car as Lindy's mobile phone rang.

LINDY

"There he is," Caleb shouted from the backseat. All eyes followed the direction of his pointed finger. The tractor in the distance worked at a steady pace as it kicked up fine brown dust behind it.

"That looks so boring," Joanna muttered as they approached Jack. "Up and down, up and down. I'm definitely not going to be a farmer when I grow up."

"What," Nate gasped, "I'll be just like Dad," he announced, "Looking after cows and running a farm and fixing cars in my spare time. That would be awesome."

Lindy stopped at the end of the row Jack was working on. She got out and hopped into the back of the car next to Evie, listening as the children kept talking. Slowly she was learning a little more about each one.

"Nursing, that's what I want to do," Joanna looked determined. "But I'll come back and work here when I have finished uni. Dad told me I'd make a brilliant nurse."

Caleb refused to be left out, "I'm going to play footy and be a racing car driver. I can't wait to drive a car. Dad can teach me everything he knows."

Evie, the only one who hadn't joined the conversation up to this point, turned towards Lindy and asked, "What work do you do, Lindy? When you're not with us, I mean."

"I work as a business mentor."

"A what?" Nate's eyebrows squished together.

"Business mentor, I help people who want to improve their business."

Nate nodded and turned back to watch his father.

"What do you think you'll like to do Evie?"

Evie stared out the window. "Be a scientist. Work all around the world. That's what I want to do," Evie watched Jack climb down off the tractor, "Learn more about medicine and people who need help, like Mum."

She never continued on that topic as Jack rounded the front of the van and jumped up into the driver's seat.

Lindy squeezed Evie's shoulder. "That sounds great." Who could tell what was bouncing around inside their heads after the last few traumatic weeks? Something deep inside her longed to help each of these children get what they wanted out of life.

Jack's husky voice interrupted her musings as he settled into the seat.

"So, who's for a picnic?"

"Yay," the children cheered.

Starting the car, Jack turned to look at Lindy, his face was relaxed and his eyes bright, there was a message but Lindy wasn't willing to delve too deeply. Not just yet, that's for certain. But her smile broke free, obviously of its own volition. Jack drove the family to the end of the huge paddock and parked next to the river by a clump of pepper-corn trees.

The children jumped out excitedly and bombarded their father with news of their school day as he helped Lindy unpack the picnic and set it all out onto the old tattered blankets, Lindy found in the linen cupboard.

"Look," Caleb said, "I got my footy back, Miss Edmund gave it to me at lunchtime."

"So, after all that you left it at school, huh," for Lindy's benefit Jack explained, "Caleb was in tears when we thought Elsa palmed off even the tattered football."

Jack tried to make a joke of it, but Lindy could see it was difficult. "Mum gave Caleb my old football she found at home a few months ago."

"Oh yum," Joanna used her fingers to tear the flesh from the chicken bones.

"Make sure you have some salad with that," Lindy enjoyed the sounds of relish coming from them as they ate.

"The food is delicious," Jack said through an enormous grin.

"This potato salad is the best," Caleb went back for seconds.

Jack picked up a serviette and wiped his son's face.

"Slow down, it isn't going anywhere," Jack's grin added no effect to his attempt to reprimand.

"Sorry," but Caleb didn't look sorry. His eyes gleamed as he grinned around a mouthful of food, he definitely wasn't sorry.

Lindy couldn't help but smirk at the exchange. "Caleb, do you want more chicken with that?"

"Umm, no just rice salad please." Caleb handed over his plate as Jack added another spoon of rice salad. The others leant over the makeshift table and helped themselves, pleasure written all over their smiling, grubby faces.

Looking at his watch, Jack stifled a groan. Work awaited him, "Ray and the boys headed home just before you arrived. They'll be out with me again tomorrow." Watching the children playing, he added, "With three more tractors we'll have it done in no time."

Lindy held Bradley's cup while he drank and turned to see Jack's eyes on her. Dropping her gaze wasn't enough to stop the rush of colour to her cheeks. The half hour picnic turned into an hour before Lindy began packing everything up.

"Awww, do we have to go?" Caleb asked.

"Yes, if you want your father home before midnight," Lindy told him as she ruffled his brown hair which looked rather dapper.

"Yes, we do," Jack said in his son's ear and earned a scowl for his efforts. He buckled Bradley into the car while the kids pitched in to help pack away the picnic. Driving back to the tractor, Jack asked, "Who had fun?"

Lindy laughed when they replied with squeals and clapped their hands, especially when Bradley joined in. He stopped the car beside the tractor, hopped out and met Lindy at the front of the car.

"Perfect, that was perfect," he took her hand in his. She tried to distract herself from the sparks bolting inside her, "What time sh... shall I expect you back?"

"Before midnight that's for sure," his crooked smile was becoming unbearably appealing. Lindy stepped around him and hopped into the car, not able to help herself but knowing she shouldn't, she watched as Jack climbed up onto the tractor.

He waved to them before starting the machine and continuing on his way. Lindy drove back up the dirt track that would be impassable in the wet. As the children spoke about the picnic, Lindy pondered Jack as master of his own domain, in charge of everything around him and content, not happy, not yet. Just content with his lot in life.

RISING PASSION

LINDY

*T*hursday morning heralded the most magical sunrise over the mountain range as Lindy made her way across the yard. What a magnificent sight! Nothing could steal her pleasure today. Being here with this family gave her comfort and kept her from over-thinking her own situation.

Jack poured boiling water into a couple of mugs as she walked into the kitchen.

"I see you beat me to the washing."

"Well, you're not here for much longer. I need to learn the routine." His tone came out harsh and rather scathing.

Lindy gaped at him.

Whoa! Hang on a minute. Where was this coming from? This wasn't her fault. She always planned to return to her family in Melbourne at some point. Lindy gave a slight shake of her head as her lips pinched together. Forcing some control, she replied, "Yes, sorry I keep thinking the same thing," with trembling hands she picked up the mug he pushed her way.

Something must have upset Jack. Thinking back over the last few days, she came up empty. She couldn't remember doing anything to cause this reaction. Maybe realisation set in, he would have to cope on his own soon. Should she ask him if there was a problem? She remembered her promise to herself, she wouldn't pander to some power seeking male even if he was gorgeous and made her insides flutter wildly.

Jack's face flushed before he turned towards the sink and poured the rest of his tea down the plughole. "Are you okay with the kids this morning? I want to get an early start." Jack asked as he stepped around the bench and headed for the back door.

Lindy watched on as he stepped outside. "I'll be fine."

Really?

Fine! Her hand trembled a little harder as she pieced together what just happened. She was not fine. And neither was the current situation. Was this why Ralph treated her so poorly? The truth was she wasn't even close to fine. Why did she tell Jack that?

The way Jack spoke to her sent her blood pressure soaring but if she could stop time and stay with this family forever, she'd do it. She was torn. Shaking her head, Lindy walked into the pantry, picked up the loaf of bread, butter and a range of spreads for the kids' lunches.

This is all for the kids, I can do it.

She repeated this mantra over and over as she went about the morning routine. Seeing he struggled with the idea of her leaving as much as she did, didn't help. His reasoning would be different.

Jack's most pressing need was her help with his children, she'd do anything for the children but her attraction to Jack was becoming impossible to hide. How could she walk out of one marriage and harbour such powerful feelings for another man the following week? The whole idea was ludicrous.

By the time they were almost ready to leave for school she pushed the distraction to the back of her mind and honed her attention towards her charges. Luckily for Jack she did. What she discovered proved to be an oversight Jack would have been kicking himself over. Lindy couldn't deal with that now, she needed to get the children to school first. Then she would speak to Jack.

JACK

Driving in the tractor, Jack's mind kept returning to his treatment of Lindy this morning. He slammed a clenched fist onto the stirring wheel, causing the tractor to veer off course slightly. He cursed as he righted the vehicle. His reaction to her was unforgivable. And even more outrageous was the fact that his treatment of her resulted from his feelings for her and not the fact that the children would need her. He was being purely selfish, and that made him a prized jerk.

He'd known lust before, that was his feelings for Elsa, but this attraction was something entirely different. His feelings for Lindy ran deep and the idea of losing her sent his heart pounding. She'd just walked out of her marriage a week ago and the torment of that betrayal became clearer when she drifted back into her memories. He never missed the sighs escaping those beautiful lips. The woman he treasured mourned the loss of others who had nothing to do with him. Her pain was for her children who had forsaken her, not her husband, but still he had no right to burden her with his affection.

Slamming his fist on the steering wheel a second time he muttered obscenities to himself. He nearly missed the ringing of his mobile. Jack juggled the phone and finally managed to answer it, hearing the familiar voice greeted him.

"Sorry to bother you."

After an inward groan, Jack replied, "No, that's fine," he took a long breath, then asked, "What's up?"

"I just dropped the children at school." She paused, Jack gripped the steering wheel. "Joanna was quiet this morning and then I over-heard Nate, Evie, and Joanna talking in hushed tones. Nate said don't bother Dad or Lindy about it, they're too busy and you know Mum never celebrated them anyway. Dad was the only one to remember." Lindy paused giving Jack a chance to process the information.

"Oh shit," he pulled the phone from his ear and checked the date, "Joanna's birthday," he cursed.

Hadn't he been praising himself, believing he was getting on top of things? Something always popped up to remind him he never would manage alone with the farm.

"Bugger. With everything happening, I completely forgot. Shit!" he said again, running his free hand through his hair and down his face.

He shut down the tractor and sat for a minute, while Lindy waited patiently on the other end of the phone.

"All going to plan I hoped to finish by mid-afternoon and come with you to pick the kids up, I wanted to surprise everyone." More to the truth, he wanted to spend time with Lindy trying to make up for his poor behaviour earlier in the day. "Now I'll need to organise presents. Oh, hell, and Ray and the boys are here helping me."

"If you know what you're buying her, tell me because I'm still in town," Lindy offered.

"Are you sure, if you do that I'll finish up here and together we can make this day extra special, not just for Joanna but for all the kids," Jack let out a huge breath knowing Lindy would help.

"Just tell me what to do." The sincerity in her voice made his heart flip again. This kind woman had endeared herself to him and his children.

"Okay, I'll message you a list." Jack and Lindy planned out the rest of the day. Now having something to strive for together, the tension between them dissolved. Before turning his attention back to the crops, Jack made a few more calls planning an evening full of surprises. Without her, his whole world might fall apart. How could he allow her to return to Melbourne?

JACK

By the time Jack pulled the tractor into the shed he was dirty, sweaty, and exhausted. After locking everything up outside he ran into the house to find his lunch and a cuppa on the bench waiting for him. Bradley was playing near his play gym yakking away to himself.

"Should I eat first?" Jack asked Bradley and laughed when Lindy walked into the kitchen with a full laundry basket of wet clothes perched on her hip.

"Shower first, lunch second," she scolded in jest but he wasn't silly enough to argue.

Pounding rivulets of water on his body, had him appreciating the gentle kneading of his tight muscles. His mind raced, divorce proceedings were underway and the safety of the children were a priority. He would take nothing less than full custody from Elsa, no matter what it took. His children were so precious and a decent life was nothing less than what they deserved. By hell or high water, he'd be the one to provide them that. He grabbed the crisp clean towel that had been sundried and breathed in the scent of lavender on his body, gentle yet enticing.

Just like Lindy.

How perfect everything was with Lindy around? Meals were delicious, on time, and plentiful. Clothes washed, darned where needed, and the rich colours shone brighter than before. He admitted to himself that wouldn't be too hard to achieve when washing as methodically as Lindy did. The house was clean and smelt fresh, not to mention no trace of fowl smells leaching out of the fridge.

His mind strayed as he stood before the foggy mirror running the cool blade over his whiskers. He remembered running out of the house early this morning, he tried to ignore the reprimand his conscience was giving him. Why was it this woman twisted him in knots? Everything happening in his house had Lindy in control and at the centre of it all. He'd never known the pain of losing someone so special in his life. Her time with them was ending. Again, a tightness gripped him and he attempted to ease the pain by kneading his chest with the heel of his hand.

He'd make her see he wanted her in his life. Not because the house was operating far better than ever before. Or that his children were happier and more organised. No, it was because of the way his heart rate quickened when she was around. Yes, Lindy needed to know his feelings ran deep for her.

He selected a pair of jeans and a T-shirt from his now well-ordered shelves, smiling again, knowing how much this woman endeared herself into his life and those of his children.

A few minutes later he stood at the kitchen bench downing his lunch while watching Lindy at the clothesline. Only Bradley's babble behind him forced Jack to take his eyes off her.

"What do you say, should we stop her from leaving us? Give this angel a reason to stay."

"Mumma, mummm," Bradley said as he rested against the pillows that surrounded him.

"Yes, mate, I wish she was your mother too," he longed for her to be the missing piece to their shattered picture of family. Parents were two people who worked in unison for the good of the offspring. United by the unconditional love they had for each other. But unfortunately, these kids weren't Lindy's offspring. He often pondered his predicament getting Elsa pregnant and by such foolish means forging his future. Her idea of a wonderful life was alcohol, drugs and night clubs which meant disaster for the family. Elsa managed to get hold of the drugs and alcohol, but none of this ever made her happy.

Watching Lindy, Jack considered how everything had spiralled southwards. It was only the incoherent babble behind him that made him admit not everything in his life was wrong. No, on the contrary, it was only one thing.

His wife.

But on reflection, the cause of the dull pain in his chest was the knowledge that Lindy would leave soon. This truth gripped painfully at his heart.

Jack rinsed his dishes and turned back to Bradley before Lindy came in and caught him watching her. His body's reaction to her matched the overwhelming desire in his mind. Was she as affected by him?

He turned his thoughts to more practical matters. With all the paddocks sown, Jack's focus could shift. He would deal with Elsa, freeing her from a commitment she no longer wanted, him and their children.

He recalled the conversation he had with Ray in the paddock on Tuesday.

"The offer I made your father still stands, the boys and I will take the farm off your hands if that's what you need to do for the children." Ray stated matter-of-factly. "The missus quashed gossip in town about you taking up with another woman. You know, she doesn't take kindly to that rubbish. Put a few women back in their place, my Marge did."

"Tell Marge I appreciate her support, Lindy doesn't deserve to be the centre of town gossip, especially after everything she's done for us."

Jack rubbed the back of his neck.

Bradley's voice bought him back to the present as Lindy walked through the door.

"Thanks for lunch," he said as she headed past him for the laundry with a basket full of clothes. "Here, let me take those," he stepped in front of her. They both stood staring at each other, unwilling, or maybe it was truly neither of them were able to move.

LINDY

Swallowing hard, Lindy stared at Jack. His broad frame, a wall of muscle she couldn't miss. He stared deep into her eyes. Pulling her eyes from his, Lindy focused on Jack's hands as they covered hers, attempting to take the basket.

"I've got it… Thanks…," but her voice stopped. She couldn't deny the attraction drawing her eyes back to his. Enormous light brown eyes that she lost herself in, and for the love of God, she was sinking deeper.

Prising her fingers from the basket, Jack placed it on the bench. Allowing him to touch her wouldn't be a smart move, but she didn't want him to go. Jack stepped closer and cupped her face with his hands.

"If you don't want this Lindy, pull away. I can't deny my feelings for you any longer." He ran his thumb over her bottom lip, tracking her darting tongue. When she didn't pull away, his mouth captured hers.

Their kiss began gentle but with a power beyond anything she'd known.

She could hear Bradley playing on the ground behind them, but nothing could make either of them stop. His touch was tender and her heart raced in response. She longed for this kiss. Now she was desperate to know whether his feelings matched hers.

Jack pulled back slightly, his eyes searching hers. His laboured breath caused a tremble to roll through her.

She broke eye contact and whispered, "Oh Jack, I walked out on my marriage only a week ago…" She wanted to say more but nothing would come. Instead, she rested her head on his shoulder and sighed. She shouldn't have these feelings for this man, but she did, and now she wasn't sure what to do about them.

"I've tried to resist but you're too beautiful," Jack kissed her again and again.

Eventually she pulled away, checking the time, her face flushed, her eyes refusing to meet his in case they couldn't pull away next time they touched.

"We need to get going."

It wasn't hard to see Jack had something to say but instead he stepped away and scooped Bradley into his arms, "How about we get the kids?" he asked Bradley as he settled him onto his hip.

Jack drove out of the driveway and onto the highway. Glancing over with a toothy grin she became aware she'd been staring at him.

"I've filed for divorce. I've spoken to my lawyer." He paused, breathing deeply. "I know this isn't ideal but time is never perfect with these things."

She looked away and stared out through the windscreen again, but words escaped her.

Jack continued, "This morning when I was so rude, it wasn't because you're leaving and I'd need to find someone else. It's because of the way I feel about you, I want you in my life. Think about giving us a chance, please?" Jack reached over and took her hand. Lindy tried not to cling to the connection. The power of their attraction was mystifying.

"There's so much to think about," her sweaty hands trembled in his large calloused ones.

"I get that but I still want to give us a go."

JACK

Back at home the children did as Lindy asked, unpacked school bags, and began their homework. Both Jack and Lindy sat around the table helping the children as they completed their work.

"Nate, what are you working on?" Jack asked as he fed small pieces of a chocolate biscuit to Bradley. Jack turned back to Nate to see an uneasy expression marring his face. "What's up?"

"Everyone's doing a project on drugs but Mr Willis said I don't need to do it because I've only just come back to school. But I think it's because of Mum."

Jack watched on as Nate's eyebrows pinched together. Having to face this so soon with his son left him feeling uneasy. Closing his eyes, he fought the urge to sigh. A decision like this was Nate's, even though Jack struggled with the topic. "Do you want to do it?"

Nate nodded. "I don't want to be different."

"Okay, let's sort this out," Jack grabbed his phone from the table and rang the school. He finally got put through to George. "Sorry to bother you George, but I'm wondering if I could ask for your help with something?"

"Of course, you can, what's up?"

Jack explained about the project, and Nate's discomfort in being excluded. A few minutes later when George came back the call was put on loudspeaker.

"Jack, I've talked to Rob, he didn't want to put Nate in an awkward position."

Jack turned to his son who was waiting patiently, "The homework everyone's researching is the side effects of drugs. Would you like to do that?"

"Yes. But do we have to present it?"

"The others will be but Mr Willis said you don't have too."

"Okay then I'd like to do the project," Nate nodded.

"Thanks Guys," Jack said. "I appreciate your concern, Rob."

"Next time Jack, I'll call first. I didn't want to put you or him under any extra pressure," It was obvious Rob cared for his student.

In Nate's room, Jack dropped onto the bed beside his son and for the next hour they made notes and discussed in depth how the family's life had changed because of drugs. They added some facts and then deleted others, especially the ones that were too personal. Then they read through and rearranged sentences of a rough draft.

"I'll show Mr Willis tomorrow and then finish it tomorrow night. Thanks for your help."

"My pleasure," Jack stood up and stretched. "Come on, I'm hungry."

Lindy was helping the others repack their school bags when Jack and Nate came back into the kitchen.

"All done?" Jack asked, looking at the girls with their bags.

"Yes."

"What's for dinner, Lindy?" Caleb asked as his tummy rumbled.

Jack didn't miss a beat. "No cooking today. We're going out. Lindy deserves a night off," Jack said as he helped Caleb put his school bag on the shelf in the pantry.

"Off to your rooms and get dressed, I think we'll go to the pub."

With cheers, the little bodies bounced down the hall.

"I'll put the presents in the car," Jack whispered to Lindy when the room was clear.

"Could you grab Bradley's nappy bag as well?" Lindy asked as she headed up the hallway to change Bradley.

JACK

A short time later they stopped at Jack's parent's place and Lindy took over the driving. Jack motioned for Joanna to join him when his parents came out of the house all dressed to go out. The moment Darla walked out with a present in her hand, Joanna looked around and grinned at her siblings. Tears of pleasure, just a couple, leaked out of the corner of her eyes.

That's when Jack picked her up and kissed her. "Happy birthday, sweetheart." He spun her around to see Nate taking a photo on Lindy's phone. Knowing they'd have these precious memories, touched him deeply.

Just then it occurred to him that Elsa would have photos of the children on her phone, so he'd insist she gave him copies of all the photos in the settlement. They were his children's memories, and they deserved to have them.

Joanna brought him back to the present when she threw her arms around his neck and hugged him tight. "Thank you, Daddy. So, you didn't forget?"

"I did, but apparently you guys were talking this morning." He didn't elaborate any further but kissed her wet cheek again.

"Daddy, I love Lindy, she's so special." Joanna turned to find everyone watching. She waved happily and pushed off her father's chest.

Jack refused to comment on her declaration for Lindy. He couldn't entertain the dangers of going there. Fortunately, his parents commandeered Lindy and the children's attention, giving him time to compose himself.

After the short drive, Jack walked beside Joanna as they entered the pub. There was a gurgle of surprise to find Ivy and Aunty Tessa, Uncle Harry and their cousins sitting at a long table. Jack watched on, his throat clogged, as his family received hugs and kisses from everyone. Joanna who was the centre of it all, wore a gigantic smile.

"Wow, this is great," Nate told his father as they all watched Joanna receive her birthday wishes. "I told Joanna you forgot."

"I did. But we can thank Lindy for eavesdropping," Jack grinned at his eldest son "Promise me something?"

Nate met his father's gaze, "Sure, anything."

"If. No, when, I forget anything else important like this you'll tell me or even message me about it."

The confused look on Nate's face made Jack smile.

"How will I message you?"

"With this," Jack pulled a small present out from under the table.

Nate gaped at his father, then at the present in his hand. "Are you kidding me?"

"I need you to contact someone if you or the others are in trouble," Nate opened the parcel to reveal a brand-new mobile phone. He stared at the phone in his hands.

"We'll set it up at home, okay?"

"Sure. Thanks." Nate turned to Ben to show him his new possession.

Jack tuned in to his father's conversation and smiled when he caught Lindy's glance. Feeling others watching him, he quickly shifted his focus.

Jack handed the rest of the presents out, revelling in the wonderful atmosphere.

"Thanks Uncle Jack," Ben and Lachie hollered in unison.

He watched on as they opened their gifts. Eyes gleaming and voices rising from his children, niece and nephews. He could see receiving presents on Joanna's birthday was awesome. Even if he had to justify the purchases to Tessa.

He'd seen for himself how Elsa only gave them crap for their birthdays, and lately she'd given them nothing at all. Now was his chance to make it up to them. The table buzzed. He sat back, taking in the children's pleasure. The only thing that could have made it better would have been to have his arm wrapped around Lindy. Sharing in this moment she'd made possible was stuff dreams were made of. He caught her eye and with a nod and a wink his smile broadened, hoping she understood what an important part she'd played today.

LINDY

"That meal was delicious," Tessa put down her knife and fork, "How good is it not to have to cook?"

"Or eat on your own," Ivy added.

Lindy heard the conversation, but was lost in the warmth of Jack's gaze as he nodded and winked at her. He'd done that a few times this evening and Lindy could only hope that no one else noticed. Only diverting her eyes when Joanna jumped up on to her lap to kiss her.

"Thank you, I love my presents."

"Happy birthday, darling. Are you only eight years old? I'm sure you're much older than that," Lindy questioned as she kissed Joanna's forehead.

"I'm sure," an indignant Joanna replied, "I have had eight birthdays, and this was the best one ever. Thank you." Joanna climbed off her lap and ran to her father. She shouldn't watch, but how could she not when the man she had the strongest feelings for was the hero his children so desperately needed.

Lindy's gaze met his again. It was the hardest thing not to admire the man opposite. She sensed Tessa watching them, her scrutiny way too close for comfort.

Tessa asked for the birthday cakes Ivy had supplied. When they arrived, Joanna cuddled into her father as the whole dining room began singing happy birthday just for her. Joanna smiled at the patrons, most of them familiar to her.

The kids happily consumed the cake, Caleb's face wearing more than he'd eaten.

"Did you enjoy that buddy?" Jack asked as he wiped away the smeared mess of chocolate. Caleb's nodding response had Jack and his father laughing.

Evie snuck up to Lindy and whispered into her ear, "Am I allowed to try the other cake?" she asked eyeing off the chocolate mud cake in front of her Aunty.

"Of course, your sister only turns eight once in her life. Tell Aunty Tessa I said you could have another piece."

"Ta," Evie hugged Lindy then turned to talk to Aunty Tessa in the next seat. Lindy pinched her lips, not wanting to smile at Jack again. His radiant smile exacerbated the warmth in her cheeks. Diverting her eyes, reality hit. Both Ivy and Tessa had witnessed the passing affection, which they continuously failed to control. Yep, they'd been sprung.

"How about another drink?" Ivy asked.

"Ummm, just water thanks," Lindy said once she shifted her eyes from Jack, again.

"Then maybe you could tell us what's going on," Tessa whispered with her eyebrows dancing up and down. Lindy focused on the children.

Tessa laughed and fortunately said no more.

UNDENIABLE ATTRACTION

JACK

Smiles were becoming a more permanent fixture on his children's faces. The way each child's personality came alive, sparked something deep in Jack's soul. Their love of the outdoors returned and Jack was proud of the respect they showed towards Lindy and feeling comfortable enough to allow Lindy to see them for who they truly were.

Jack, who sat at the head of the table for meals, revelled in the warmth and contentment that took hold in the old farmhouse once again. It wasn't hard to see Lindy was the reason for that. Often in the evenings, the two of them shared some quiet time, initially they used the time to converse on the happenings of the day and plan the next. But now Jack longed for the opportunity to be with Lindy, share a hot drink and hopefully devour one of her delectable treats, and then her.

Now sitting in silence in his favourite armchair and Lindy on the couch with her legs tucked up under her, Jack released a sigh. He devoted so much time to planning his family's future and agonised over what steps would ensure the children's safety. He rubbed at scratchy eyes and then rested his heavy arms across his chest.

Harry and his team spoke to him on several occasions determined to have the facts straight over the Bradley incident. The knowledge that the interrogation was over meant he could put it all behind him. Now he needed to talk to someone about the path forward and maybe Lindy was still distant enough to not have a bias against the mother of his children.

"Can I run something by you, I need a second opinion?" Jack asked when he finished his drink.

"Sure, if I can help," Lindy leant forward, placing her empty mug onto the coffee table next to his.

"It's about Elsa," he paused and forced himself to breathe deeply, "I've been in close discussion with my lawyer about making her an offer, one I hope she accepts. We can come to an agreement if she signs full custody of the children to me with no visitation rights until she cleans herself up. In exchange, I'll set up a trust to provide for her future."

"Do you think she'll go for that?" Lindy asked.

"I don't know, it's a long shot but I can't trust her with the children's safety, not after what she did to Bradley." What happened still gave him nightmares. "I'll give her the money to get rid of her. And she has to sign divorce papers into the bargain. I'll never regret my children but I so regret marrying that woman," he shook his head, and sighed heavily. The pain was still there and probably would be for a while to come.

"That sounds reasonable."

"I just need everything between us to be over." Jack dropped his head onto the back of the leather chair, staring up at the ceiling. "But my question to you is, am I doing the right thing for the children? I mean…" Jack stopped. Took a moment and then began again, "She still is and always will be their mother."

"I think Joanna will be the one to suffer the most from not having Elsa around. She asked me tonight if there were any photos of her." Jack could feel Lindy's eyes on him as she continued. "Joanna said there were some photos on Elsa's phone, she asked if maybe you had some."

Jack pulled out his phone and searched. Handing it over to Lindy, he said, "We took this one on Elsa's birthday in April. She looks good here."

"She's pretty," Lindy said studying the photo, "Gosh, Evie looks so much like her."

The strain of that reality was met with a heavy sigh. He wasn't sure he'd cope if Evie took after her mother regarding addiction.

"I'll show Joanna this photo in the morning. I've asked for copies of all the photos she has on her phone in the settlement."

"Maybe Joanna would like a copy," Lindy suggested, still looking at Jack's phone.

"Yeah, maybe, how about I let her decide which one she wants?" though Jack wanted to protect his children from further pain, he decided a photo of their mother shouldn't put them in harm's way again.

"You're a great listener," his voice was low. "I needed to get that off my chest. I haven't spoken to another soul about this other than my lawyer in the past couple of weeks." He rubbed his hand down his face and expelled another rush of breath.

"You've done an amazing job. Just in the couple of weeks I've been here, I've noticed a change in all the children. Nate is slowly accepting he doesn't have to protect the others every minute of every day. Evie smiles and laughs on cue, she's not over thinking everything. Joanna has found her spunk and is arguing with her siblings when they annoy her and Caleb, well, he's the family clown and revelling in the roll. I've seen his mind ticking over just before he gives those funny one-liners. The kid's a comedian and the others love his efforts to joke and tease them. And Bradley, well he loves you and follows you with his eyes everywhere you go. You're his rock and security blanket and I can see his delight when you come home.

"They're the only ones you have to please. Your love has given them the strength to put aside what's happened, you encourage them to be who they're truly meant to be. Jack, if there's one thing I've learnt recently it's that you'll never please everyone."

The last statement referred to her own children. He couldn't imagine the pain of it. Neither spoke for a long while, but the silence was easy to bear, Jack wasn't ready to venture to bed, not yet.

He had one more question in his heart that needed answering, and only Lindy could do that. He spoke again, working hard to hold back a frown that threatened, "Have you had time to think about what you will do when you leave here?"

At that moment Jack couldn't bear to hear her say that she'd be returning to Melbourne. An icy chill crawled up his back. What would happen when she left him and the children and return to her life as a businesswoman? Could he stand it? His heart hammered but he tried for nonchalance as he waited for her answer.

Had her eyes just watered? He watched the movement of her throat as she swallowed, then got up from the couch, grabbed the cups and walked out to the kitchen. The slump of her shoulders told him Melbourne was highly likely. He had to give her an alternative. But what could he offer? Elsa was yet to agree to his terms and then if she did, he had big changes ahead of him. There was no way he could keep the farm as a single dad and this second chance made him realise he wanted to be the one to raise his children.

Jumping up, Jack followed her into the kitchen and without hesitation turned her around to face him, his hands resting on her shoulders.

"Talk to me. What's wrong?" his gaze darted over her face as he bit down on his bottom lip, hoping she'd confide in him.

A ragged breath escaped, and she leant in to him, her head resting on his shoulder. The shiver passing through his body was epic, but right now Jack wanted to know if she planned on going home.

His lips collided with hers to show the depth of his feelings.

Jack relaxed slightly when Lindy took charge of the kiss. Her arms wrapped around his waist and her lips dancing with undeniable passion. Nothing could have prepared either of them for the intensity they experienced with each other. Jack's arms travelled around her back and up to her neck, as if holding her in place. He wanted her more than he ever believed possible. Their lips danced and tongues tangoed for an age. Eventually they came up for air, Jack searched her eyes deeply.

She didn't say anything. When Lindy gave him a small smile, he took that as encouragement, Jack reached for her again, cupping her cheeks, and taking more of what he yearned.

LINDY

Just the sight of this man had Lindy yearning to be with him. There was a bond with Jack that she never experienced, ever, in her married life. Even though the first few years with Ralph were wonderful, this connection with Jack was unfamiliar. In her first marriage their relationship turned sour when Ralph became incapable of making love to a woman, he only took what he wanted, her needs didn't matter.

Lindy couldn't deny her attraction to Jack, being honest with herself, Lindy could practically hear the zapping sparks which flew between them since the first night at the pub.

"Will you answer my question now? You can't kiss me like that and not say anything."

Although sleep beckoned, this question deserved an answer.

She pulled back and a thrill went through her at his usually light brown eyes now dark and pleading.

"First let me say, I have children back in Melbourne and even though they don't agree with my decisions, I plan to make sure they're okay, even if they will have nothing to do with me. And then there's also my career."

"But…"

She stopped him with a raised hand. This was her time to speak. He needed to hear her out. "I've spoken to my lawyer," she paused, chewed on her bottom lip before continuing. "I'm seriously considering selling the business. The young man I have been mentoring, would be the perfect candidate to buy me out."

A smile crept across Jack's lips. He gently caressed her shoulders and continued down her arms.

"It's all in the hands of my lawyer at the moment."

Had she said too much?

"What does this mean for us?"

"Nothing has happened between us yet, other than some amazing kisses, and yes they were amazing!" Lindy gave him a shy smile and inwardly cursed the heat as it scorched her cheeks. "Country life agrees with me, if it's not this town then I'll settle down somewhere else and enjoy a quieter life and become a part of their community."

"We need you here, you understand that, don't you?" Jack took hold of her hands.

Lindy didn't want to be needed, she wanted to be loved. Truly, deeply adored. The reality of raising another woman's family didn't scare her, but the idea of going through life unloved, sent her heart crashing in her chest.

Maybe by staying here she was setting herself up again, just as Ralph had done. She'd never cope with the intense pain a second time. Actually, the intense pain was more from her children, their rejection of her decision had cut deeply, and somehow Ralph's betrayal was an insignificant second.

"Before those kisses I would have been happy to stay just for the children and a friendship. I won't lie to you, Jack," Lindy shook her head, "Now I need more. There has always been an attraction between us, but both of us are in a tough place at the moment. I don't know that our circumstances are the best foundation to form a relationship."

Before Lindy could continue, Jack kissed her again. He pulled back smiling, "Definitely sparks, a magnitude 10.0 on my Richter scale."

"Not possible."

Jack laughed, mirth twinkling in his eyes.

"Will you hear me out?" Jack bent down to meet her eyes. His voice hushed now. The seriousness of the conversation was not lost on either of them.

Only when she nodded, did he continue.

"When I was in town on Tuesday fetching the part for the tractor, I was chatting to Deano at the farm supplies. He was telling me he's thinking about selling. Business is good, but he wants to retire. So, we discussed it further, and I have expressed an interest. If I sell this and give Elsa the agreed sum, I can purchase the farm supplies and buy a place in town for the kids and the horses."

"Horses? Nate said Elsa sold them," Lindy raised a questioning brow.

Jack's laugh was bitter. "She did…to my mate," Jack pushed back from her and ran his hands down his face. "He rang me when she made him the offer. We schemed, and I paid him the money. He bargained her right down, and he's taking care of them until I'm ready to collect them again." Jack scoffed, "She sold five horses and gear for a thousand dollars three weeks before she left."

"You've known all along what she was up to?" Lindy heard the alarming tone in her voice.

"If I had known she was capable of what she did to Bradley, I would have run her out of town myself. I just prayed she'd get herself in deep enough that I would get custody of the children. They were my major concern." He turned away but not before a deep pain shone through. Lindy wasn't sure whether the pain was a result of his actions or his wife's. It was intense.

"Nate endured so much when I wasn't around and he protected the others, except for the Bradley incident. It took only weeks for her to sink into her own demise." Jack ran his free hand roughly through his hair. "Anyway, as I was saying, I want you to be a part of us. You have shown me how wonderful it is to have someone special in my life."

Jack couldn't help it, he stole another memorable kiss.

"Are you sure that's what you want?" Lindy refused to misunderstand his meaning. Her future lay in his hands and Lindy wouldn't walk away with questions.

"You deserve deep love and affection." Jack told her. "I can't contradict what my heart is feeling. I love you."

"But…" Lindy was certain her eyes were the size of small plates.

"If you don't love me, that's okay," Jack said, not breaking the connection.

She finally stammered out, "I care for you. So much." Her head pivoting, as if to deny the words as they were spoken. Her mouth fell opened with some sort of clarity, "Are you saying I wasn't the only fool here?"

Although Jack was friendly and caring, him reciprocating her deepest feelings never entered her head as a possibility, only sheer hope. But declaring her love for this gorgeous man was a declaration her mind and heart couldn't comprehend right now.

"Are you calling me a fool woman?" he teased.

"Yes, we've known each other less than two weeks." Her hand trembled slightly as she caressed his face, she couldn't see him clearly through her tears. Though this time they were tears of pleasure.

The kiss they shared this time had all the makings of a future together. Lindy was finally honest with herself. Yes, this was where she wanted to be, well not on the farm but with this family and this wonderful man. Wherever Jack planned to take them she was desperate to be there, to be a part of his life. Lindy could only hope nothing anyone said to him now would change his mind. "Please tell me you won't wake up in the morning and run from me."

"If there's one thing I'm not, it's a coward," Pulling her in close, he added, "And just to confirm, I'm not the reason you're thinking of selling the business, am I?"

"No, I need a change."

JACK

They stood in an embrace, as their eyes met and bodies melded. Jack pulled her closer, caressing slowly and gently up and down her back. The comforting gesture helped settle him. Eventually he bent his knees so they were eye to eye.

"Let's get this straight. We're talking about a future together. Marriage and family. Lock, stock, and barrel. I don't want to scare you, but I need to know that's what you're agreeing too. A future with me."

Lindy tried to hold his gaze but her tears made it difficult, "You realise we're both insane." She closed her eyes when he laughed, forcing a few tears to escape. She swallowed hard and then regained her composure and spoke. "Oh Jack, I wish. That's what I want. You and the children and hopefully mine might accept my decision…one day. But I'm uncertain that I need this right now. I rushed into marriage with Ralph because I didn't know better."

"Did you ever love Ralph?" Being judgemental wasn't his purpose, but understanding the woman he cared so much about was vital.

Leaning back onto the end of the kitchen bench Lindy gripped it tightly with both hands and released a sigh.

What was she thinking about? Had she never challenged her feelings for the man she married? The strain on her face told a tale, one he was desperate to understand. He watched her mull over the answer.

"I loved him, in fact I believe he loved me. But when I announced my pregnancy with Cameron, our second son, something shifted. It was like he could not love another child. Liam seemed to be his limit."

"So, what about Sophie?"

"He wasn't as harsh on her but being a mere girl, she would never amount to anything in her father's eyes." Lindy gave a sharp laugh, "I remember him coming into the hospital and telling me. You've got your girl. That's it. No more children. And he made sure there wasn't, he had a vasectomy."

Trying to school his puzzled expression, he said, "I don't want to rush you but I have to know if you believe we have a future together. Where do you see your life going?"

Lindy shrugged and then shook her head. "I wish I knew."

MAKING CHANGES

LINDY

Friday morning rolled in and Lindy was still thinking about what occupied her mind the night before as she drifted off to sleep. The conversation with Joanna had Lindy analysing any setback for a girl who desperately wanted to see her mother again. Even though neither she nor Jack could fathom why Joanna wasn't as fearful of the woman as the others, they still understood her request. What could they do to prevent Elsa from hurting the child any more than she'd already done?

Getting out of bed with a sigh, she got ready to start her day. When Lindy entered the kitchen at the usual time, Jack walked down from the bedroom and greeted her with a kiss.

"I was thinking, I'll take the children to school," Jack filled the kettle with water, "I've gotta be in town all morning. There's a nine-thirty appointment with my lawyer to discuss the outcome of talks with Elsa. Then I'm meeting Deano from the farm supplies. After that I'll drop by the real estate office in town to see what's available." Jack packed Caleb's lunch box and drink bottle into his bag, "Lastly, I'll pop in next door and see Ray."

Lindy loved the way the man multitasked. It shouldn't have surprised her, considering the balancing act he'd undertaken living with his wife. Also, something else Lindy noted about Jack, when he decided on a way forward it was hard to miss that sparkle of hope glistening in his beautiful brown eyes.

"Okay, Bradley and I will take it easy this morning and just clean the house."

"You call that taking it easy?" he chuckled as he poured the hot water into their mugs.

The well-practised and relaxed morning routine was full of laughter. With Jack not having to rush out onto the farm, his presence encouraged the children to keep moving. With all the seed sowing done, Jack could step into the daily grind.

Lindy chatted and coaxed the children through their morning and then waved everyone off from the veranda with Bradley on her hip.

"Housework to do for me and playing in your play gym for you. We're both so busy," Lindy cooed as she tickled him under his chin. After settling him down on the floor, she systematically worked from one room to the next, taking Bradley as she went.

Her conversation with Jack last night was playing on her mind. He'd been so open. It would have been so easy to just take the opportunity before her. But she was in Chester's Run to work things out and not plunge herself into a situation similar to what she'd just escaped from.

Truthfully, she didn't believe for a minute Jack was anything like Ralph, but when she married Ralph, she couldn't believe he would turn out as he did either. A loud menacing grunt forced its way out, causing Bradley to yelp and shy away.

What a stupid thing to do!

Abandoning the housework Lindy walked slowly towards Bradley, her voice low and gentle.

"Hey little man, did I scare you?"

Bradley's eyes were bulging and fixated on her.

Picking him up, Lindy headed outside onto the swing and settled him on her lap. The warm Spring breeze brushed across them as they swung back and forth.

"Hey Bradley, I didn't mean it," she whispered as the swing rocked forward then back, her hand caressing his hair and cheek. Never once did he look at her. It took about ten minutes before he glanced up and then his little body moulded to hers.

What a hard lesson, but one she'd never forget. Lindy didn't want to think about the truth of what these children had been through and how a throw away response or grunt would set them off. None of them needed to remember those dark times.

JACK

After dropping off the children, Jack first stopped at his lawyers'. Hoping Elsa accepted the offer he'd made, he walked into Mac Senior's room and waited to see the father of one of his old school buddies.

"Morning Jack. Come on through," Mr MacDonald led the way down the hall.

"Morning. Thanks." Jack followed the lawyer into his office and took a seat opposite his large, mahogany desk. Nothing but complete order greeted him. Something about that told Jack of the man's attention to detail, that's how Jack did things. Knowing this man worked on his behalf comforted him.

"Well, we have wonderful news. Elsa agreed to all the terms after consulting her lawyer. Might I say it was good of you to give her access to representation. Well done."

"Thanks. I don't wish for her to rot in jail but I need to protect our children," he swallowed hard at the way the compliment unsettled him. That wasn't Mr MacDonald's intention but it didn't sit well with Jack at all.

"We've got fourteen days to complete a trust," the lawyer said as he handed over the signed agreement for Jack to see. "Oh yeah, here are the copies of all photos and I handed over the USB for her as you asked. Once she's cleaned herself up, her lawyer will contact me when all medicals have been passed. Then as you promised we will make a time for visitation."

"Do you believe she'll get clean?" he attempted to disguise his inner turmoil.

"You know her better than me, but let's just give her a chance. Remember, all access is supervised," the lawyer clarified, just as he'd done on the phone to Jack previously.

"Yeah, you're right." Jack should have been celebrating, but he couldn't stop the shiver race through him when he reflected on his ex. Something shifted, maybe a seed of discontent. He wasn't stupid enough to believe he'd seen the last of Elsa and her problems. For now, he could only hope his instincts were off this time.

JACK

Next stop, the Farm Supplies. As Jack stepped through the door the older man was serving customers. "Morning Deano."

"Hey mate, just give me a minute to help these guys and I'll be right with you."

Jack got chatting to a man while they waited.

"Sorry to hear about the missus. A shitty thing to happen."

"Thanks Ivan, hopefully everything will settle down for us all now." The man nodded and stepped up to the counter when Deano called him.

As he left, he stopped in front of Jack again. "See you later," Ivan shook his hand. "If there's anything Katie or I can do, you know where to find us."

"Means a lot, thanks."

He waited, looking around at the premises.

"Well come on through, the paperwork's in the office," they headed down a short hallway. Deano handed him the paperwork and quietly waited while Jack skimmed through the information.

Closing the folder, Jack asked, "How long will you need for settlement?"

"Me missus said as soon as possible but I think sixty days will be perfect. Gives me a chance to fix those things I mentioned to you in the wood store and clean out the junk."

Jack glanced around the building again. Finally, he spoke, "I think this is exactly what I need, have to put the kids first now. This will bring us into town and the kids can play sport again."

"How is your missus going?"

"She's not my missus anymore mate. I wish her well but we're officially through." Jack didn't look at Deano, he didn't want anyone to see his relief at moving on without her.

"So, you'll be looking for a place in town then?"

"It's the best way forward. Something with land. I'm heading to the real estate office next to see what's available. We might have to rent something till I can find exactly what I want."

"Good luck with it all." Deano hesitated, "Hang on a minute, don't see that bastard in town. Here, try this bloke," Deano searched through piles of paperwork. Jack waited patiently, "There it is, the little bugger. Here, the missus is using this guy to sell our place and her sister in Deans Brook swears by him. Real decent bloke, not like that idiot up the road."

Jack took the paper Deano offered. "Thanks. Better than Stefan?"

"Much...decent bloke and knows his business. Definitely a better option." The men walked towards the front of the store.

Jack turned to shake hands, "Thanks for everything, I appreciate the opportunity."

"Don't worry mate, you're not the only one who's happy about this. The missus is beside herself. Just you take care of those kids. I'll be waiting to hear from you."

"Will do. Thanks again."

Jack headed back to the lawyer's office to give him the paperwork. A pleased expression settled on his face, knowing he'd completed two of his four tasks for the day. He noted the time, it was getting late. There was still so much to achieve today.

JACK

Once he was back in the car Jack dropped his head onto the headrest. None of the properties Michael Evans showed him were suitable. He needed to hear Lindy's voice.

"Hi Jack," she answered.

"How's everything?" Jack tried to keep his voice upbeat.

"Okay. Bradley's asleep." He heard hesitation, "How'd everything go?"

"Lawyer and farm supplies better than expected. House hunting was rather disappointing, unfortunately."

"Oh, I'm sorry Jack," And she was, he could hear it in her voice.

"Let's hope I have more luck with Ray and the boys."

"You'll work it out."

"Is everything okay?"

"Yep. It's all good." Lindy answered almost too quickly.

"Well. I'll let you go," Jack didn't know how else to keep the conversation going. He needed to be there to see her face, to understand what the problem was. If there was in fact something wrong. They hadn't known each other long enough for him to understand the situation from what he'd heard.

"Okay then. Good luck with Ray."

When Lindy ended the call Jack could only stare out the window. It was beyond amazing to be with her. How was he going to convince her to give them a go?

JACK

Last stop. Ray's. Jack prayed nothing had changed from the last conversation. He drove past his driveway looking up towards the house, Lindy was there looking after Bradley. Was she missing him like he missed her?

Continuing up the road for a little way, Jack turned up Ray's wide driveway lined with a mass of gum trees on either side. His memories went back to a time when he and his mates would ride their bikes up and down this driveway for hours. Welcome cups of cordial and cake or biscuits back at the house, always went down a treat. Ray and Marge's was like his second home. The realisation he and Elsa never provided his children with the security he took for granted growing up, sent a knife through his heart. He wasn't altogether blameless in this. If he was honest with himself, Jack Saunders believed himself a coward.

"Arvo Jack. Good to see you mate," Ray walked towards him across the gravel driveway.

"You too, thanks for your help the other day," Jack took the man's outstretched hand.

"Our pleasure, what brings you out here?"

"Does your offer still stand, same price?" Jack kicked his boot into the fine dust on the path.

"Yeah, you bet. Are you ready to talk?" Ray's face lit up.

"Spoke to Dad last night and he's more than happy to sell. Old Mr Mac will draw up the papers as soon as you're ready."

Ray nodded to Jack when he noticed dust rising on the track from the back paddocks, "Excellent, let's include the boys."

The four men stood together, nutting out the details. A pang of something surged through him, but tough times called for change and his commitment to his family was too important. The farm had to go.

"Done." Ray said when they all agreed. "How about we take over the paddocks now and you move out when you find something?"

"Great, include rent into the contract," Jack offered.

"Nah, that's unnecessary. Take the time you need." Ray didn't hesitate.

"I can't do that."

"Fine, put it in your bloody contract, after a year you can pay $200 a week rent," Ray's right arm flew.

"No, I'm not taking advantage of you. You could rent the house out, I can't expect you to do that." Although Ray's generous nature would give Jack a chance to organise himself and not rush him into an unsuitable purchase, he understood how hard living on the land could be.

"Okay then no deal," Ray's tight, straight face stared back at Jack, the man never wavered.

"You can't be serious."

"Mate, we don't need the house," Ray's youngest son Troy said. "The place will be mine but I'm staying with Bert for now so do as Dad said. Anyway, you'll find something before then, don't worry."

Jack nodded, they were right, "Sold. Thanks guys, I really appreciate this."

"We'll come over and have a look at the machinery. I'd like to take that off your hands too. I know you keep it all in top nick," Ray added as an afterthought.

"Whenever you want. Just call me," Jack told Ray as one of the farm dogs came up and sat by Troy.

"Well, I'll be in touch. Thanks again…for everything," Jack shook hands with each of them and headed back across the driveway to his car. Home was waiting.

ALL TOO MUCH

JACK

The clatter of spoons against bowls drew Jack out of his self-imposed funk. He smiled at the eager destroyers of the humble apple pie. With everything happening recently, Jack sensed it all taking its toll. If he could have got away with missing the family dinner, he would have. But there was a depth of the unknown which kept him afloat. Maybe it was Lindy or even knowing his children were safe. Something kept him from plundering over the edge.

Catching Lindy's eye, his lips turned up in the corners. Slightly. "Umm, it's safe to say they didn't like that," he told Lindy.

"That's fine, I won't do dessert again," she answered.

"What! No way." Nate cried.

"Oh Dad," Evie admonished.

Caleb and Joanna's mouths were full of pie and ice cream so they could only shake their heads and grunt their disapproval. Jack grasped for the relaxed, cheerful atmosphere around the table. He had to hand it to his family they were keeping him from a downward spiral with just their presence.

Nate pushed away his empty bowl, glanced first towards Lindy and then his father. "Dad, can I ask you something?"

Jack gave a measured reply, "Sure buddy, you know you can ask anything."

In an instant the mood around the table turned sombre.

Lindy and Jack looked at one another and then at Nate.

Nate drew in a breath and clasped his shaking hands, "Will Mum ever come home to us?"

Jack ran his fingers through his hair, searching for the right words to explain the situation to his children that wouldn't scar them for life.

"No mate, your Mum and I have agreed to go separate ways, but you guys will stay with me. The most important thing is that you're all safe and happy. You are happy, aren't you?"

The enthusiastic agreement around the table had tears welling, but Jack swallowed hard holding them at bay. Well, all agreed sighed except Joanna. Her desire to see her mother was never far from Jack's mind. He saw the dedication Lindy showed when she dealt with Joanna's need to reconnect with Elsa.

"Oh, thank goodness," Nate smiled at Lindy, the woman who brought structure, security and not to mention unconditional love back into their lives. "Dad, will Lindy stay with us, we don't want her to go away. We were all talking about it, Lindy belongs here with us. Don't you think so?"

Jack didn't know where to go with this. His eyes darted from his children to the woman who'd shown him something much deeper than a man's desire.

"I hope she'll stay," Evie reached for Lindy's hand. "You're happy here, aren't you?"

Even the normally endless chatter from Bradley stopped, Lindy met the tense expression of the children.

"Everyone, hang on a minute," Jack held up his hands. "You know Lindy has a family back in Melbourne."

"But we know she loves us and she's...special," Evie's voice wobbled.

There was no doubt this woman was special.

"That's a decision for her to make. We need to understand Lindy needs time." Jack told his children.

"Dad, can I ask you something that's private?" Nate's questioning tone was barely audible.

Knowing this could end up anywhere, Jack pushed on, "Anything mate?" Jack loved how opened Nate learnt to be.

"Do you love her?" Nate didn't meet his father's gaze.

Jack's head dropped, unsure how to proceed. His heart raced thinking of Lindy. For the first time in his life, Jack understood love, true love...between him and Lindy. He placed a gentle hand under Nate's chin, lifting it so their eyes met, "We all know Lindy is wonderful. Look what she's done around here to help us."

"The kids at school say you're living with her, that's why you had Mum arrested. But don't worry, I told them the truth." Jack's jaws clenched, "Mr Tuttenham broke us up as Mickey grabbed my shirt. He took me and the boys into his office and they said rude things about you and Lindy. Mr Tuttenham told them off and sent me back to class. I don't know what happened but I don't think those boys will pick on me again."

"Did they hurt you?" the colour drained from Lindy's face.

"No way, I can beat them in a fight." Nate was more than confident in his abilities.

Lindy's brow furrowed when she caught Jack's smirk. "Lindy is very important to all of us, and she's a very special friend. But don't believe lies people say, okay?"

Nobody responded.

Jack's mobile rang. Struggling to dig the phone out of his pocket, he read the caller ID, it was George Tuttenham. He excused himself from the table and walked into the lounge to take the call.

LINDY

With the eyes of the children on her, Lindy got up from the table to clear away.

"Thank you, Nate." She leaned over the table to gather up the empty pie dish and server.

"What for?" Nate asked, puffing out his cheeks and releasing a rush of breath.

"You stood up for me today and that means something. Something amazing. But I don't encourage fighting. Your dad is working hard to protect you. Please be careful."

"I know it was right and made me feel good. And anyway, I didn't start it!" Nate answered.

"I know love, but I don't want anyone to hurt you guys. None of you."

The nods from the children as they helped clear the table told Lindy they understood. A knowing grin spread on Nate's face, he believed in the cause. He had taken a stand for what he believed in, and Lindy couldn't fault his loyalty.

"You did the right thing, trusting your feelings. The same way you did for Bradley. You're all very special to me, never forget that and remember your father needs your help and support at the moment." She took a step away from the table and stopped, "And also remember I'm here for you all, okay? Whenever you need to talk, I'm here."

Disappointed they'd lost the easy feel of the evening, Lindy ushered the children off. She needed to talk with Jack and make sure he was coping with everything. She didn't miss the distant stares from him earlier.

"Come on, time for showers and bed," she turned towards the sink, but there weren't any footsteps and she turned back to see the children watching her. Without giving it a thought, she put down her load and gave each of them a hug and kiss before sending them on their way.

The children were in bed reading forty minutes later.

"Lindy, can you send Dad up to say goodnight," Caleb called as she left the room.

Lindy agreed before walking into the girl's room to help Joanna with her letter to her mother.

"Okay, what have you written so far?" This was the fourth letter she and Joanna had composed together. Even though each letter was only short, it never failed to pull at her heartstrings.

Joanna read.

Dear Mumy,

Today at schol I played with Rosey. She asked me if I can play netbal. I hop I can.

Lindy explained to Joanna her mum probably wanted to hear about things she was doing.

My reading is geting beter and so is my handwriting se

I wil write again son

Love

Joanna.

"That's beautiful," Lindy didn't even attempt to correct the mistakes. That was part and parcel of a child's progress. Lindy watched on as Joanna selected her coloured pencils for the picture she drew with every letter. A stick figure of herself with her mother. The first day the smile on the drawing of Joanna was huge. But as the drawings continued, Lindy noticed how the smile diminished.

A few minutes later Joanna packed everything away, "Can we post this tomorrow?" she pointed to the envelope.

"Absolutely. Your mum will love it." Lindy picked up the envelope, "I'll leave this in the kitchen."

Joanna looked up at her with a smile. Lindy kissed her goodnight and then Evie.

"Lights out in ten," she called to them all. Ten minute's reading helped settle them after such an active day. With a sigh, she walked towards the lounge to find Jack.

JACK

As he left the dining room Jack took the call, "Hi George."

"Jack, Sorry to ring you so late, but we had an incident at school today and I wanted to let you know what happened."

"I was just talking to Nate about it, he explained his side of the story to us."

"How is he? The boys didn't believe him when he told them what Elsa had done to Bradley."

"He's more worried for me and Lindy."

"I can't stop gossip, but I set some parents straight today," George replied.

Jack's heart ached at how the lies would affect Lindy. He paused before replying. "Thanks, I appreciate that. Lindy doesn't deserve the gossip after everything she's done for us."

"There are some things which are no one else's business, mate, you need to move on. Forget about the nosy gossips and do what's right for you and your family. For all of you." There was a hidden meaning there and Jack breathed easier knowing George understood his plight. George's show of support was appreciated, considering a few weeks earlier they could barely cope with the tragic events of their lives.

Understanding his friend's message Jack replied, "She's very special but both of us have things to work out."

"Good for you. I won't keep you, I just wanted to let you know Nate did you both proud today."

"He told us as much, thanks for the call. Means a lot."

Jack hung up his phone and stared at the ceiling. With his mind a jumble, he focused instead on the lack of cobwebs which used to invade the corners of the lounge. There it was again, another reminder of Lindy's dedication, love, and devotion. He sat for a long time lost deep in reflection.

JACK

Not sure how long had passed, Jack opened his eyes to see Lindy leaning against the door frame.

"George. To tell us about what happened," he held up his mobile phone.

"The children are waiting for you to say goodnight," she told him and turned towards the kitchen.

By the time Jack returned, the dishes and kitchen was tidy, but Lindy wasn't there.

He found her in the lounge.

"Sorry about all this. Maybe I should move back into town."

He could see how affected Lindy was by the gossip, the children's welfare was always number one where Lindy was concerned.

"You're not going anywhere. We have done nothing to upset the children and even if there was nothing between us the gossips would still have their say. Anyway," watching her closely, he added, "Do you know what?"

"What?" she asked as he slid onto the couch beside her.

"So much happened this week, a month ago I couldn't have coped with any of it." He pulled her closer. "I'd run and hide when I could, hoping Elsa would lay off the kids. The more they came to me, the more aggressive she got. Instead of looking for help, I buried my head in the sand. That realisation hit me today. I tried to convince myself I was doing the right thing. I was as much a crap father as she was a bullshit mother." He ground his back teeth, his pulse thudding at his throat.

"No, how could you have foreseen she would physically hurt the children. If you tried to act against her, she would have got the kids, where would that have left you...and them?" She gripped his arm.

"I keep trying to convince myself of that but I can't. She took drugs and even though I didn't know what concoction, I couldn't ignore it was happening. I convinced myself if I didn't give her money, she'd stop." Jack threw his head back and groaned. "How bloody foolish was that? How can a father do that to his kids?"

"You were desperate," Lindy reasoned.

Waving his hand towards the kitchen, he continued, "You've seen it for yourself. She sold everything she could. Even the bloody horses. The bitch sold her children's horses to feed her addiction," he swiped at a tear and dropped his head into his hands.

"Shit."

He clenched his fists, squeezed his eyes shut. A tremor bored its way from the depth of his soul, Jack allowed a blackness to engulf him. He sunk further down into the couch releasing a low whine, sounding almost dog like.

LINDY

This was something she'd never experienced. Jack was a broken man. The focus which drove him recently cracked. Now here was a man desperate for help. She came to the realisation that this exact step was what she and Ralph bypassed. Something in that comforted her. There was hope for Jack to survive this.

Lindy knelt before Jack and rocked him in her arms. He sobbed uncontrollably. When the wailing began Lindy messaged for help.

Harry, Tessa, please help. Jack has just hit rock bottom.

Only Tessa replied.

Lindy I'm coming with Mum and Dad hang in there.

Thanks.

Ten minutes later a car pulled up in the driveway. Jack hadn't registered they had visitors, so Lindy stayed with him. The door opened and Harry came into the lounge.

"Close the hallway door over please," Lindy wanted to keep as much of this from the children as possible.

Harry came back as his partner walked inside. "Terry, Lindy Kemp. Lindy, my partner Terry." They greeted each other with nods as Harry sat next to his brother-in-law and tried to ease his pain.

"Hey mate, talk to me."

But Jack was rocking.

Terry walked to the front door when they heard a second car.

Harry nodded to his father-in-law as he entered the lounge room. He got up and made room for Tony and Darla to sit with their son. Lindy gave a weak smile as they slid beside him. Still she couldn't move away. Jack's hold on her was intense.

She lifted his head off her shoulder, "Jack, everyone's here to help," she dropped a kiss on his forehead unable to resist touching him.

After an interminable silence, Jack shifted his gaze from Lindy and took the tissues Tessa offered him.

"Thanks. Sorry for all this," he struggled to inhale the breaths he desperately needed.

Lindy told the family about the conversation with the children at dinner, also mentioning the phone call from George. Jack let go of Lindy and sat back, dropping his head onto the back of the couch. His eyes were closed, but she could tell he listened as she spoke.

"Now he has expressed how much of an awful father he's been. This man is blaming himself for what a drug-affected woman did to his children."

Harry stood before him. "Jack Saunders, look at me." Harry's tone was gruff, "You did what you could whilst trying to protect your kids. There's no way the courts would have taken the children from her with the minor things happening. You had no proper evidence of neglect or abuse. You did the very best you could for the kids, so don't you dare blame yourself."

Tessa paced, trying but failing miserably to control her emotions.

Jack took his father's hand and lent his head on his mother's shoulder. "Thanks for coming, I need you guys right now."

"Don't thank us, Lindy's the one we should thank. I can't imagine if you were home alone with no one to lean on," Darla smiled at Lindy.

She'd never experienced anything like this, watching a father, a genuine family man, be ashamed of something beyond his control. Sure, there were things that could have been dealt with differently, but under the circumstances Jack did the best he could.

Elsa went to substantial lengths to push away all his mates and their partners, and eventually Tessa and Harry and his parents. Lindy remembered how Jack spoke of the way Elsa no longer welcomed his family at the farm. Watching Jack and his parents now, she could see pain written all over their faces.

JACK

Silence settling around them was one of comfort and maybe even a sense of achievement. For the first time in a long while, Jack believed in himself. Before Lindy, his plan was to get it right for his children, but now something inside him demanded love, unity, comfort, and peace. Jack looked at Lindy, what he'd dreamt of with her lately could become their reality. Would she see things the way he did? There was only one way to find out. Jack slipped his hands into Lindy's and rested his forehead to hers.

"Thank you," he whispered.

Tony eased himself up off the couch. Gesturing towards the kitchen as he asked, "How about a cuppa, love?" Jack smiled as his father led Darla, Harry, and Tessa into the kitchen to join Terry who made himself scarce earlier.

Looking down into the stunning blue eyes which attracted him from the very first time they crossed paths, Jack drew in his first controlled breath in a long while.

An angelic smile stretched across her face. Oh, this beautiful face, this smile, this woman. Yes, there was no question, she was everything to him. Jack rested his forehead on hers again and pulled her closer.

"So, Ms Kemp, please tell me, where you've been all my life?" his voice rough and low.

Lindy placed her hand over his heart, "Right here. It's just neither of us had met yet. I don't care what anyone says about us. We've done nothing to be ashamed of, I see that now, especially when we fell in love."

Jack pulled back so he could see her face and those beautiful blue eyes. "Did you just tell me you've fallen in love? With me? For real?"

With her eyes locked to his, she could only nod as her hand toyed with the gold chain around her neck.

"Talk to me," Jack's face now radiated a warmth he didn't feel sitting around the table for dinner with his children. The words she'd spoken fractured the dark cloud he'd been carrying. Light and hope seeped through the moment Lindy declared her love.

JACK

Jack caressed Lindy's face, "I love you Lindy Kemp, until I met you, I never understood what true love was." He added with a laugh, "And we haven't even got to the good stuff yet."

Hearing footsteps, Jack looked up to see Tessa hightailing it out of the lounge back towards the kitchen. He listened as voices wafted into the lounge.

"What?" asked Harry.

"I don't think the words 'fond of' or 'like' come anywhere close to what's going on in there. I see wedding bells." No one spoke.

Jack began to chuckle softly as Lindy buried her head into his chest. Trust his sister not to hold her tongue.

"I don't think I can show my face around here again," Lindy said as she looked up.

Jack kissed the tip of her nose. "Yes, you will. I'm not giving you up out of pure embarrassment," He gave a low chuckle as he watched a blush invade her beautiful face.

They heard Terry speak, "How about I take the car home tonight and you pick it up in the morning?"

"Sounds good to me," Harry replied, "See you tomorrow," he followed Terry out.

Jack watched Harry reappear into the dining room as Tessa walked into his arms and rested her head on his shoulder and only moving when a sob rang out.

Jack and Lindy looked at each other. At first, they couldn't make out who it was. They headed quickly to the doorway. Sliding open the glass doors between the lounge and hallway.

"Hey buddy, are you okay?" Tessa asked as she settled down next to Nate.

"Will they?" he sobbed.

"Will they what?" Tessa looked up to meet Jack's eyes.

"Will Dad and Lindy get married?"

"I don't know," Tessa grinned at Jack. "Do you like her?" Tessa pulled him into a tight hug.

"I think we love her as much as he does. I feel safe when she's here. I know she hasn't been here long, but if Lindy goes away…" Nate couldn't finish the sentence before he broke down into noisy sobs again.

Jack pulled Lindy close and kissed the side of her head. The discomfort of earlier forgotten. "Hey, mate," Jack squatted before his son.

"He has questions that need answering."

Jack saw the rush of colour on his sister's face but instead of chastising her as he normally would, he scooped the tall lad into his arms, pulled him into a tight hug and let Nate cry it out. Lindy wrapped her arms around father and son. For Jack, it was the perfect place for her to be.

He looked up to see his parents' tears. They were experiencing his hardship right along with him. Out of the corner of his eyes he watched as Harry comforted Tessa. He was grateful when Harry guided his sister and parents back to the kitchen.

Jack didn't miss Harry's next words, "They'll get through this, no one expects it to be easy but they'll work it out."

Jack said a silent prayer of thanks for his brother-in-law's confidence in him and his amazing family. They hadn't always seen eye to eye but they only wanted what was best for Jack and the children. He rocked his son until Nate managed to calm down.

Jack led both Nate and Lindy into the kitchen. "We all need to talk, everyone take a seat." He'd regained his control from earlier. His voice sent a more composed message.

I've got this.

The family settled around the table. Jack pulled a chair out for Lindy, they exchanged a knowing look as Nate took the seat next to hers. Jack couldn't hide his grin as he took the seat next to his son. There was something calming about the depth of love that rolled off Lindy in waves, and that smile was so encouraging.

"Today was a big day," He sighed and then continued, "I went to see Old Mr MacDonald. Elsa has accepted my offer. She's signed divorce papers and full custody of the children to me," the moment the news registered, Darla dropped her head while a slow smile stretched across Tony's face. "We've agreed on a settlement and she's moving back to the city to be with her family while she waits for the trial."

There was a uniformed sigh which echoed around the table.

Lindy asked, "Nate, do you understand what your father has said?"

"Yes, I think so. She's gone for good."

"Well not exactly. If she cleans herself up, she will be entitled to supervised access. But that won't happen for a while yet," Jack explained.

"What if we don't want to see her?" Nate's wide eyes met his father's.

"Then we'll cross that bridge when we come to it."

Harry spoke up giving a professional point of view to comfort his nephew. "The law will consider your wishes, buddy." Nate nodded to his uncle and shifted his eyes back to his father and waited.

"I spoke to Dad," Jack lent back in his chair, "We're selling the farm to Ray and the boys. The price is reasonable. It's in Old Mac's hands now," Tony nodded, emphasising his support for Jack's decisions.

Tessa's eyes widened, "What will you do?"

Jack smiled. Plans were already in place. "Deano is selling the farm supplies, we've been in discussion this week and those papers are with the lawyers as well. Hopefully, I'll sign on Monday."

"Wow, that's fantastic. You've been busy." Tessa's pride shone.

"So, finding a house is paramount, I'll move the family into town and live a normal life. We could stay here but I don't want this anymore," Jack waved his hand around indicating the house and property. "We all need a fresh start."

"What sort of place are you looking for?" Harry asked.

"Well, seeing as we still own five horses and all the tack, I think something on the outskirts of town would be perfect, ten to fifteen acres and hopefully a house with rooms for all the kids. I plan on us all being there for a long time," Nate's tears slowly descending over the curve of his cheeks.

"Hey, what's wrong?"

"You said we still have horses, but we don't. She sold them." Nate didn't say 'Mum'. What pain must he be feeling to have already disowned Elsa as his mother?

"Well funny story that," Jack tried to ease the tension. "She sold them to Bernie. He rang me as soon as she made the offer. Bernie has kept them safe for us."

With that, Nate dropped his head on Lindy's shoulder, not bothering to contain his tears. Lindy pulled him into a hug which wasn't missed by anyone.

Jack understood how important this news was for Nate. To hear the horses, were safe and still theirs was probably beyond any of his wildest dreams. Lindy held Nate, rocking him gently. His heart lurched as he saw her dabbing at her own eyes. This woman had so much love to share.

"I'm sorry buddy, I couldn't tell you in case your mother found out," Jack scratched at his cheek and bit his bottom lip. He knew how much time and effort Nate put into brushing, cleaning, and riding with his siblings over the years. He'd taken on the responsibility of them himself. Nate loved, cared, and protected the horses, especially when his father was busy on the farm, just as he did with his siblings.

"When can we see them?" Nate wiped at tears again.

"Is tomorrow soon enough? Bernie will let you ride them, I reckon." This brought a smile to Nate's face. One of pure joy.

TRUTH TO TELL

LINDY

The bright orange sunrise peeked through the corner of Lindy's curtains. This time of morning brought peace and comfort before her day began. Rolling over, she stretched and enjoyed the blissfulness only an early morning offered. She considered the day ahead. So much promise, she could only imagine how excited, and in a small way, upset the children would be hearing about their animal friends. Nate would be up early this morning knowing they would see the horses. Her memory replayed the conversation with his father right before she put him to bed for the second time last night.

Throwing back the bedding, she tossed her legs over the side and settled her bare feet on the timber floor. As the cold seeped from her feet up her body, Lindy drew in a deep breath of fresh crisp September air and began her day.

After tidying the bungalow, she began the trek over towards the house. The curtains at the backdoor were swaying in the morning breeze. Lindy looked around to see where Jack could be, his car was there. She turned and saw the shed door was opened. Changing direction Lindy walked over to say good morning. As she ventured closer, voices echoed out to greet her.

"Does Bernie have everything Dad, all the tack and cleaning gear?"

"Yes mate. Bandy's coat is looking as shiny as ever. I promise Bernie's taken excellent care of them."

"What time can we go?"

"Morning," Lindy called as she stepped through the shed doors.

Jack's smiling eyes met hers. She listened to the conversation from Nate and noticed something cross Jack's handsome face. Not even his early morning stubble could hide a realisation, had he also deduced they'd miss their early morning cuppa and cuddle because of Nate?

"Morning. So, Dad what time?" Nate questioned his father again.

Lindy came up beside them.

"When everyone is up and Bernie is ready for us."

"Oh! Come on," The words rushed from his mouth, both clear and piercing.

"Nate," Jack warned, "Help me finish putting this together, next we'll start sorting out this shed." Jack put his hands on his hips and surveyed the years of equipment and junk, "No, on second thoughts, get your boots, let's go out and check the watering systems first."

"Okay Dad."

While Nate ran back to the house to find his work boots, Jack put the next few minutes with Lindy to good use. Pulling her into his arms he began systematically placing kisses beginning with her forehead, over her eyelids, the tip of her nose and finally settling on her lips. The deep kiss they shared stopped suddenly. In the far recesses of her mind, Lindy had a vague memory of heavy footfalls echoing across the back-yard. Fortunately, Jack broke their connection because Lindy showed no sign of letting go.

She gripped the bench as Jack stepped away and turned towards the door. Breathing deeply, she remained rooted to the spot until the guys left. Ralph never affected her the way Jack did. Once the Ute pulled away Lindy placed one unsteady foot in front of the other and headed for the kitchen, slowly calming herself.

LINDY

Saturday morning was the perfect excuse to let the children sleep in. The only place they needed to be was Bernie's and since Nate was the only one who found out about the horses, the others wouldn't be in any rush to begin their day.

After a strong cup of tea and many minutes lost in sweet memories, Lindy began packing food. She gathered some cooler bags and organised a picnic lunch. Even though her knowledge of horses could be written on her palm, Lindy was aware, once the children met up with their equine family again, there would be a struggle to get them home before the sun went down. The next hour Lindy prepared, baked, wrapped, and packed. By the time Evie and Joanna walked into the kitchen, it was just after eight.

"Morning," the girls called as they walked happily into one of her warm embraces.

"Morning girls, did you sleep well?" Did they know what had transpired last night?

"Yep, nice to sleep in and just wake up because," Evie replied as she crawled onto a stool at the breakfast bar.

Okay, so Jack must have got to Nate before he could inform his siblings.

"What's the bags for?" asked Joanna.

"Your father was thinking of a picnic lunch somewhere," okay, so Lindy stretched the truth just a little.

"You mean like the one the other week when you took us down to eat with Dad?" Evie grinned.

"Yes, something like that." Lindy hoped her face didn't give away the white lie.

"Awesome, that was so much fun," Joanna bounced on her stool.

"There goes Bradley," Evie pushed herself out of her chair. "Do you want me to get him for you?"

"Thanks love, that would be great, I'll just get the cake out of the oven." Lindy pottered around the kitchen, listening to Joanna reliving their earlier picnic.

"Did you make roast chicken and salad again?" Joanna asked.

"Not this time, today we're having sandwiches." Lindy said but couldn't say more. Evie stormed into the kitchen with her baby brother lodged on her hip and a note scrunched up in her hand.

"Where's Nate? I'll kill him." The ravaged look on Evie's face was in total contrast to five minutes earlier.

"Why love, what's wrong?" Lindy stepped towards her. Evie's eyes were full of unspilt tears. What could Nate have done to upset her? Especially considering he was out with his father.

"This note," the balled-up piece of paper landed on the bench but before she read it, Jack drove back into the yard. Evie thrust Bradley at Lindy, oblivious of his broken arm, and marched outside with a full head of steam. Lindy and Joanna just stared after her.

JACK

When the Ute stopped at the backdoor, Evie let loose. "Nate you're horrible, why would you make up those lies about the horses?" she yelled as he opened the car door.

Jack's head snapped around to see a flush of colour race up his son's neck and face.

"What did you do?"

"I wrote a note last night," Nate sighed, "I forgot about it when you told me not to say anything this morning," they both turned back to Evie, her face red and mouth twisted in a snarl.

Jack jumped out of the car and cut her off before she could reach her brother.

"What did the note say, love?"

On a sob she replied, "He said we still have the horses." Evie's body shuddered as she tried to breathe. "That's so mean," her last state-ment was spat out in Nate's direction.

By now Lindy and Joanna watched the scene unfold from the patio. Bradley wriggled on Lindy's hip as Caleb walked out, rubbing the sleep from his eyes.

Jack picked up Evie and carried her inside. He could feel her tears through his T-shirt as her head rested on his shoulder. He cuddled her close and directed the others to sit at the table. Evie remained on her father's lap, still quietly crying.

Once everyone settled Jack began, "Evie, Nate would never tease you about something like that, what he wrote in the note is true."

Wiping her palms down her face, Evie's lips pinched.

"I had to make you all believe your mother sold the horses, that way I could keep them safe," Jack explained how their mother sold everything to Bernie, "He's taken excellent care of them." Jack swallowed hard and took in Lindy's nod, "Hey, we still have our horses," The ones Jack handpicked for each of them, broken them in and trained himself.

Lindy strapped Bradley in his high chair and made breakfast for everyone while Jack spoke to the children.

This story broke his heart last night when he explained it to Nate. This morning Jack's tension ebbed with the children's delight.

"Well how about I ring Bernie to see if we can head over?"

Jack listened to the chatter around the table while he talked with Bernie, he walked back into the room announcing, "As soon as we finish breakfast and the housework we'll head over to Bernie's."

By the time the morning routine was complete, Jack and the boys went out to pack the Ute, "Nate, you grab that lot there," he pointed to fold away chairs lying beside the Ute, "Caleb, you can help me with the food."

They worked as a team.

"Dad, where shall I put these?" Nate stood holding all the riding gloves.

"Give them to their owners. Remember, we're all responsible for our own gear."

Not being able to suppress his pleasure, Jack turned for the last esky of food. Talking horses with his children was inbred, so not doing it lately was akin to having a limb severed. The topic of horses was something they always connected with. Looking over the packed Ute, Jack smiled, Lindy took such care preparing an awesome spread for the day. Elsa never had been this generous and practical for others.

With everyone ready, the family piled into the cars and headed into town.

HORSE REUNION

LINDY

"*T*his is so exciting," Joanna squealed as Lindy followed Jack's Ute. She listened as chatter oozed from the girls. Bernie must be a great guy to do what he'd done for Jack and the Saunders family. Understanding Bernie's love of horses equalled Jack's in every way, she wasn't surprised.

She recalled the conversation last night after everyone had gone.

"We grew up together and spent a lot of time riding and learning about horses," Jack told her.

Lindy turned and followed Jack up a long driveway, and spotted a farmhouse in the distance.

"There's Bernie and Nola," Joanna yelled, twisting in her seat as Lindy brought the car to a stop next to Jack's Ute.

"Morning Bernie, Nola." Jack said as he got out.

"Jack." Bernie shook his hand. "Well, I reckon you've got some hyper kids there," Bernie looked as excited at this reunion as the Saunders were.

"Nola, Bernie, this is Lindy," Jack said as Lindy walked towards them.

She shook hands with them both.

"Hi, lovely to meet you."

"You too. Welcome to our little corner of the world," Bernie's grin was friendly.

"Now I was thinking of doing a barbie for lunch, are you all up for that?" Nola asked and Lindy smiled at her correct assumption, knowing full well Jack wouldn't be able to get the children home before evening.

"Well, actually Lindy prepared a picnic," Jack showed too much pride as he mentioned her.

Heat rushed to Lindy's cheeks when Nola raised an eyebrow. What was with her inner teenager surfacing? Shifting her gaze to the children, Lindy released a slow breath when Nola didn't linger. "Great. Let's get it in the fridge, why don't you lot head down to the horses. Our kids are already down there getting ready. They were so excited to hear you were coming."

"That should do it," Nola said as the last of the containers finally found a home in the overloaded fridge.

Lindy and Nola followed the eager horse lovers down to the arena and adjoining paddocks. The excited squeals and chatter made for an entertaining experience. Lindy spied Bernie in the thick of it, but Jack was nowhere to be seen. Turning slowly, Lindy spotted Jack on a camp chair next to Bradley, who chewed on a biscuit.

"I've got this," Jack said when Lindy walked up beside him.

Using a firm voice, Lindy argued, "No. I've got him. Off you go."

"You've had him all week," Lindy could see Jack was torn between enjoying this occasion with his children or staying close to her. Did he think she needed protection from these people?

"Jack, go," Lindy replied as she stared him down.

Nola laughed. They looked at her and then at each other.

"Don't you say a word," he hissed, pointing a finger in her direction as he walked off. This fun, teasing man was a far cry from the man she comforted the previous evening. Nola's laugh followed him as he headed to the arena to join his children.

Once Nola, Lindy and Bradley settled under the shade of a vast peppercorn tree, an interrogation began. "Okay, I've seen more affection from him towards you in half-an-hour, than his wife of twelve years. What's going on, girl?"

Lindy let out a short laugh and turned her attention to Bradley and the mess he was making.

"Now I understand Jack's warning."

Nola threw her head back laughing. "Do the children know?"

"No." She sighed. "We both have so much to sort out," Lindy's eyes took in everyone but settled on Jack as he worked with his children. They all revelled in horse life.

"From the city, aren't you?"

"Yep."

"Can I ask what happened?"

Lindy gave a slow nod, more to herself than Nola. Yes, she was ready to talk about it all. Lindy explained what happened to her a little over a fortnight ago. She retold the tale of the letter she received and the confrontation with her husband of twenty-six years. When Lindy finished speaking for some strange reason peace washed over her. A heavyweight, figuratively, lifted.

"Do you realise you never showed emotion just then?" Nola pointed out.

Lindy stared off towards the surrounding mountains.

"No, I didn't. But it feels different somehow. Maybe I'd already checked out of my marriage and never accepted it until now."

"So, where do you two go from here?"

"Straight shooter, aren't you," Lindy teased but answered. "We've talked, Jack's had to make a lot of changes this week. It's been…" Lindy sighed, "I need to go home and finalise everything. I'm still deciding what to do about my business, sell or work remotely." Bradley whined and kicked his chubby legs, trying to kick off the blanket. Lindy prepared his bottle and lifted him out for a cuddle. She supported the bottle, and he snuggled down happily.

"I've known Jack a long time. We all went to school together. Bernie and I got married after we finished the final year. Over the years Jack spent a lot of time around here riding horses." Nola gave Lindy a weak smile, then was quiet. "I don't know how much he's told you about Elsa, but she never fit in here. Of all our friends from school, Jack's the only one who stopped coming around," Nola grimaced, "She wouldn't let him."

"He told me losing his friends was when it all became obvious," Lindy dropped her eyes to the sleeping baby in her arms. "An addiction can be so destructive."

"Yes, and the harm to others can be devastating. Hopefully, he's young enough not to realise his own mother did that." Nola indicated Bradley's broken arm.

Lindy's gaze travelled from Bradley to the other children and then to Jack.

"He's a wonderful man, if you two are meant to be I can promise he's capable of loving deeply. You can see it in the way he treats the children," Nola nodded towards the arena.

"And me," Lindy was horrified to realise she'd spoken aloud.

The smile on Nola's face told her she enjoyed that more than she was letting on.

JACK

The horses were cuddled, brushed, and cuddled some more, then saddled up. The buzz was electric. Jack turned once again to see Lindy. She covered Bradley's pram from the sun and flies and left him in the shade while she and Nola walked towards the arena to watch the children's first ride. Jack and Bernie helped the riders into their saddles and settled back on the rails to watch. Lindy came up behind him, Jack could sense her care not to touch him but he longed for connection. There was a need to be as close as possible while they watched this reunion of horse and rider.

"You okay?" she whispered.

Jack swallowed hard and nodded. He wasn't game to speak just at the moment. Knowing the kids were happily occupied he passed his hand through the fence and took hers for comfort. He let out a deep breath he'd been holding and just settled in close.

"So, do you ride, Lindy?" Bernie asked

"No, never really had the chance. Like every girl I always dreamt of owning a horse."

The children's laughter and hollering from the centre of the arena kept the adults entertained. Even though the children were all experienced riders, Jack understood Lindy's concerns.

"So, the children are all old hands?" Lindy tipped her head towards the horses.

Both Jack and Bernie chuckled, "I'd have them on a horse before a motorbike, that's for certain." Bernie stole Jack's thoughts.

"Really?"

"Too right. Horses are a powerful piece of machinery but they have a heart. There's nothing more inspiring as the moment horse and rider become one," Bernie spoke from his soul.

"What do you reckon Jack, let's get her up into the saddle?"

Jack turned to Lindy. "Would you like too?"

She shrugged her shoulders and turned to check on Bradley.

"Don't worry about him," said Nola. "I've got him covered."

"Come on," Jack encouraged. The idea of the family having this one hobby they could all share had Jack silently wishing she'd agree. He waited patiently for her response.

"Okay, but I can't afford to get hurt."

Jack and Bernie laughed as they walked off to saddle up a horse for Lindy.

LINDY

"You sure you don't mind?" Lindy asked.

"No way, if you're staying with this family you'll have to learn at some stage, so why not start now," Nola grinned.

Lindy couldn't believe her childhood dream would come true. The large chestnut beast should have had her running for the hills, but knowing Jack was there made the situation almost enticing.

Jack passed her a helmet.

"Here you go, woman. Now for your first riding lesson. Just rest your foot here and pull yourself up," Jack stayed with her until she mounted with her feet in the stirrups. Jack remained close by her side.

"Why are you smirking?" she whispered from up in the saddle.

"Because I get to touch you without this all looking suspicious," his smile lines enhanced his handsome face.

"Don't be too sure. Nola's onto us." Lindy whispered.

Laughing, Jack said, "She doesn't miss a trick, that one." He waved at Nola. She was watching way too closely. "Right now, I could just keep walking with you up there and find a nice quiet patch somewhere, just you and me."

When he spoke like that, Lindy's body turned to jelly, "One day soon, I hope."

"Me too, the tensions too much," Jack waved at the children heading their way.

"Lindy, do you ride too?" Nate asked as he pulled Bandy to a slow walk beside her.

"Not until now I haven't." Lindy's eyes were on the head of her horse and her hands were gripping tightly to the reigns.

Jack put his hands over hers, "Relax, the horse is getting mixed signals from you."

Oh, hell, that made it worse. She trembled from his touch.

"Maybe Bernie should teach me, you're too much of a distraction," she whispered down to him again and received another roar of laughter for her efforts.

The reality of being up in the saddle was more enjoyable than Lindy expected. Lindy rode around with Jack by her side for about twenty minutes.

After Nola and Lindy had given them all a quick snack to sustain them until lunchtime, Bernie and Jack took to the saddles of their own mounts and followed the children, who were excited to be in the lead on a trail ride.

The women's gazes followed the nine riders as they disappeared down the track, they settled back with Bradley kicking and playing on his rug.

LINDY

The chatter of excited voices and clip-clop of hooves on the gravel path warned of the impending arrival of the mob. Nola cooked sausages on the barbie while Lindy cut up the sandwiches as the riders dismounted and settled the horses.

After washing their hands, they devoured the sandwiches and sausages in bread while the conversation about horses and riding the trail flowed. Next came cakes and slices which Lindy made. Everyone gobbled these down with gusto as the children spoke of their first horse ride in ages.

"Are you interested in getting on the horse again?" Jack asked Lindy when he scored a spare seat next to her.

"I hope so. Well, if I'm not continuously distracted from the task," Lindy's teasing tone made Jack laugh. Both of them were comfortable together and happy to banter around Jack's friends. "Bernie, could I have a tour of the stables, please?"

As Jack intended on having stables at the new place, this would be a great chance to study the interior.

"Sure, come on."

Lindy got up to follow Bernie and found the hoard trailing them. Inside the stables, Lindy listened to Bernie's explanation of how his setup worked.

"Come on, let's feed the apples to the horses," Joanna told the others as she dug into the bucket hanging on a hook. The children ran off, laughing and talking.

"Did you enjoy the ride?" Bernie sounded as eager as Jack regarding horses.

"Yes. Very much," Lindy smiled.

"Jack speaks highly of you."

"Thanks," Lindy's smile deepened. "He's wonderful." She couldn't help but notice the smirk on Bernie's face.

"I think you're both amazing if you can support each other while going through your individual torture." Then Bernie added, "It was Nola who told me what happened to you, not Jack."

"I can see you care about Jack and the children," Lindy watched Nola and Jack in deep conversation.

Bernie hitched his thumb in their direction, "I hope she does a number on him. She's been meaning to set him straight on a few things."

"Oh God, no. He doesn't need anything else right now," Lindy headed towards the door, but Bernie stopped her.

"Nola and Jack have always been close, even at school. I remember punching him smack on the nose one afternoon on the way home because I found him talking to my girl."

"You punched Jack?" Lindy's eyebrows raised as she turned to look at Bernie.

"Yep, blood gushed out everywhere. I lapped up the hero status for all of two seconds until Nola put me in my place. Geez, did I get told. They have a friendship capable of surviving anything," Bernie ran a hand down his face, "Well, anything except Elsa." He shook his head, "She got in the way of their friendship and Nola's gonna let him know how disappointed she was."

"Does she need to dump this on him right now?" the knowledge of the previous evening was fresh in her mind.

"Probably not, but he needs to hear her side of it," Bernie frowned.

"What is it?"

"Things happened with Elsa in town, Jack needs to hear it from friends before he hears it from anyone else."

"Why Nola?" but even as she asked the question, she was beginning to appreciate the bond between these two.

"They have a special friendship and we're here whenever he needs us. The horses were probably the best thing I could have done for him and the kids. For Nola it's..." Bernie shrugged, "It's more personal,"

Lindy understood he'd accepted their friendship and she respected him for that.

Her gaze lingered on her man closely, assessing any discomfort, but she allowed a smile to settle again. He looked reasonably settled as he and Nola chatted away.

JACK

"You were a fool with that one," Nola spoke without reservation. Her lips pressed in a tight grimace saying more than words could have ever construed.

"I know but once she was pregnant, I rose to the challenge and took care of my son. If she would have given me Nate as a baby and left, I would have been better off, but she refused. Now I have five beautiful children, who are all mine," Nola flinched at his harsh tone. "Even Bradley. Don't worry, I know what the town's thinking."

"You're sure Bradley is yours?" Nola couldn't meet his eyes on this topic.

"Definitely."

"You know what she was up to in town then."

Jack only nodded. He never really loved Elsa, she was just a lot of fun to begin with. When responsibility set in, she couldn't handle it. From the very start Jack organised and took care of everything, including the children, where he could.

"At first it hurt, but then I was happy to stay home, I never asked her what she did. I'd moved out to the bungalow after she fell pregnant with Bradley and stayed there until she took off after what she did. You know he's the spitting image of my dad as a baby," Jack explained as he picked up his son and cuddled him close.

"Oh, I didn't realise. That's a relief."

"I missed our chats and hanging out with you guys," Jack moved on from the previous topic which still unsettled him, "When Bernie rang about the horses, I was grateful I could still count on your support."

Lindy and Bernie stepped out of the shed, walked over and leant on the rail of the holding yard watching the children and the horses. Jack followed her closely.

"Now that you've found true love, what are you doing about her?" Nola asked with a smirk.

She was being downright cheeky. "None of your bloody business, woman," he mocked.

"She's wonderful. Don't let her get away."

"We have to be careful. Nate's already been in an argument at school about my new lover moving in before Elsa left town," Jack rubbed his hand over his face.

"You mean even though you and Elsa separated a year ago, you can't be with your girlfriend. Especially when you both need each other right now." Nola shook her head. "Do you love her?"

Jack relished being with his best friend again. He wanted what she and Bernie shared, true love, respect, and friendship. The sweetest smile smoothed his previous irked expression. "Now I understand why Bernie punched me in the nose that time. I'd do the same thing to protect Lindy. And it's not just the way she cleans the house, cooks and looks after the children."

"You're sounding like a real chauvinist," Nola gave a gurgle of laughter. "Does your family know?"

"Yep they keep telling me to move on."

"Do they like her?" Nola's voice was low as she reached for Bradley's good hand.

"Very much so."

"Yep true, how could they not?"

"Well, you just answered my next question."

"Yes, I like her. It has to be about you two and the children. She deserves and probably needs support and comfort after what she's been through."

"Did she tell you?"

"Yes. How could her husband do that to her and why would another woman stoop so low? I'll never know. But what gets me is her own flesh and blood not contacting her, that must really hurt."

Jack glanced at Lindy as she talked and laughed with Bernie. Close to them, the children spent precious time with their horses.

"I have a good mind to call them but I need to stay out of it. I think I'll only make it worse," Jack couldn't help another glance Lindy's way, "If we're open about our relationship how do you think that will affect the children?"

"Well, as you said, Nate's already dealt with one incident so really that will shut others up. I'm not saying nothing will happen but it will blow over in no time."

With that in mind, Jack got up and gently swung Bradley onto his hip and walked over to the fence, with Nola following close behind.

Bernie and Lindy were listening to the children talking about the morning trail ride. Jack approached Lindy and slipped his arm around her shoulder. Pulling her close and holding on tight. The children just kept talking, oblivious of the embrace.

"Who's for one last trail ride?" Jack looked at his watch, knowing the children would hate to leave.

With squeals of delight they set about readying themselves. Lindy reached up to take Bradley from Jack and dropped a kiss on his cheek. But before she could pull away, Jack had his hand behind her head and pulled her in for a more intense kiss. Lingering longer than acceptable with the children around.

"How about I take this ride with Bernie?" Nola offered.

"Thanks Nola, but I'll go. Lindy and I can finish this later," All the time he spoke, his eyes never left Lindy's. She swallowed quickly. Jack kissed Bradley and then Lindy one last time, before climbing the rails to prepare his horse for the ride.

He sensed her eyes tracking his every move and that warmed him. It was so natural to show how much he cared for her in front of his friends.

AT A CROSSROAD

LINDY

The fun of Saunders family life highlighted everything Lindy lost and ran from. At mass when the children sat quietly listening to the sermon and Jack cuddled a sleeping Bradley, Lindy closed her eyes and allowed the loss of her family to engulf her.

Jack and the children had become her world, but deep in her heart Lindy missed her own family. She couldn't help but wonder what her young adults were all doing now, or why they hadn't tried to contact her. Maybe she should head back home and attempt to get them to hear her side of the story.

Jack pressed her about doing as her brother Mal suggested and showing them the photos. Those darn photos shattered her safe cocoon. She still mulled over who sent them. They were no clearer to finding out the sender's identity, even with Mal's contact. Whoever it was never wanted to be discovered for some sick or sordid reason of their own.

Once the children were in bed, Jack coaxed Lindy into the lounge room with a steaming cup of herbal tea. With the glances Jack gave her, she knew he'd sensed ominous clouds hovering. It had been hard work keeping her feelings at bay, but she couldn't ignore her loss forever.

"Hey why the sigh, sitting with me isn't that much of a hardship, is it?" he asked with a flash of his slightly crooked smile.

"No." Lindy answered, accepting the cuppa he made, she forced a smile for him. "Oh, I want this more than anything and I understand you need to move on, for the children's sake. I get that," Lindy added, rushing on, "I really do," She pinched her lips together and clenched her jaw.

"You've changed your mind? This is a life decision." Jack rubbed the back of his neck. "You and everyone else needs to understand Elsa and I have been estranged for over a year, for you it's only been just over a month."

Lindy dropped her head, she couldn't look at him, "I'm so scared about a future without my children."

"Just call them. Maybe try Sophie again," he suggested.

Lindy shook her head, there was a distance growing between them, though she didn't want to, she couldn't stop herself. Jack was challenging her and Lindy didn't like it.

"You're unsure of where you're heading or what you want?"

"No, not that." Lindy paused, trying to decipher everything swirling inside her. "I'm not scared about our future together, rather I'm scared of the unknown with Ralph and my kids."

"I have a suggestion, just hear me out," Jack began. "Why don't I call Sophie and find out if she wants to talk to you. I'll tell her you've been waiting for her to return your call and we'll see what she has to say."

"No, I want to be face to face and see her. Then I'll understand why she didn't return my calls."

Jack sighed, "Okay, tell me what you want?" He drew in a long slow breath as some of the colour drained from her face, "Exactly what you need to move on."

The genuine request shattered her heart. The problem was she didn't know what would give her the freedom to move forward.

She turned to face him, resting her hand on his chest, "You. You and the children. That I know for sure. Absolutely no doubt in my mind."

"Okay so…"

"My life's a mess at the moment. My kids. My head. When I'm not thinking about all that I'm so happy."

"I need to know you're happy, and I hope the kids and I can give you that," Jack ran his thumb down the side of her face, he gently placed his lips on hers and kissed her. Pulling back, he said, "We love you so much."

The tenderness in his touch healed her heart momentarily. He made her want things sorted. She treasured the strong connection they shared. Maybe calling Sophie would change everything, perhaps she could move on and find what she was seeking.

"All right, I'll ring," untangling herself from Jack, she reached for her phone.

They both sat in silence as the phone rang, Lindy held it to her ear while she focused on a stubborn mark on the opposite wall she hadn't been able to remove.

Hi this is Sophie, though I appreciate your call I can't come to the phone, please leave a message. Thanks, bye.

Hearing her daughter's voice ripped through her, especially when it was a recording.

Lindy hung up the phone and sat in silence. Okay, so maybe not knowing if Sophie would take her call would have been easier. Jack wrapped his arms around her again and she sunk into him.

"Hey come on. I should have given you more time to sort yourself out. I'm sorry."

"I used your troubles to forget about mine," Jack blinked rapidly and had gone still, Lindy registered the moment he drew back. She didn't miss the veins in his neck bulging.

"Lindy," Jack's expression was unrecognisable. He paused for a moment, then with the words came his hesitation, "I have to ask, do you want to return home…for good?"

Lindy's voice rose, "How could you even think that? After what we've shared. Seriously," Lindy pushed out of his arms, off the couch and walked out. She shook her head, wondering what possessed him to ask such a question. There was no explanation why he'd even entertain such a notion.

Outside the night sky displayed the jewels city folks never experienced, the bright stars shone in their millions. Lindy's tears cascaded down her cheeks while her eyes focused on the beauty above. How could she blame Jack for all this? He didn't deserve the caustic tone she'd used. She wandered around in circles as the sky and the stars became her constant. Her mind raced, lost halfway between the house and the bungalow, the dizziness made her realise her own foolishness. Pulling her eyes away from the stars, she tried to focus on something at eye level.

Standing there, looking confused, lost, and unsure was Jack. Not sure how long he'd been there, Lindy's head tilted to one side and her arms opened wide in invitation.

A low sigh escaped his lips as he stepped off the patio and made his way over. His muscular arms encased her, and she released a low moan.

"I'm sorry for asking. I panicked." Lindy snuggled in closer to him, "Hey, you don't have to do this by yourself, I'm here with you," Jack mumbled into her hair, "I need to make plans to take care of the kids, but if you need more time and have to go back to Melbourne and return later, I'll understand. Just as long as you return. I can't, no," Jack shook his head, "We can't, the kids and I can't live without you."

The plea pierced her heart.

"I don't know what I need, other than you, all our children and to make some tough decisions," Lindy shivered in Jack's arms.

The heat of his body made no difference to the arctic chill in her bones. She squealed when he picked her up and carried her back into the house.

Settling her on the couch, Jack arranged her so they were looking at each other. "I'm sorry."

"You have nothing to be sorry about. My life was turned upside down by my husband and by someone I've never even met. I can't understand what benefit there would be for some stranger to cause me such pain."

"You'll probably never know who sent the photos, whoever it was, did you a favour."

"You're right. Through them I discovered the truth. Whatever their motives were." Lindy's grip tightened around Jack's neck. She was hanging on to the security that was Jack.

"Good. Now, let's focus on a direction for you."

"What do you mean by a direction?"

"You need time, so maybe we should plan out how the next few months will go. I'll advertise for someone to help me with the children, you can't make these decisions whilst looking after us."

"Are you trying to get rid of me, Jack Saunders?" Although she tried humorous, it was an accusation which she could see stung.

"Please understand that the possibility of losing you even for a short while is like an arrow to my heart, but I get you need to sort things out. I love you, never forget that, when you're ready to come back, we'll be waiting."

LINDY

Tossing and turning between the thick flannelette sheets, Lindy woke to find her body entangled. The little quality sleep she managed was trapped among snippets of restless dreams and nightmares. Her mind whirled with activity. Jack was in all bar the nightmares. Would Lindy accept the strongest voice in her head telling her to 'follow her heart'?

Being honest with herself, packing up and selling the home that had been hers for the past twenty-four years wouldn't be a hardship. As with the business, Zave was taking care of that for now. Deep down there was no question. Her young protégé was capable of taking over, not to mention the fact she lost heart in the day to day running of the enterprise.

The sticking point was her children. She couldn't reconcile the fact that she would be so far away from them. She bit her lip, in only a few short weeks so much of her life had changed.

With everything else in Jack's life, he still gave her his time and took an interest in her and how she coped. She understood the children were his first responsibility, and he loved them dearly. It comforted her to know she was a close second. This man evoked a sense of desire, protection, and love. She'd identified with such nerve tingling and heart racing caused by her connection and love for Jack. Thinking of him intimately caused her to blush.

With her own family, life had been a balancing act and not in a pleasant way. She devoted herself to her children, worked hard in her business and somehow found solace, though Ralph always undermined her efforts.

Lindy forced herself to sit up when her chest tightened.

For Ralph she was only the woman to run the house, provide him with children and raise them on his behalf. Had he laid foundations early in their marriage that the children were only a burden, therefore her responsibility? The gut-wrenching feeling forced her to trawl through her years of marriage, looking for the point where Ralph represented more than the figurative head of the family.

For the first time since the fateful day she received the photos, Lindy's heart pounded, muscles quivered and jaw hurt from the grinding of teeth.

If her children were so shallow, she must have failed them somehow.

She had a chance to take control of her life and be happy. Lindy had a right to find what her first marriage lacked. A true connection, commitment, and a wonderful future. Jack was not the person to determine her fate, that would be her own vocation. She smiled and conceded that would result from a successful partnership. Her first marriage was never a union, maybe she'd been too young and immature to demand more of Ralph.

How could she have been so foolish? Lindy analysed the evidence before her. In some way she failed her children, but definitely not her husband. It distressed Lindy to realise the painful admission, over the last twenty-six years as a couple they failed. Oh yes, Ralph failed her. His arrogance was to blame. Her purpose had been to keep everyone happy, no matter the costs. Those costs were the loss of her marriage and children who were now adults and apparently had no respect or time for her.

Life was always about grappling from one day to the next, fitting into Ralph's demands and expectations for how things happened. But now, life was about her and alternative possibilities. The metaphorical light bulb moment added clarity. Time to move on.

The need to sell the house in Melbourne became crystal clear. The time arrived, Lindy needed to let go of her old life as Lindy Kemp and embrace the chance to be loved and cherished as Lindy Saunders. Jack, Nate, Evie, Joanna, Caleb, and Bradley were her family now. The fit was perfect and the love overwhelming.

Yes, the town of Chester's Run had become her future.

Only when her big toe caught the leg of the chair in the lounge and she cried out, did Lindy realise she was up and moving. The pain forced her to sit, with her mind spiralling, she grabbed her foot and deliberated over her next step. This place wasn't home, it was however, the passage marking the time between her horrible marriage breakdown and a genuine chance for a fortunate life.

Jack and the children brought her such joy. Lindy was absolute in her knowledge if any struggles cropped up they'd deal with it together. Being part of a genuine couple, one where both partners' feelings were important, made Lindy smile. People needed to know her decisions and plans for the future. Lindy treated this decision like a business deal when in fact it was so much more important.

Not thinking about the time, Lindy picked up the phone and scrolled through her list of favourites. There he was, her father, always her sounding board for anything in life. She and her dad had a connection from her early childhood. She could remember talking to him about most things, those she couldn't talk to him about became her mother's domain.

"Hello," a sleepy voice answered.

"Oh hell, I'm sorry I didn't realise what time it was," tears threatened just hearing his voice.

"Hey love. Is everything okay?" his strained voice only emphasised how much she was loved.

"Dad…" she tried to swallow down a large lump as tears slowly descended.

"What's wrong?" in the background Lindy could hear her mother speaking.

"Oh hell, how do I say this?"

"Just tell me love. You know we're all here for you." Duncan's voice was barely above a whisper, she hated to do this to her parents.

"Dad, I know this will sound ludicrous," Inhaling deep, Lindy tried to form words that would make sense. "I'm in love." Not wanting to hear an awkward silence between them she pushed on, "He's wonderful, caring, open and a great family man. This one will make you happy," Lindy caught her breath, "He's an absolute gentleman."

"Hey. Hang on there. Slow Down."

"Sorry Dad. I know this is foolish, but he's wonderful and I'm about to change my life in ways that just a few weeks ago were unfathomable."

"Is this the man you're working for, the one with the five children?"

"Yes. Jack, Jack Saunders."

JACK

The conversation with Lindy the night before left Jack a little shaken. She needed time, and he understood that. He even accepted her trepidation about the swiftness of their attraction. But could he really survive without her for an extended period while she settled things back in Melbourne?

Not being able to sleep, he walked out the back door and sat on the swing, the fresh morning air washed over him helping to cool his body and calm his nerves. Feeling more settled he got up to go inside as Lindy's voice and then sobs floated out into the darkness. Unsure of whether to leave her be or investigate further he stopped, overcome by indecision. Eventually, he edged closer to the bungalow.

His mother taught him about the evils of eavesdropping. Such poor gain and he should turn and walk away. That was until Lindy said, 'Dad' and then she announced her feelings to her father.

Jack stalled.

His heart was about to burst, he turned back towards the house, better not to intrude on her private conversation. But when the echoes of her loud sobs returned, Jack had to find out what was wrong.

Ignoring his inner voice, Jack opened her door.

"Lindy, are you okay?"

The small light in the sitting area blinded him momentarily. Once his vision cleared again, Lindy was looking directly at him. Her raised brows exposed sharp, expressive eyes studying him carefully. Their gazes locked as she tried to hold a conversation with her father. Her blue eyes watching his every move. He walked in and sat next to her on the two-seater couch and gathered up her free hand in his.

"Dad hang on a minute, Jack's just walked in," Lindy handed him the phone with shaking hands, "My father," she whispered.

Taking the phone, he swallowed hard, "Morning Sir, Jack Saunders here."

The silence stretched on longer than Jack wished. He swallowed again. Finally, the other man spoke, "Is she okay, Jack? Lindy means the world to her family."

"I hope she is. Sir, please understand I love your daughter deeply," he softly squeezed her hand in his, not sure what else he could say to convince her father.

"We don't want to see her hurt again."

"I have no intentions of anything but loving her and making us both happy. Sir…"

"My name's Duncan."

"Duncan, would you and your wife like to come up and meet my family? That will give you an opportunity to talk to Lindy and see for yourself how happy she is." Jack put his arm around Lindy's shoulder and smiled as she leant into him.

"Well, thank you. We'd appreciate that. And seeing as there's no time like the present and my wife and I are awake, how about we set off just after sunrise?"

"That sounds perfect…Duncan."

"Thank you. Could I talk to my daughter again? We'll see you later this morning."

"See you then," Jack handed the phone back to Lindy and listened to the rest of their conversation.

He couldn't wipe the smile off his face.

She'd told her father she loved him. What the hell? The words from her sweet lips replaying over in his mind, *'he's a wonderful, caring family man.'* Wow, she told her father that and only after a few weeks. A knowing smile followed by a warmth spreading through his body. Jack vibrated with pleasure.

JACK

Stepping out the front door, Jack did a double take when he saw a dark SUV with six adults getting out. "Morning," he called trying to appear relaxed, it took a conscious effort not to swallow hard.

"I'm Jack Saunders."

"Duncan and my wife Charlotte," Lindy's father stated. The pair shook hands and Jack gave Charlotte a peck on the cheek. "This is our youngest son Danny and his wife Barbara," Duncan waited for Jack to greet them, then continued. "And our oldest son Mal and his wife Adele."

Once Jack greeted everyone, he gestured towards the house, "Come on in."

In the kitchen Jack put on the kettle and offered everyone a cuppa. "Tea or coffee?" But before anyone could answer, Lindy walked in with Bradley in her arms.

"Oh my God, you're all here." She rushed over to greet them. Jack offered to take Bradley, but the little fellow burrowed deeper into her shoulder. Lindy carefully greeted her guests with a shy Bradley clinging to her. "Hey Bradley, this is my family." He didn't move, only snuggled further into her hair, making everyone laugh.

"I know little one, we're a bit too much to take in first thing in the morning, aren't we?" offered Adele as she took her turn to greet her sister-in-law, "Lin, you look wonderful."

Lindy smiled. "Thanks, I'm feeling great."

"I can see why," Barbara whispered in Lindy's ear.

With Barbara's smirk and Lindy's flushed cheeks, Jack raised a questioning brow. No reply was forthcoming. Instead, Lindy just took Bradley's bottle Jack prepared and she quickly turned back to her family.

"Where are the other children?" Charlotte asked as Lindy led them out to the patio.

"Yesterday was a huge day, we were down at Jack's friend's farm where the family's horses are being stabled so we let them sleep in." She smiled at Jack.

Jack arranged the drinks on the table and went back into the kitchen for the food as he readied himself for an interrogation.

"Anything I can do to help?" cooed a sweet voice, one sister-in-law, he wasn't sure which one.

"I'm Adele, Mal's wife."

Jack laughed. "Thanks, I'll remember that." He handed her a plate of toasted sandwiches as he picked up the tray of pancakes with all the trimmings.

"Don't let them get to you, they really are the most wonderful family to be a part of. Loyal. I think for the Chapmans', loyalty is the family's badge of honour, just a tad more important than their devotion to one another," Adele added with a smile, "And I rarely warn people about my husband, Mal may be a cop but he is a husband, father, son and brother first and will do anything to protect all of us."

"I'm glad to know Lindy had such a supportive team behind her when her marriage imploded."

Walking to the door, Adele made one last comment, "You've got a wonderful one there, she's probably one of the best. Take care of her."

He nodded. He'd discovered for himself how amazing she was. If that was a challenge set down by her family, he was in. All in. They would understand how precious she was to him.

He settled into the chair next to Lindy as Bradley finished his bottle and attempted to climb over to his father.

"Morning," Jack said as he reached for his son.

For a while the conversation flowed, Jack and Lindy answered questions put to them, some about the farm, others about the children.

Finally, the conversation turned personal, "Jack, can you tell me the full story about how all this came about?" Mal pointed to Bradley's arm but meaning so much more.

Jack was ready. Mal was the cop, and Adele's warning somehow calmed him.

But before he could reply Lindy sighed, "Mal!"

"It's okay love, I understand where he's coming from," the best explanation to date flowed from Jack, fully accepting responsibility for the events of his previous life. They all leant forward slightly, listening as he spoke. No one's expressions altered. He straightened his back and looked them all in the eye as he continued, "That's the bungalow over there, which is where Lindy stays," finishing his recount, Jack sighed inwardly looking directly at Mal, "Go on Mal, I can see you have more questions?"

He could only smirk as he spoke. "You'll laugh, but I rang the local sergeant to find out about you this morning."

Jack did laugh. Hard. And so did Lindy.

"He informed me you were best friends through school and his brother-in-law so he had to vouch for you."

That raised a chuckle from the others around the table.

LINDY

"Mal seriously," Lindy fumed, "Stop!"

"You know me, I just need to know you're safe. Where you're concerned, we all seem to be protective," he wiped jam from his lips with a paper serviette.

"You mean overprotective," she countered, practically snarling at him.

"It's just so soon." Mal continued, eyeing Jack carefully.

"Son. Enough," Duncan's voice sounded a warning, as he settled his mug on the table in front of him. A warning you never crossed unless you were a fool, no matter what your age.

"Sorry Dad," Mal was on notice.

Changing tact, Duncan asked, "Jack, do you have family in the area?"

"Yes, Mum and Dad bought a house in town when I took over the farm and there's my sister Tessa, she's Harry's wife," he met Mal's gaze when he added that. "I also have a cousin, Ivy, who owns the local bakery in town. Everyone else passed away or moved on gradually over the years. There's just us left now."

Before anything else was said, Jack's girls made their way to Lindy's chair quietly.

"Good morning sweethearts," Lindy greeted them the same way she did every morning since arriving. She hugged and kissed them both and pulled Joanna onto her knee. "Evie, Joanna, this is my family."

Both girls nodded and smiled shyly, "Good morning." Evie said in a voice only a little above a whisper.

Before anyone could reply the boys exited the backdoor and stared at the visitors.

"Nate, Caleb, come meet Lindy's family. This is Nate and Caleb," Jack introduced each of the six adults. After everyone said hello Caleb's chin quivered and tears gathered in his eyes. Pulling him close, Jack whispered in his son's ear, "What's the matter, buddy?"

"They're not here to take Lindy away, are they Dad?" Caleb gulped as he wiped tears from his eyes with the back of his small hand.

Lindy looked at her parents. That statement told them how much these children would miss her if she left, not that she ever wanted to leave.

"I'm not going anywhere, sweetheart. My family wanted to meet you, that's all."

Caleb turned to Lindy, threw his arms around her neck, "Do you promise you're not going away? Because I really want you to stay with us." His little arms gripped tighter. "I love you, Lindy."

Swallowing the lump in her throat, Lindy hesitated for a moment.

She dropped a kiss on Caleb's forehead and whispered back, "I love you too." She ran her fingers over his bed hair, "I love all of you. I promise, I'm not going anywhere." Lindy gripped the hand Jack offered and watched as the children turned their attention to the table. With the help of the adults they gathered plates and dished up a hearty breakfast.

The morning passed quickly, and when Jack suggested he invite his family over and put on a barbecue lunch Lindy jumped at the idea, "That would be great, maybe invite Ivy too," Jack dropped a kiss on her lips and stepped into the lounge to make the calls.

PLANNING A FUTURE TOGETHER

JACK

By the time Lindy put Bradley down for his afternoon nap on Monday, Jack stood in the kitchen in search of food. His chair scraped along the lino floor as Lindy entered. On the table were two plates of cold meat and salad, along with a note pad and pencil for the strategic planning needed to combine their futures. He poured them each a glass of sparkling water, something he'd never tried before Lindy arrived, and focused on the notepad.

Jack began, "Now, these are all the things we'll hopefully achieve by Christmas," before him was a page full of dot pointed items. "Also, I promised Troy this morning we'd be out as soon as possible." And as Troy and his father previously stated, they were in no hurry to begin renovations on the farmhouse. But with Jack and Lindy agreeing to move on together, he wanted their joint life to start now.

Jack pushed the list he prepared last night towards her. The day with their families only helped strengthen his resolve about beginning their life as a couple. Any reservations from Lindy evaporated. Jack sat in silence as Lindy read through his list.

"Do you mind?" she picked up the black pen.

"Go for it."

She added a few things, crossed out 'buy' and wrote 'pick up' next to lists of kitchenware and furniture.

"How long did you work on this? You've considered everything," Lindy placed the pen next to the pad and pushed them both back towards Jack, who was sitting next to her with his arm resting over the back of her chair.

"I couldn't sleep after you went to bed last night, you know that saying about a kid in a candy shop…" he paused not sure he should say anymore.

"You can look but can't have any, just yet," she finished for him on a laugh.

"Something like that," he replied gruffly, a grin turning up the corners of his mouth. Looking to change the subject quickly from them deciding not to sleep together yet, he asked, "Are you ready to discuss where you're at?"

Lindy drew in a deep breath, "Well first things first, I need to decide whether I sell the business or work remotely."

"Which way do you think you'll go?" her answer wasn't important, but he'd prefer to know as not. The necessity of her having 'business trips' maintained an invisible tether for her to Melbourne. And even though he could manage the house and children, he didn't want to spend nights without her. Holding his breath, Jack waited for her response.

After a lengthy pause, Lindy spoke, "Our lives are here. For me, selling makes more sense, but I don't want to let go of it fully. I'm considering a compromise might be better. I'll put it to Zave and see if he wants to buy into the business. A partnership. I'll be working from here but I can still mentor Zave. I won't need to travel to Melbourne regularly or anything like that."

Jack couldn't hide his smile, "You must have some interest or job so it makes sense. I don't think Bradley will be enough for you."

"You're probably right. This way I'll still have my mentoring and thanks to Harry, as of next week I'll have two new contacts and there's still work with Ivy. For now, that's enough to keep my hand in the game." Lindy told Jack.

"I get we have so much on, but this is my mess. I'm scared you'll get bored with just being a homebody."

"At the moment, the way things are is perfect for me. And besides, Harry mentioned he could get me more clients, I can do that when I'm ready," She reached out and squeezed Jack's hand as she encased it with her own, "Just remember you and I are in this together. I'm here with you for the long haul. And I have no doubt you'll be available when I need help and guidance."

"I am. Just promise me if you change your mind, you'll tell me. Communication will be vital, especially with five kids in tow. Eight when we sort out your three."

"Don't hold your breath about my lot. I can't understand what they're thinking so I have no plans with them at the moment," Lindy's face closed over. A look that often passed over her when she spoke of her children.

"How about I ring Zave and finalise the future of the business?" Lindy pushed herself up from the table.

Before she walked away, Jack pulled her onto his lap and kissed her. When they both came up for air he whispered, "You mark my words, all eight of our children will be around the dining table with us. There will be love, peace and friendship, you'll see." He kissed her again before hurrying her along.

"Haven't you got a phone call to make?"

PERFECT FAMILY HOME

JACK

"Morning Doc," Jack said as they followed him into his office. It had been eight weeks since Bradley's cast was put on and he prayed today Bradley would be rid of it. Lindy pushed the pram as the toddler talked away to himself. When he was like this, he reminded Jack of Caleb. He supposed it would be funny to have two boys who chattered away needlessly, maybe they could occupy each other instead of annoying their siblings.

"Let's have a look," Doc pulled the pram a teeny bit closer. "Has he been using the arm?"

"Yes, more and more over the last week." Lindy told him.

"Good," he took out the old X-rays and had a look. "I'm happy to take it off today, it's looking much stronger."

Jack nodded. That was the best news. Bradley was delayed slightly in speech and movement before the incident with his mother. His speech had come a long way with Lindy and the children chatting to him whenever they could. As for his ability to get around, that was hampered by the bulky cast he'd worn for the past eight weeks.

"Okay, could you hold him please, Jack, and we'll get started?" The doctor called in his nurse. Lindy and Jack kept Bradley busy during the procedure, which only took about five minutes, Bradley watched on, even leant forward investigating the new phenomenon.

When his arm was free, he oohed at seeing it again. He clenched his fist and flexed his fingers.

"Hahaha," he looked at Lindy. "Mumma ook."

The way Bradley trusted Lindy mended another piece of Jack's heart.

"Yes, look, there's your arm. It's all better." Bradley held his hand out to Lindy and Jack handed him over, noticing the doctor watching the two of them closely.

"Thanks for that, Doc," Jack said as they headed towards the door.

"My pleasure," the doctor said, offering his hand, "And you little man, it's time to make up for all the lying around you've done. Next time I see you I want you at least crawling."

Bradley laughed at the attention.

On the drive back to the farm Lindy sat in the back with Bradley as he chatted away moving his arm. "I can't believe how happy he is with the cast gone."

Jack looked in the review mirror as his son took the food Lindy was handing out to him.

"Yum, yum, yum," Bradley said even before putting the sandwich to his lips.

"Now we can get him to walk," Jack was eager for Bradley to become independently mobile.

"I think he should crawl first."

"He was crawling before the incident, though not far."

"It won't take long, just make sure the children stop doing the legwork for him. They need to encourage him to move around for himself." Lindy was right, and he was eager to see Bradley walking.

JACK

"Hey Jack," Darla called from the kitchen. "How'd it go?"

Lindy handed an over excited Bradley to his grandmother who cooed at him, "Look at you, your arm's free," he laughed and looked back to Lindy.

The two women greeted each other with a kiss and headed into the house with Jack following. After he dropped Bradley's nappy bag in his bedroom, he walked into the lounge to see Bradley sitting up playing with his toys. "Is Dad in the shed?"

"Yes love. The skip arrived about an hour ago."

"Thanks Mum. I'll be with Dad if you need me," he told Lindy, then kissed her and Bradley.

As he walked down to the shed, he could hear the two women chatting away. They'd been working together to get things sorted since Jack sold the farm.

"Hi Dad," Jack walked into the shed.

"Jack, how'd he go?" Tony asked.

"Great, he's a two-armed bandit again," Jack told his father.

He pulled out the next box of odds and ends and began sorting. They chatted away as they continued the sorting process.

A short time later his mobile rang out.

"Jack Saunders," he said as he rested his tall frame against a workbench covered in his father's treasures.

"Hi Jack, Michael Evans here. Think I could have a house that might interest you. I know I've shown you a few places lately but this one I think will suit all your requirements."

"Okay Michael, I'm all ears," Jack listened and smiled at his father.

"Well, how about I show you? I'm with the client now, they've just put the property on the market. I've told them about your situation, they're happy for you to come through straight away. How soon could you be here?"

"Is half an hour quick enough?" Jack was eager to investigate the new possibility.

"Perfect." Michael gave Jack the address and promised to be waiting.

As Jack pressed the end button on his phone he looked at his father.

"Dad, we've got a house to look at, do you mind if Lindy and I head into town to check it out."

"Not at all. I'll still be here going through this junk when you return," Tony answered, laughing at the never-ending task.

Jack found Lindy and his mother sorting out the laundry cupboards. "Michael Evans from the real estate office just called, he's got a place for us to look at. Mum, could you look after Bradley while we duck into town?"

"Sure, that's fine. Don't rush back, we're not going anywhere."

Jack checked his watch, "We shouldn't be too long. Thanks."

Lindy got up off the floor and brushed herself off, "Give me five minutes and I'll be ready."

As Lindy walked across to the bungalow, Jack headed for the kitchen to grab his car keys and met Lindy out by the Ute.

"Where's the house?"

"Michael said it was just near the ones I was looking at the first time. He said the owners have just put it on the market. They're giving us first dibs." Jack smiled. The idea of his family finding a home had his insides vibrating. He needed a miracle to find a house with everything they were looking for.

JACK

Following the directions, Jack pulled up out the front of the original Chester's Run homestead. Admiring the facade of the Bluestone house he turned to Lindy, "It'll be way out of our price range."

He turned up the drive and parked next to Michael's car. They got out as Michael walked towards them from the front door.

"Morning. Hope I didn't drag you away from anything too important," Michael asked Lindy as he shook her hand.

"Only if you call cleaning out cupboards an important task," she laughed.

"Good, I don't feel guilty," Michael's manner was friendly and open. Jack could see she was as relaxed with the man as he was.

"So, the homestead's for sale?" Jack asked, nodding towards the house.

"Exactly. The owners have kept it for two years since the wife's parents died, but they never really get up here much. So, it's on the market. I know it's not the done thing but come inside and meet them," Michael led them through the large wooden double doors which set off the rest of the stone building.

Lindy and Jack followed him into the kitchen where a couple were sitting at the breakfast bar having a coffee and staring at the view across the valley.

"Steve and April, this is Lindy and Jack."

"Hi Jack, it's been a long time," April watched Lindy. He couldn't miss the confused look on April's face. He hated having to explain himself. He watched on as April's eyes shifted from him to Lindy and then their clasped hands. In the past she'd known Elsa vaguely and being away, wouldn't have caught up with the gossip.

"April this is my girlfriend Lindy. April and I went to school together." Jack forged on, hoping no further explanation was necessary. "Didn't you and your sisters sell this place a few years back?"

April shrugged. "No, the others sold it to Steve and I, but it's just too much. We're settled in Melbourne and we don't use it enough. Steve travels a bit and the kids have their hobbies."

"Yeah, I get that. I'm selling the farm and looking to move into town so the children can start some sport and activities."

"Can I ask what happened with your wife?" April questioned.

No, she wasn't letting this go.

Jack drew in a sharp breath, "Let's just say things went from bad to worse when she broke my youngest son's arm back in September. I have full custody and need to make changes for my five children."

"Do you have children too, Lindy?" April was getting over inquisitive.

"Yes, I do, but mine are all grown. They live in Melbourne."

Before April could ask any more questions, Michael interrupted the conversation, "How about I show you through the house and see what you think?"

"Perfect," Jack nodded and followed Michael out into the hall.

"So, as you saw from the front it's a double story, has all the original features inside and out. Eight bedrooms and two bathrooms, three of the bedrooms have ensuites. The common areas are finished to a high spec and top-quality appliances in the kitchen." Michael kept talking as he led them through the downstairs first and then they made their way upstairs.

Jack could see Lindy studying the features closely, just as he did. She smiled when Jack wrapped his arms around her from behind. They gave each other silent nods of approval.

"Loads of ideas for that room," Lindy said. The volume of her voice rising as she spoke.

The house displayed the history of its era. Open fireplaces and high ceilings restored and decorated, Jack was very conscious of the expense and upkeep of an old property, but this place was beautiful.

Next Michael led them outside, he showed them the original stables which could take up to eight horses. Jack marvelled at the solid wooden barn, noting the work it needed. He ran his hand over the rough hand sawn ironbark structure which was as solid as the day it was built. "Wow, there's definitely history in these walls," Jack looked around, enamoured with the property.

The land surrounding the house was covered with lush green grass, which Jack deduced would be brown or non-existent in summer. But with a rounding yard and tack room for all the horse gear, this place was practically calling to his family.

"What's over there?" Jack drew Lindy's attention away from the land and the shed.

"Well, that's what made me think of you," Michael headed off towards the lovely stone structure. It resembled something like an outbuilding from the old working homestead.

Michael opened the front door and stepped aside. The grand entrance door, a replica of the main house, opened to a sizeable living area with the kitchen and dining room. Michael highlighted the open plan with the light streaming in from the windows.

"Wow, this is beautiful. So masterfully done. Liam would love the architecture of this place," Lindy walked through a second time, taking in the feel of the historic building.

Jack noted this was the first time she'd mentioned her children in general conversation.

Once back outside, Jack turned to Michael, "Okay what's the damage for this place?"

Michael laughed, "Look the owners are conscious of the things that need doing so I think the price is beyond reasonable considering what you'll get," he lowered his voice, "They're keen to sell." Straightening up again, he gave the price. One hundred thousand above what Jack had set as his limit.

Jack shook his head, "This place is perfect, but that's over my budget."

"Just remember Jack, it's got everything you asked me for, and then some."

Running his fingers through his hair, Jack cursed. He could tell how much Lindy connected with the property, but he still had to pay for the business out of the money his father would give him from the sale of the farm. He wanted a decent amount in the bank for any future emergencies.

"Sorry love, it's too much." It shattered Jack to have to tell Lindy.

"Michael, could you just give us a few minutes, please? We're not holding you up, are we?" Lindy had agenda written all over her face.

"Take your time," Michael walked away, leaving Lindy and Jack to walk around again and talk in private.

"What's your budget?"

"This is a hundred thousand too much. I've paid the money to Elsa and there's the business. I won't put too much financial pressure on us."

LINDY

"Have you factored in my contribution?" Lindy raised a brow.

"I can't ask you to pay money towards the house."

"Why in heaven's name not? I intend to live here. Or have you forgotten about that?" Her manner was light but her muscles were rigid. They were a couple, a partnership. Jack needed to understand decisions like this were made together.

"No, I haven't forgotten, but there's only you and there's six of us."

"Tell me, other than the money, what's wrong with this place?"

"The stables need a bit of work. The structure looks sound, but cosmetically the inside needs a makeover."

"Anything else?"

"You know there's nothing. This place is perfect." Jack spun on his heels taking in the rounding yard, the stables and he cast an eye over the bungalow and finally rested his gaze on the rear of the stone house. "Bloody perfect. Shit!"

"I have money. Please don't get caught up with details. You and the kids need this. We as a family would utilise every inch of this place," she turned on the spot, "There's everything here for the children. Have a good think about it." Using her trump card Lindy added, "Not to mention, if you're correct that is, there are also my three. This place would be perfect," she didn't beg, but hell, she considered it.

Jack wrapped his arms around her and led her towards the front of the house, they walked together arms wrapped around each other in silence. Lindy and Jack both turned, taking in the house and land as a package.

The gardens needed to be planted out. Lindy considered a display of annuals would brighten up the beds leading to the house. The stone building with sash windows were stunning and from a historical view-point the architectural features of the old homestead were its strength.

Observing aloud, Jack said, "The garage must have been added on later. The entire thing is done so well, you'd hardly notice. The garden needs a bit of work though. Mind you, it wouldn't take much to get it up to speed," Jack couldn't stop his eyes from roaming the property.

"I was thinking the same thing. A combination of annuals through these perennials would really brighten the gardens up. Let's bring the kids here this afternoon and then we can talk price with Michael," the children's lives had changed so much recently, she was sure they'd appreciate being included in a decision with something as grand as this.

The front door opened and Michael walked out. "How did you go?" He asked.

Jack took Lindy's hand and walked towards him. "Would it be possible to bring the children here after school? Lindy and I would both like them to see the place first. Then we can discuss price."

Lindy focused on Michael, hoping to see a hint of negotiation in his eyes.

"Let me talk to Steve and April. Just wait here for me."

When Michael walked through the door, Lindy stepped into Jack's open arms, "This would be perfect, I could see us all living here. The paddocks out the back are great for the horses and the children could all have their own rooms. They could share when your kids come to visit. I'm sure they won't mind that."

"Don't hold your breath on my lot coming up. I'm not, even though I miss them." Lindy couldn't hold back the moan.

April and Michael walked out towards them. April began, "Michael said you'd like to bring the children through?"

"If you don't mind us coming back after school's out? Did he also mention that the price is steep?" Lindy's gaze flicked between Jack and April.

"Yep, he mentioned it. Steve and I will negotiate on price, but like you, we're limited to how far we can go. Steve agreed, you should bring the kids after school, we'll all sit down with Michael and try to nut this thing out."

"Thanks, we'll be here around four if that's okay."

"See you then."

Jack and Lindy said goodbye and walked towards the car, as Jack reached for the handle to open Lindy's door, April called out.

"Jack, be prepared to give me a bit of movement, Steve and I would love you to have this place. Lindy, it was lovely to meet you. See you this afternoon."

"Thanks, you too. See you later." Lindy climbed into the car as Michael followed April into the house. "You realise once the children see this place, we don't stand a chance of walking away?"

"Are you sure you want to put in?" Jack asked with furrowed brows.

Were they really doing the right thing?

"Absolutely. This would be the most wonderful place to be a family." A smile crossed her face.

"What's with the smirk?"

"Do I get my own house? I rather like the bungalow."

Jack's laughter rang out, "No. We can't afford it. We'll have to rent it out."

This changed the smirk to a burst of laughter from Lindy. She treasured the banter that came so easily between them. She'd never had this easy camaraderie with Ralph, just another plus in Jack's favour.

LINDY

The visit proved as predictable as Lindy expected. The children and Jack's parents took in the house's grandeur. His parents studying the finer details with rapt attention.

"Lindy, this place is beautiful," Darla walked beside her as they went from room to room.

"Tony knows of its origins, look at him marvelling at the features. He's like a kid in a candy store." Darla's smile matched Lindy's.

Jack let go of Lindy's hand when his father called.

"See that?" Tony said, pointing to the open fireplace, "That rock was quarried locally. Imagine sitting here reading."

"When you go missing, we'll know where to find you?" Jack joked.

"A bedroom for each of the children?" Darla asked, passing him in the corridor upstairs. "And please don't tell me you're sticking Lindy out in the bungalow?"

Lindy blushed and turned away with ears straining to hear Jack's response.

"Mum," Jack hissed, "We can't marry yet, so we'll live together until our divorces come through."

"Jack you need not spell it out for me. I know love when I see it. You both need each other. Don't worry, everything will fall into place," Darla's head dropped to one side, "Now about this property. Decision made?"

Stepping out into the hallway Lindy heard the rest of the conversation and gave Darla a gentle smile. Lindy turned her attention back to admire the old sepia photographs hanging from the picture rails.

Her body moulded to Jack's when his arms encircled her waist, "Mum said you and I have a house to purchase," he whispered. "Are you ready?"

"Definitely. I agree with your mother, time for wheeling and dealing," Lindy said as she leant into Jack. She eyed the ornate trimmings. "Love the dark wood on these stairs," the runner covering the stairs brightened their way and Lindy took in the intricate patterns and burgundy border.

In the kitchen they found April, Steve and Michael watching the children running around the backyard with Tony looking on. They looked at home in the vast garden, Jack swallowed hard before clearing his throat.

"Jack, Lindy. Do we have something to discuss?" Michael asked as he clapped his hands together.

"Hopefully we can come to an agreement," Jack replied, his speech slow and measured. Even with Lindy's input, Jack wanted some negotiation from April and Steve, even a little would help their bottom line.

After much discussion and compromise on price by both parties, Jack and Lindy were congratulated as the new owners of the Chester's Run Estate. A divine twenty-acre property with everything the family could ever want. Jack glanced sideways at Lindy, giving away nothing to an outsider, but to Lindy his beautiful light brown eyes shone.

"Well congratulations, I believe we have ourselves a deal," Michael said, holding the pen out for both Jack and Lindy to sign. "Settlement will take place early in the new year," An understanding that April, Steve, and the family had one last chance to say goodbye. "I believe we're all done here."

Michael replaced the lid on his pen. He stood up with signed contracts in hand.

"Call if you need anything, otherwise I'll be in touch."

After Steve had seen Michael out, he joined the others in the kitchen. The Saunders children had just come inside to hear the delightful news.

"Really Dad, is this going to be our new home?" Evie's eyes gleamed.

"Looks that way. What do you think?" Jack picked Evie up and gave her a cuddle.

"How about you go upstairs and have another look while I get everyone a drink?" April suggested.

The next comment quietened the room.

Caleb asked, "Dad, Mum won't be allowed here, will she? This isn't her house, is it?" Nobody said a word. What do you say to a child traumatised by his own mother?

Finally, Lindy stepped in front of Caleb and as always placed the children's needs as top priority, she scooped him up in her arms with a slight struggle and pulled him in close for a hug. "No matter what happens Caleb, your father and I are here and will always take care of you. You'll be safe." As an afterthought she added, "I promise." And she truly meant it.

Caleb wrapped his arms around Lindy's neck and hugged her. "Okay Lindy."

As he slid to the ground and took off after his siblings Lindy vowed no matter what happened, Elsa would never cause Jack's children any discomfort if she was around to prevent it.

CURIOUS PAST

LINDY

*A*fter the purchase agreement was signed, everyone worked knowing the time on the farm was coming to an end. With a moving date to work towards, all available hands joined the cause. The overloaded skip was removed and replaced while the sorting and clearing out continued. Both Jack and his father encouraged the children to join them after homework and snacks.

"I'm all done," Nate told Lindy as he closed his homework book.

"Who's turn to set the table?" she settled a freshly changed Bradley into his highchair.

"Yum, yum," Bradley screeched, banging his hands on the table. Darla settled in beside him with his bowl of mashed veggies and gravy.

"Mine and Caleb's," Joanna answered as she stood to pack her finished reader into her schoolbag.

"Okay Nate, off you go. Joanna and Caleb set the table please then you can join him." Nate ran down to the shed to spend time with his father.

"Evie, are you nearly finished?"

"Not yet, I'm doing my project." Evie took notes from an old library book. Lindy peered over her shoulder, "I'm allowed to do my anything of local interest project on the history of Chester's Run Estate."

"Hadn't you finished that?" Lindy asked, with furrowed brows.

"I had, but when I told Miss Mackenzie we bought the new house she said I could use this project to make up on marks I lost when we weren't at school." Evie spoke of the time when they missed weeks of school earlier in the year before Elsa left.

"When's it due?" Lindy asked, not wanting to rehash that agonising time in the children's life.

"Miss Mackenzie gave me till next Friday. She took me to the library today, and we found these two books, she asked if I could use the internet for more information. Here are the websites," Lindy took the offered piece of paper from Evie's outstretched hand.

Before reading the note, Lindy suggested, "How about you work up at the bench so Joanna and Caleb can set the table. I'll help you while I'm finishing dinner."

"All right," Evie moved her books and pencil case to the breakfast bar and settled down to work again. These children had come a long way in the weeks she'd known them.

LINDY

After a late dinner, Darla and Lindy took care of the showers and baths while Jack and Tony did the dishes. Jack walked up the hall in search of a clean Bradley to feed him his bottle. They'd spoken of doing away with the use of bottles, but decided to leave that until after they had settled into the new house. Delaying the loss of the bottle till after Christmas wasn't going to be an issue. Another few months would at least help him cope with the changes to come.

Once the other children were in bed reading, Evie settled down at the table with Darla and continued her project.

"Nanna, I don't understand this thing about horseshoes. In this book it says that the early town's people engraved horseshoes." Evie was still poring over the words as she spoke.

"Here love, let me see that."

Evie turned the book towards her grandmother.

"Oh, Tony come here," Darla called into the lounge.

"What's up, love?" He asked, hitching up his pants as he walked towards them.

"Read this," Tony dug his glasses from his shirt pocket and read.

A grand tradition existed for years in Chester's Run. From the first joyous marriage between Samuel and Beth, the townsfolk partook in a newfound ritual. On the wedding day, the local blacksmith or smithy would engrave the lucky couple's names into a large horseshoe. Signifying the union between the couple.

The article went on.

Unfortunately, these artefacts of our past have been misplaced but the records show an undetermined number of locals took part in this ritual which became a well-loved tradition beginning with the first young couple Samuel and Beth Inglis.

This information piqued Lindy's interest.

"I don't remember anything about that," Jack called out from the lounge.

"Yes, I do." Tony replied, "It's scratchy at the moment, I'll have a think about it."

"How long ago was that book written?" Jack asked.

Tony flicked to the front pages, "Published in 1957," Tony offered. "Hmmm, leave it with me. I vaguely remember my parents talking about the horseshoes. Maybe this is what they were referring to."

Moving on, Evie continued to impart more knowledge on the adults. "Dad, did you know a really mean man built the estate. His name was Roger Inglis. Miss Mackenzie said it was a sad story, but that I'm too young to understand what he did. She said it has a happy ending though." The adults glanced at each other but remained silent.

What might they discover about the history of the Chester's Run

Estate with more research? Lindy thought, history had been one of her passions.

"Another half an hour, Evie," Jack called. "Then it's time for bed."

HER CHILDREN

LINDY

*W*ith baking dishes piled up on the sink, tonight's dinner in the oven and food on cooling racks, Lindy was hard at work finishing things before Bradley woke from his afternoon nap. She jumped when her phone rang. Even though the ringing of her phone wasn't unusual, it happened less often these days. Reaching for a tea towel, Lindy wiped her hands answering the call before it woke Bradley.

"Lindy Kemp," she answered.

"Lindy, how are you? It's Flo."

"Flo."

"Can you talk?" Flo's kind voice asked.

"Yes, how are you?"

"Good. Before I go on, I have Ralph here. Please don't be angry with me but he wants to make sure you're okay and asked me to ring."

Lindy sucked in a breath and replied, "Flo, I have nothing to say to him," Lindy looked up when she heard Darla arrive.

She waved and turned to look out the window. This was one call she needed to concentrate on.

"All correspondence between us goes through the lawyers," her tone was harsher than she'd meant it to be. Well, in her defence the call caught her off guard.

She heard Ralph in the background. "Ask could we just talk? Could I come around to see her?"

Lindy tensed, she wasn't sure talking to him was a good idea. Eventually with a sigh she said, "Put him on Flo."

She heard the phone change hands and then waited for him to speak.

"Hi Lindy," the tension in his voice was full of nerves and lacked the arrogance of the past.

"Why weren't you the one to call?"

"I didn't think you'd speak to me," he answered honestly.

"You got that right," Lindy tried for a harsher tone that didn't eventuate, hell she was all over the place.

"We should talk. Maybe dinner," he quickly added, "Bring whoever you like."

Lindy sensed a shift, Ralph wasn't attempting to lord it over her like he usually did. She wanted to ask about their children, but maybe he didn't know they hadn't been in contact. Hell, maybe this was about one of them. Before she could think better of it, Lindy asked, "Are the kids okay?"

"I don't know. None of them will take my calls."

"If it's any consolation," Lindy said, her voice gentle. "I haven't heard from them since the last time we spoke."

"That might be my fault, I fed them some lies about you."

"You what?" The truth of his words landed heavy in her heart, heavier than she could have ever believed. Those children were her life and Ralph manipulated a rift between them.

"I was angry. You took away my life."

"A life you didn't want or deserve. Don't worry about it, I'll ring them," she snapped. "What do you want from me?" The muscles in Lindy's neck tightened when she added, "I've moved on with my life."

"Oh," the shake in his voice gave away his surprise. "Umm, are you happy?"

This was the man she'd married, the one who disappeared when she announced she was pregnant with their second child. The night came back as if it was only yesterday. Lindy cooked his favourite meal. Mongolian beef followed by the Ultimate Chocolate Cake, which had been his favourite. She almost laughed, knowing she'd never cooked those dishes again.

In answer to his question, she couldn't help but smile, "Yes. So happy…for the first time in years. And you?" She tried to hold the snarkiness from her voice.

"I've been a fool, I want you back. I want to explain it all to you and your parents. Please give us another chance." That tone wasn't consistent with how he'd spoken with her for most of their marriage.

Tears threatened, in the early years of their marriage Ralph was always this caring.

"Sorry, you and I have nothing in common. I'll meet with you, but only to appease your conscience."

And as if flicking a switch, his voice now held that air of authority she was used to. The compassionate man vanished. "Message me with the time and place, you have my number," Ralph hung up.

How could she blame him? Her comment was horrible. Lindy never took cheap shots, not even at him. It just wasn't in her nature.

Thinking back to what he'd admitted, Lindy tried to catch a rush of tears. Why did he cause her such pain? What lies had he told the kids? Lindy dropped her head into her hands as the emotion of the call took over.

But she wouldn't crumble. Her children were told lies about her, she would rectify that immediately. Without pausing she placed a conference call to Liam, Cameron and Sophie and waited for them to answer. If Ralph lied to them, she wanted to be the one to set them straight but not as much as to hear their voices, each of them.

"Mum," Sophie called out, the emotion in her voice thick and the background noise reminding Lindy she was probably at work.

Seconds later Liam's voice echoed through his car, "Mum, is that really you?"

Then the unmistakable sound of silence. Cameron never coped well with separation from his mother. Lindy expected at least he would've called.

"Cameron, are you there?" Lindy asked, her voice thick and her chest tight.

"Yeah, I'm here," there was no joy in his soft voice.

She tried to speak, but words disappeared amid her tears and sobs.

"Mum, we don't believe what he told us. We've been waiting for you to return our calls." Sophie explained.

JACK

"Jack, come quick." Darla ran across the yard as Tony and Jack rushed out from the shed.

"What's wrong?" Tony rushed to grab her as she stumbled, stopping her just before she crumbled to the hard dirt.

"Jack, it's Lindy." Darla puffed, but before she could fill him in Jack bolted for the house.

His heart was in his mouth, pounding like a battering ram on a castle gate. What else did this woman have to endure? He approached the door to the kitchen with hesitation. Lindy's head was in her hands as she stood by the sink.

"Tell me everything. What's happened?"

He noticed the phone clutched in her white knuckled hand like a lifeline. Wrapping her up with one arm, he took the phone in the other and saw the names on the screen. It was her children. These must be happy tears. Jack whispered, "Shall I talk?"

She nodded as her sobs eased.

Jack put the call on loud speaker and introduced himself. "Your mother is fine. She's so happy to hear your voices."

"Who is this?" a male voice asked.

"My name's Jack. Your mother is just catching her breath. Are you all well?" Jack would not explain the relationship to them at the moment. And besides, it was their mother they longed to hear from.

Finally, she took control of her emotions. "I rang and left messages for you all. I was desperate to hear from you."

"You rang from the home phone and we've been calling that. And your mobile is turned off." Liam explained.

"I have my mobile," Jack could see how confused she was.

"Oh, hell!" Lindy fought back more tears, "This is the work mobile, your father has my other phone. He threw it and smashed it a few days before everything happened. And as for the home phone, I haven't been home since I left your father."

"So, who's this Jack?" Liam wasn't letting this go.

"Liam, I'd like to explain all that in person," Lindy said, before adding, "Your father just called," this she said to her children but also to Jack. "He wants to meet with me, so I'll come down soon."

Jack shuffled his feet, itching to pace or scream. He was desperate for more details but he didn't force the issue.

Lindy made eye contact with Jack and whispered, "I told him I've moved on and am so happy with my life."

A smile exploded on his face as he pulled her into his arms, dropping a tender kiss onto the top of Lindy's head.

To her children she said, "I've gone away for a while to sort myself out. Let me plan to meet with your father and then I'll be in touch soon."

"When's soon?" Cameron asked. His voice frantic.

Jack mouthed, "Within the hour."

"I'll sort it out straight away and contact you all within the hour. Will that be soon enough?" but Jack could see Lindy didn't look convinced about the time frame.

After she hung up, they held each other tight as Bradley's demanding wail rang out.

Darla headed down the hallway.

"Thanks Mum," Jack called as Tony entered the kitchen looking at his son for guidance. Jack rocked and comforted Lindy, and smiled.

"Dad, are you and Mum able to help Tessa with the rugrats tonight and tomorrow? Lindy has a date with her children."

Moving Lindy back to meet his gaze, Jack saw both pleasure and pain lingering in her blue eyes.

"Of course we can. Stay in Melbourne as long as you need," Tony told them.

"Jack, maybe we should take Bradley," Lindy was over thinking things as usual.

"No love, it's fine. You need to concentrate on your family and settling things with Ralph. Tessa and Mum can handle him for one night. We'll head to Melbourne and sort this out."

TRUTH OF BETRAYAL

LINDY

*A*s Jack turned into Lindy's parent's driveway, the front door opened and Duncan and Charlotte walked out to greet them.

"Hey love," Charlotte called as Lindy's car door opened. "How was the trip?"

Lindy walked up the porch steps, rubbing her left arm absentmindedly. She forced a smile and walked into her mother's welcoming arms.

"Hi Mum. The trip was fine." Charlotte was a tad shorter than her daughter, who stooped slightly to rest her head on the older woman's shoulder.

"Jack, good to see you," Charlotte kissed his cheek and turned to lead them inside. "The children will be here soon. It was wonderful to hear Sophie's voice again."

"Hi Dad," Lindy kissed his leathery cheek. "Thanks for putting us up for the night."

"You know you're always welcome. Jack, good to see you again."

Duncan stood aside and waited as Jack and Lindy followed his wife through the door and up the hallway to their appointed bedrooms.

The doorbell chimed. Charlotte stood from the stool she'd perched herself on and cursed under her breath.

"When have those children ever had to knock in this house?"

Lindy laughed, "I think they've upset her now."

Cameron's desperate voice echoed down the tiled hallway.

"Mum," he called.

Watching from the kitchen doorway, Lindy could see her children walking towards her. All three of them.

"Oh Cameron," she cried as he rushed forward and scooped her up. His trembling arms embraced her tight. Unable to hold back her tears, the two stayed together for a long while. Cameron incapable of controlling his emotions, was holding onto his mother for dear life.

She formed a special connection with each of her children. With Cameron she shared a love of reading and studying and took extra time teaching him to socialise. The pair could talk for hours about a topic of interest to them both. When Cameron left home, at his father's insistence 'to become a man', their tie diminished. Though they still spoke to each other every day, it wasn't the same. Maybe he blamed her in some way. The strain on that bond affected their relationship in other areas. Having her son in her arms once again, Lindy treasured the closeness she missed.

Sophie and Liam watched on, both waiting their turn. Sophie wiped at a stray tear or two.

Lindy gestured to Liam and Sophie to join her and revelled in having her children in her arms again.

"I never believed him. I promise, but we couldn't find you," Sophie said through her tears. A perfect completeness blanketed them, one she hadn't basked in for a long time.

Seeing a need to take control of the situation, Lindy pulled back, "Now, let me look at you all." Her gaze travelled over Cameron, he'd lost too much weight. She began mentally making plans for her contact with him. Sophie was paler than usual, but hopefully that was only from the stress of the moment. Liam was quieter, something that could never be said about her eldest son.

"Are you going to introduce me?" Jack asked.

Stepping back, Lindy used Jack's interruption to gain some control. Her heart raced as the hairs on her arms rose. Clamping her eyes shut, she drew in a breath. *Steady. Steady.*

Was this a dream? One hand still held fast to Cameron, ensuring it wasn't.

Stepping closer to Jack she wrapped her other arm around his waist. "Liam, Cameron, and Sophie, this is my boyfriend, Jack. Jack my children, Liam my eldest, Cameron and my daughter, Sophie."

"A pleasure to meet you all. I just hope you don't make a habit of making your mum cry whenever we see you," Jack teased, making everyone chuckle and in turn easing the tension gripping them all.

The newcomers greeted their grandparents with hugs and took the chairs their Nan offered while she bustled around the kitchen to finish dinner.

"Are you okay, Mum?" Sophie's voice was strained.

"Yes love, I am. But things have changed guys. I hope you're able to accept that. Jack and his children are an important part of my life, just as you all are." There was truth in those words. She'd been lost, without realising it, until she'd met Jack. Nothing would convince her to give him up now. Not even her own children's disapproval.

"You mean you're not coming home?" Cameron's choppy voice broke her heart.

"No Cameron," Lindy's chin dipped as she shook her head. They all knew change wasn't easy for him.

Sophie's shoulders relaxed, and she nodded her encouragement to her brother. "See, I told you she was okay," she reassured him,

"Cameron, I should have tried to contact you again, but I was hurt and stubborn, I'm so sorry. But I promise we'll work something out."

"Come on, Charlotte let's dish up dinner." Jack helped Duncan set the table whilst the others helped Charlotte dish up the evening meal of roast lamb and veggies. Lindy's appreciative sigh made Jack laugh.

After the day's events it was only now as her tummy rumbled that

Lindy took a mental note of what they'd eaten so far today. It wasn't much.

The conversation around the table seemed to jump from one topic to the next. Lindy caught up on what the children had been up to and filled them in on how she was spending her days. Then a question nagging in the back of her mind had Lindy asking, "Why didn't you call your uncles or grandparents?" her hand sat on Jack's knee beneath the table, she wasn't certain she wanted to hear whatever excuse they came up with.

Sophie looked to Liam and back to her mother. She swallowed her mouthful.

"I pulled into the office car park behind Grandpa and another guy the afternoon it happened. I wanted to talk to Flo." Sophie explained, "When I couldn't get you and realised Liam was overseas, I wasn't sure what to do. I left and called Flo later and she told me Dad took a leave of absence."

"Ralph took a leave of absence from his beloved business?" Lindy's eyes bulged. But then it occurred to her, maybe it wasn't the business he loved so much, as the women he came into contact with.

LINDY

Liam looked to his grandfather and back to his mother, "I didn't understand what was going on and you weren't answering your phone so we steered clear until we found out the truth. We knew for certain you hadn't gone to an asylum as Dad claimed."

"Your father said what?" Duncan roared.

"Dad," Lindy warned while still trying to get her head around why her father had been to Ralph's office. But that was a question to put to him in private.

"Can you tell us what really happened with Dad?" Sophie asked, setting her napkin beside her plate. "Initially we believed what he said about you but as time went on, it occurred to us none of it stacked up. So, we called home and your mobile, but you didn't reply. And the house keys don't work either," Sophie added as an afterthought.

Lindy was reluctant to explain about the mail she'd received and then about visiting Ralph in his office. But Jack and her parents were correct, the children had a right to know the truth.

"Are you kidding me?" Liam spat.

"I packed up and went away for a few weeks, which seems to have become rather permanent," Lindy shared a smile with Jack. It was as if a bolt of lightning hit her, Chester's Run was now her home.

Cameron started clearing the table, silent as ever. Lindy was fully aware he was taking it all in and processing it at his pace.

"You okay, Cameron?" Charlotte asked when she followed her grandson into the kitchen. Lindy noticed the emotion dancing across his gentle face.

"I never believed him for a minute," Cameron stacked the dishes into the dishwasher. "I hate the man."

That broke Lindy's heart, and she struggled with her emotion, too choked up to speak.

"Hey love," Charlotte's understanding voice comforted him as she held the gentle giant in her arms, "Promise me you'll come here for dinner all the time. I've missed you guys so much." Tears welled in Charlotte's eyes, her mother treasured all her grandchildren. It didn't take a genius to know how deeply she'd missed these guys.

Jack took over clearing the table and began washing the dishes as the family tried to find some understanding. They talked and asked questions, and Lindy answered as best she could.

Sophie checked her watch, "Well, we'd better go, I'm on an early shift in the morning. What time will you leave here tomorrow?" she asked Lindy and Jack.

"We'll be back in Chester's Run for dinner, so mid-afternoon, I'd say." Lindy smiled when Jack nodded his agreement. There was a telepathic connection between them, Jack understood she would like to see her children again tomorrow if they could manage it.

"How about you all come over for lunch, say about midday?" Charlotte suggested.

"Yep, and I'll be staying for dinner," Cameron clarified, which brought a smile to Lindy's face. This was Cameron's safe place.

"Thanks for dinner, Grandma," Sophie said as they shared a hug.

Liam pulled the keys out of his pocket, shook hands with his grandpa and Jack, then hugged his mum and grandmother, promising to be back the following day.

Lindy saw them out while Jack finished clearing up dessert dishes and cups.

With the kitchen clean, Lindy and Jack followed Duncan and Charlotte into the lounge.

"I believe you have something to tell me," Lindy said to her father, "Why were you at Ralph's office?"

"Funny story that," Duncan said, half of his mouth a grin.

When the silence stretched out, Lindy added, "Well?"

"Ralph didn't take a leave of absence. Hang on, let me go back to the start."

Lindy's brows raised and her face contorted.

"What are you on about?"

"Remember when Ralph started the company?"

"Of course, I do."

"Did you ever wonder how he got the financial backing for the business?"

"You own part of the business?" Lindy was enjoying this conversation.

She snuggled back into Jack to hear more.

"No," Duncan couldn't hold back his delight, "You do. My plan was to invest in the company and once it paid me back, the ownership transferred to you and Ralph. You own the majority share, it's a seventy/thirty split."

"I own seventy percent of Ralph's business?" her voice was a shrill.

"Anthony and I have been overseeing the company from day one. Flo has been working for us, keeping abreast of the day to day stuff."

"Did you know he was seeing other women?" Lindy questioned.

"No. That he was very good at hiding. But it explains why we lost a few important contracts over the years," Duncan added, "When you told us what happened, Anthony and I decided it was a smart business decision to have him stood down, so Liam took on the role of overseer in the interim."

"Does he know I own majority stakes in the business?" Lindy wondered whether that was why Liam came today. He'd always been self-absorbed like his father.

"No. All communication goes through Flo. And that's why Liam had no idea that it involved me."

"Oh my God, I love that woman."

"She's had your back for years."

Did Flo know what Ralph was up to? But really what did it matter now? After tomorrow, she'd just let it all go.

"What'll happen with the business now?"

"Your husband was big on signing agreements, but hopeless at negotiating what was best for him. He gets thirty percent of the business or he can offer to buy you out."

"I want nothing from him. I have my nest egg to live on. Zave and I have agreed that he'll buy half of my mentoring business which will allow me to be a silent investor, to a degree. I'm opening a branch in Chester's Run when everything settles down for us, just to keep my hand in it."

"I thought as much. My suggestion is to sell Ralph the business and give an equal share to the children. Set them up. Liam could start his own business somewhere else, Flo won't hang around with Ralph, so she could help him. Cameron could find his own home to live in and work from. Better than that dump Ralph put him in. And Sophie will want a business of her own soon. You could help them all out."

JACK

After the cries of goodnight and laughter from his children, Jack hung up. His mind shifted from the welfare of his family, who were delighted to spend the night with their grandparents, to the woman beside him. He wrapped his arm around Lindy.

"Tonight's all ours. Let's relax and enjoy it."

"I can't believe I owned a majority share of the business, that's probably why he didn't leave," Lindy concluded, still reeling from the truth. The slight tremble in her hand was clearly caused by her surprise at that discovery.

They were sitting together in the back lounge, just the two of them. Jack's eyes roamed her adorable face. He sighed inwardly when her wine glass met her lips. He was lost in her beauty.

"I can't tell you how much I love you for what you said to your father."

"Whether or not I need the money, I want nothing from his business," Lindy leant into him. "But Dad's right, it'll probably set the children up."

"I'm so proud of you."

"Thank you," Lindy smiled at him, "Let's not talk about this anymore."

"Okay, but I'd just like to say how much I liked your children. Apart from Sophie being a spitting image of you, they all resemble you."

"In a good way I hope," Lindy teased.

"Yes, in the best way possible," Jack studied her for a long minute. She was such a sophisticated lady. The delicate movement of her mouth and throat enticed him. That action had his mind wandering, so before he allowed it to race away, he squeezed her hand and smiled. Jack put his glass down and sliced a few bits of cheese, he selected a biscuit and turned to face her. "Your mother is a treasure."

Lindy let out a laugh and looked up at him, "Yes, she really is."

"Open up," he whispered. He didn't miss the rush of colour creeping into her cheeks, in fact it sent a warmth through him. Hell, this woman was stunning. They took turns feeding each other a selection of nuts, fruit and then more cheese. Talking and laughing in soft tones, he would always treasure the memory of this moment. Knowing this was a pot of gold among a painful task, they could at least enjoy their time together. He longed for total intimacy but was more than satisfied to spend the evening with her in his arms here on the couch.

She deposited her glass onto the coffee table in front of them and turned to look at him. The intensity in her bright eyes was a delight, as well as her next move. Reaching across she took his glass easily from him and placed it on the table beside hers, then taking his hand she stood up before him.

Momentarily, he was lost in the depths of her beautiful blue eyes, her voice husky as she whispered, "Your room or mine?"

Her ears turning dark red at her boldness.

Jack found he was drawn to her even more in this moment. Pushing himself to his feet, he looped his arms around her waist and pulled her in close. Her lips were soft as he began to kiss them, he revelled as her body slumped against his. He cupped her face as their lips met again. Standing together, the heat rose between them. Jack didn't want to fight this. His love for this woman made their decision simple. He'd finally get to lie with her tonight. His heart skipped a beat.

"Mine, so you have the option of leaving if you need to. Because there's no way I'm going anywhere once I have you beside me," the rawness in his voice spoke of a need he had for Lindy. She reached deep down into his soul from the very moment she comforted his battered baby.

Lindy led the way down the hall towards the bedrooms and paused outside her open door.

"My room, because you need to believe I want this as much as you do. Tomorrow morning, I want to wake up in your arms. I'm in love with you Jack Saunders, and nothing will change that."

Without another word, Jack backed her into her room and kicked the door closed with the heel of his boot.

LINDY

Waking up next to Jack was more wonderful than Lindy could've imagined. Her mind retraced the joy they shared last night. As Lindy lay listening to Jack's even breathing, she recalled the reason they were together, here in her parent's house. Lindy's body tensed at the harsh memory of who she'd see today.

Jack's sleepy voice startled her, "Hey, what are you thinking about?

Hope that sudden tension in your body is not because we're here together?"

Lindy rested her chin on his chest, looked into his eyes and gave him a weak smile.

"No. Never." With a sigh, she added, "I just remembered what we're doing here. I'm so nervous."

Jack pressed his lips to her forehead, "We'll do this together, just like we will with everything for the rest of our lives."

"Thank you. Whatever Ralph wants, I'll listen to him and then move on."

"Your father said last night that Mal's coming over," Jack told her. And Lindy could see he was trying to ease her discomfort.

"Hey, I'm here with you all the way. You and I will get through this, we're a team. I'm not foolish enough to believe any of this will be easy, but I honestly think everything will be all right."

"I wish I had your confidence."

"I love you and we'll get through this together, no matter what Ralph says," Jack dropped another kiss to her lips.

"I keep thinking of our life back in Chester's Run. I miss the children."

"Good. Keep thinking of them, I can't wait till we can sit around the dining room table with all our children. That's my goal for us. Just keep hold of that dream and of how much I love you," Jack pulled her closer as she met his kiss with the same intensity they'd shared last night, "Come on, let's tackle this day."

With a groan from Lindy, they set about preparing for Ralph's visit and whatever came of it. It was comforting to know Lindy would see her children for lunch and they still had Jack's children waiting for them when they arrived back at the farm later.

JACK

Jack noticed Lindy jump as the doorbell chimed. Her face paled, so Jack took her hand in his and gave her an encouraging smile. Now it began. Lindy sat at the kitchen table while she waited for someone to appear.

Ralph entered the kitchen and took in Lindy and Jack sitting together. He nodded briefly before greeting Charlotte with a kiss.

Jack could tell this man was used to owning a crowd when he stepped before them, though today he didn't appear comfortable in this environment.

"Morning Lindy," he mumbled, looking her up and down. Jack held in a groan, the normally confident woman vanished. The timid woman before him was alien. Maybe this was the wife Ralph created during their marriage. If that was the case, Jack didn't like what it did to her. Realisation set in, he remembered meeting her family. This Lindy was so despondent. Her eyes blinking rapidly, something Jack had never seen.

"Morning Ralph," Lindy offered as she met her ex-husband's gaze. Lindy squeezed Jack's hand, oblivious to the fact she hadn't introduced them.

"Hi, I'm Ralph," he extended his right hand.

Jack raised himself out of his chair and took the offered hand.

"Jack Saunders," Ralph was a tall man and stood an inch or two taller than Jack.

Realisation had Lindy quickly apologising, "Sorry I should have introduced you..." but before she continued her brothers called a greeting from the front door. They showed themselves in, kissed Lindy and shook hands with Jack before greeting their parents. Mal nodded to Ralph, pulled out a chair and after leaning back waited for the show to begin.

Danny was subtler. He spared a few words for his former brother-in-law.

With the silence stretching out before them, all eyes were on Ralph. They waited eagerly for what he wanted to say.

Ralph squirmed in his seat. Good, Jack liked that the man looked uncomfortable.

LINDY

Ralph sat forward in his chair, his elbows resting on the table, then pushed back. He rolled his bottom lip into his mouth, eventually parting his lips with a pop.

Good, he was just as nervous as she was.

"I asked to meet with you," Ralph began, "Because I found out who sent the photos." He paused as if searching for something, whether it was courage or the right words Lindy wasn't certain. "Jeez this is all wrong."

"You bet it's wrong. The way you treated my sister—"

"Mal!" Duncan warned.

Lindy could imagine her father was just as eager to hear what excuse Ralph had to weasel himself out of the current situation. She kept her eyes on her ex-husband, taking in the deep lines on his face. The face which was once handsome was now haggard and plain. Being honest with herself, Lindy saw their union for what it now was, their life as a couple was over. He was nothing to her but the father of the children she'd raised.

"What do you want to say?"

"Maybe I could speak with you in private?" Ralph suggested glancing at Mal.

Jack squeezed her hand and gave her a slight nod.

With the support of Jack and the men in her family, she'd get through this.

Standing up, she gestured to the backyard and Ralph followed.

Without an audience Ralph spoke more freely. "I'm not proud of what I did to you. In fact, I can't believe I took the word of a playboy without even seeking your side of the story."

"What the hell are you talking about?" Lindy was close enough to hear his words but far enough away to feel safe.

"Wes and Pat."

The name of Ralph's old friend and boss sent shivers down her spine, as the memories of that fateful night came rushing back. Lindy's mind reeled. She released a groan when the vision of the horrible man flashed before her. The man who caused her so much discomfort all those years ago. The memory of being shoved back against the wall in the hallway of their old home was plaguing her all over again. Lindy never hated people, some she just avoided, others avoided her and the rest were never important.

But Wes. She hated.

With a passion.

The man was a bully and a mongrel.

"Why are you bringing them up now? We haven't seen them for years." Lindy said, as a cold clammy shiver went up her spine.

"Why did you take a disliking to him?" his eyes bored into her. "Tell me, I think I know the truth but I need to hear your version."

"But what does any of this have to do with the photos?"

"Just indulge me," he pleaded, his hands deep in the pocket of his jeans.

Wrapping her arms around herself, Lindy drew in a sharp breath.

"You were away on one of your trips. Wes came over just after I'd put Liam to bed one night. I had a bottle of wine and two glasses on the table," Lindy took a few steps away and turned back towards him, "Wes taunted me, his scathing remarks accusing me of expecting a lover. But it was Danny and Barbra who were coming over."

"Why only the two glasses?"

"Because I'd just found out I was pregnant with Cameron. I didn't drink with any of the pregnancies, remember?"

She was aware the door was open, Lindy looked in and saw all eyes on them.

"Shit!" Ralph said and paced.

"Why shit?" she shot at him forcefully. "If you don't believe me, speak with Danny." Her arms flayed toward the dining room. "He can vouch for it all. Especially what happened next."

"Next?"

"Wes tried to force himself on me. I screamed out when he pushed me up against the wall in the hallway and then Danny was there pulling him off me," her arms had a mind of their own, crossing over her chest.

"That's why you wanted to move?"

Lindy could only nod.

"Why didn't you tell me?"

"I tried but the night you returned home you were angry and I didn't know how to start the conversation," Her voice dropped, "I was scared and Wes warned me you'd lose your job."

Ralph stormed towards the house, "Danny, is that what happened?"

"Exactly. I rang Mal and this Wes character was threatened with attempted rape," Danny puffed out his chest and folded his arms.

Lindy caught Jack's eye as he nodded further encouragement and what she took as his support.

They all watched on as Ralph dropped into a chair on the patio, his head resting in his hands. "That was the beginning of the end for us. I could see it was only a matter of time. I waited for you to cheat again, but you were excellent at covering up what you did or it wasn't happening."

"What do you mean cheat *again*?" her previously barely audible voice rose.

"Wes taunted me about how good a lay you were."

"And you believed him?"

"When you told me you were pregnant with Cameron, I put two and two together."

"And got six," she snapped. And why shouldn't she. It was obvious he'd been unfaithful and going by his attempt at openness it had been going on for a while. "So that's when you began sleeping around?"

"Not straight away, no. It ate away at me and then I decided if you can't beat them," he shrugged his shoulder, "Join them," his eyes avoided hers.

"I'd been nothing but loyal to you, Ralph. There was never anyone else during our marriage."

"But there is now?" Ralph asked, looking in at Jack who stared straight back.

"I love Jack. Nothing will change that for me."

Ralph nodded.

"So, what's this got to do with the photos?" Lindy questioned when her mind circled back to where they started.

"The girl you saw on my knee, Casey, she's pregnant. From what I can tell she had three goals, first was to get photos of me with other women, second she wanted you out of the way before she told me."

"And third?"

"To get me to pay for this child of hers," Ralph said with a snarl. "I had three beautiful kids and stuffed that up. I don't need the responsibility of ruining another child's life."

"I suppose I should say congratulations," her words were sharp but Lindy couldn't help it.

"It's not mine. I had a vasectomy, remember?"

"How could I forget!" Lindy's hands raised and then dropped to her sides with a thud. "I was still in hospital with Sophie. In fact, I was cradling her in my arms when you announced there wouldn't be any more children. I still can't believe how quickly you had it done," Lindy snapped, "So, you rejected Cameron and Sophie, thinking they were never yours."

"More I didn't trust you they were mine."

"Nothing like a firm slap across the face with your harsh words," Lindy headed for the house. She'd heard enough.

But she stopped. She wanted to know how this Casey got all the photos.

"Ralph," she said, turning back towards him.

"Yep?" he asked, his dejected face turning up to meet hers.

"No, on second thoughts, it doesn't matter," Lindy continued towards the house. Although it intrigued her, it wasn't any of her business.

Best let sleeping dogs lie.

JACK

Watching on, Jack heard the conversation with her ex. How could anyone believe she'd be disloyal? The accusation stung him.

As she walked to the door, delivering her final blow over her shoulder, Jack stepped up and pulled her into his arms. Her body shook and her eyes didn't meet his. Jack's heart ached on her behalf. Both Ralph and Elsa were self-centred people who didn't consider anyone else. Hopefully that would only bode well for his future with Lindy. Neither of them were anything like the people they'd married.

"You okay?" he asked.

Lindy nodded and followed Jack as he led her from the room.

He sat her down in the back lounge with her mother. The men's voices were rising. He wanted this man gone for Lindy's sake.

"Can I leave you with her?" Jack asked Charlotte as he looked towards the door leading back into the dining room.

"Just make sure they behave," Charlotte told him, taking the seat next to Lindy and holding her hand, "Especially Mal."

In the dining room Jack took a stance beside Lindy's brothers, his feet apart with hands on hips. But instead of seeing a formidable foe, he encountered a dejected soul.

Ralph was now inside and had dropped into a chair. Jack concluded the man must have been lamenting his own foolishness.

Ralph stood up, "Lindy and I have things to finalise but today is not the day for that." He looked to Duncan, "What do we do about the business? She can buy me out if she wants it."

"That's for her to decide," Duncan answered.

"Why didn't you tell her she owned a controlling interest?" Ralph asked.

"My accountant and I had full control of the finances so you posed no threat to my daughter's investment," Duncan told him with a shrug and missed the open-mouthed stares from his boys.

Jack noticed how pale the man now looked. Ralph believed she was innocent, Jack supposed hearing Lindy deny it all only made his situation worse.

Ralph turned to Jack and held out his hand, "I probably don't need to tell you how special she is. Take care of her and make sure she's happy," he looked at the other men, her father and brothers, their dislike of him clear.

Ralph only nodded before heading for the door.

When it closed, Jack watched her father sink into a chair.

"Why didn't you boys tell me what happened?" He was pale. He'd held himself together until Ralph left, now it was all too much.

"I asked them not to," Lindy stood at the door leading to the back of the house.

Jack walked over and pulled her close. "You are the strongest woman I know," he said resting his forehead against hers.

"Maybe if I was stronger and told him," Lindy replied with a guttural growl. "I could have saved my marriage and my children from so much rejection," Jack held her.

Right now, Lindy blamed herself for everything that ever happened between her and Ralph. That's what he'd done for such a large part of his marriage also. He'd become the unwilling pawn in Elsa's games. So, no, he had nothing to say. Instead he just held her close as the others processed what just happened.

JACK

Over lunch the family finally talked, really talked. Jack's skin tingled hearing the things Lindy's ex-husband said to or about her. The man had a vivid imagination.

"Listen, what's done is done and none of us can change that." Lindy began, "I don't blame you for doubting my actions. The entire thing was so outrageous, even to my own eyes and ears. But I promise you nothing could convince me I should go back to that life." Lindy leant into Jack and continued. "As a mother I was happy. How could I not be? I had three wonderful children, it was easier to make my life all about you guys."

"Mum, he said and did some horrible things. How did you tolerate that?"

Lindy nodded at Sophie's observation.

Jack wrapped an arm around her, unable to accept the way she used to live, and by the look on her father's face, he too, was struggling.

Lindy reached out her hands to her children and gave a sad smile. "I convinced myself it was the right thing to do."

"Where do we go from here?" Liam asked.

"Forward," Jack said without hesitation. "Both families will move forward. Together." Sophie sized him up. Her disbelieving gaze seemed to stare right through him. Even though he believed he'd survive her scrutiny, a tingle scurried down his spine. He'd have to prove himself to Lindy's children.

"I can only show you that your mother means the world to me Sophie, and I won't do anything to make her suffer. You have my word just as your grandparents do."

Sophie nodded, accepting his words, but actions speak so much louder than hearing heartfelt promises.

LINDY

"I love you Mum," Sophie pulled Lindy into a tight hug. "I'm so sorry for everything. Take care."

When Lindy turned to Cameron, she recognised the insecure man. Being by himself now would be hard, so she vowed, "I'll ring every night. It will be just like it was before I left, you'll see I'm right."

"Thank you," he replied, swallowing hard and shifting uncomfortably from one foot to the other.

"Don't worry Mum," Sophie interrupted, "We'll keep him sociable as always. We'll all be fine," even Cameron chuckled at Sophie's comment.

Liam stepped up pulling his mother into his arms, "This entire thing has made me face reality. I'm sorry for my selfish ways. I followed in Dad's footsteps more than you could know. But I promise to change. You scared us when you took off, we actually believed Dad had done you in but," he shrugged, "Uncle Mal would have raised hell if he didn't know where you were."

"Where do you go from here, Liam?" Lindy asked her son.

"Forward," Liam said, "I'm quoting a wise man." Liam looked at Jack as they all laughed. "Will you allow me to be a part of your life?" Liam's gaze was on Jack who nodded looking directly back at him. He gave a small nod of his own, "We'll be in touch. I'll be there for Cameron too, I promise." Liam shoved his hands in his pockets, "Oh hell, I nearly forgot. Flo asked me to give you this," Liam pulled out a little envelope, and he turned to where his keys were and gathered a bag off the bench, "Your SIM card from the old phone and a brand-new phone. Apparently the last one was beyond repair."

"Thanks love," Lindy took the bag. "I know you've all got each other and remember Jack and I are only a phone call away."

"You have my number," Jack confirmed with the three of them. "Call whenever you want."

Lindy kissed them all goodbye a second time and then thanked her parents for everything.

As Jack pulled out of the driveway, she sucked back the tears. There was bitter sweet realisation. For the first time in her life Lindy put her needs ahead of others. Conceding she was entitled to be happy. Looking at Jack's profile, she had to acknowledge that with this handsome man she found purpose and meaning in her life.

As the sun set on another warm November day, Jack drove down the driveway of the farmhouse. Lindy swallowed hard, she'd missed his children. She glanced across and noticed Jack watched the front door just as eagerly. The door swung open and all the children spilled out onto the front veranda waving like crazy. Nate appeared last leading a toddling Bradley along, his walking wasn't confident but it was impossible to keep him down any longer. Lindy couldn't contain her pleasure. She missed them all so much. Looking over to Jack she watched as his face split into an enormous grin. They were both so happy to be home in Chester's Run.

WEEKEND AWAY

LINDY

"Here, I'm all packed," Lindy dropped a small suitcase at her feet, "I still can't see why you don't tell me what's going on."

"Nothing's *'going on'*" Jack made quotation marks in the air.

"Nate, can you put Lindy's bag in the back of the ute?" Jack asked.

"Sure."

"They're here! They're here!" Evie and Joanna yelled from the front door.

"Who's here?" Lindy looked up at the kitchen clock. It was eight o'clock on a Thursday morning, Lindy shook her head.

Jack gave a cheeky grin.

Well, Lindy would just step out the front herself and see who'd arrived.

"Pack enough for three days," Jack told her before she'd even got out of bed this morning. He'd walked over to the bungalow at five. Even that was too early for both of them.

But as Lindy walked through the lounge to the front door, she only saw the tail end of a car going around the back. She turned and headed for the back door and heard the greetings of delight before she actually saw who'd arrived.

"Hi Mum," Cameron and Sophie stood there grinning like loons.

"What are you guys doing here?" Lindy's hand automatically going to Caleb's shoulder as he cuddled in close to her.

"Well, when we were here last time, we decided you needed a bit of a break," Sophie started explaining, "So, Cameron and I are babysitting the rugrats while you have a weekend off."

"But you're here," she looked to Jack, pleading with him. She'd missed her children so much.

"Yes, and when you get back on Sunday, we'll have time together then. We won't be leaving till Monday afternoon." Cameron reassured her.

"Now say goodbye to everyone and we'll see you Sunday for lunch at the bakery," Sophie insisted.

Lindy looked at the children and then Jack. "So, we're going away for the weekend?"

The young ones giggled and Jack just smiled his broad smile, with a message that said he couldn't wait.

JACK

The drive took less than an hour but for Jack it wasn't the destination, more the time they spent together.

"When did you organise this?" Lindy asked as they drove the almost deserted road. Her hand entwined with his.

Jack looked at her then back at the road. "Sophie and Cameron rang the other day and made the offer."

"Will they be all right?"

"Tessa has promised to help and Mum and Dad will be there every day." Jack looked over at her again. "Relax, they'll be fine. Liam's going to arrive after work tomorrow, but he'll leave either first thing Monday morning or Sunday afternoon. He's got an early meeting Monday he's trying to push back."

"Really?"

"What?" Jack asked.

"Liam never puts himself out for anybody," Lindy said.

"You mean the old Liam. This one will prove to us how responsible he can be."

"You enjoy his company, don't you?"

Jack turned and smiled at her. "Yep, I do. He's a smart guy, channelling his cockiness is more the issue. He has a determination I've seen in someone else I admire." Jack squeezed her hand.

"It surprised me to hear he picked Cameron up and took him out for dinner. Liam never did things like that."

"Cameron told me all about it the following day."

"Cameron?" Lindy said, with both brows raised. "My son, the one who doesn't talk to people. Wow! Today is full of surprises."

"The very one. He's great. You remember the time I rang him when Caleb stuffed up your laptop?"

Lindy nodded.

"Anyway, no more talk of children or family. This time away is all about us."

Pulling into the parking lot of their hotel, Jack checked his watch. "Good. Let's check in and maybe we'll go for a stroll."

"It's not even nine. Isn't check-in at two or something like that?"

"Normally yes but I grovelled, and they relented. Come on, let's go."

Lindy followed Jack to their suite and her mouth fell open, "Oh wow! This place is beautiful. Are those our mountains?" Lindy walked out onto the balcony.

"No, we're another range over," Jack walked up behind her and dropped a kiss to her neck.

Back inside, Lindy ran her finger along the handmade dining table with edges still resembling the tree it had been cut from.

"This piece is so rustic. This place is beautiful."

Jack couldn't hold back his pleasure, "Good, my choice lives up to your standard. Now come on, time for a walk and then we'll come back for lunch and maybe even an afternoon siesta," Jack kissed her nose, pulled her to the bedroom to unpack their belongings.

LINDY

"I don't think I can remember being so relaxed," Lindy said as they both sat quietly. "The walk to the gorge was wonderful. Could we bring the children here one day?"

"You bet. I want to do things like this, even horse trails and weekend camping. This place is our backyard and I want us to use it. Harry and Tessa would love to join us, and maybe even Bernie and Nola. Could you imagine the fun we'd all have?"

"Would your parents come too?"

"Not sure they'd camp, but they'd definitely meet us for lunch. I'm glad you liked it though. I agreed with Sophie, you needed time to yourself. I asked them if they wanted you to themselves for the weekend, but they insisted you and I get away," Jack pulled a face, "Who was I to argue?"

Lindy smiled and shook her head.

"Besides, soon it'll be Christmas and we'll be packing the houses up and moving into the homestead. This is as good a time as any."

Lindy took Jack's hand across the table. They had chatted, planned, walked, and talked together most of the day. It was an unfamiliar experience not having the children around interrupting a conversation or wanting something from either of them.

"I know this will sound funny but I miss the children."

"Haha, here I was thinking how peaceful this is. I can start an idea and follow it to the end without interruption," Jack chuckled.

Just being 'Mum' was the chance she never had with her own children, her opportunity to be there, to be present, to be a full-time mum. Not fitting it around her business commitments or Ralph.

"I get that but I love our noisy household, busy kitchen, relentless bath time routine and endless taxi gigs. The children playing, laughing, and even fighting. But most of all, I treasure you and I working side by side keeping everything going. I can't wait for the next chapter of our lives," she squeezed his hand and smiled at him.

"I promise we'll make sure we take time out like this for ourselves. After everything settles down with the move and the business, we'll get away again."

"Just promise it's somewhere local, not where we have to drive for hours to get there."

"I promise," Jack sat back as the waiter came over with their food.

"Thanks," they replied together. Conversation ceased as they ate slowly, Lindy admitted to herself, she enjoyed the peace and quiet, relishing every mouthful of the meal she didn't have to cook.

"Spoke to Deano this morning," Jack said a few minutes later. "Seems everything's on schedule with the Farm Supplies."

"I can see you're excited about it."

"I am. Having more control of the hours I work and being able to be with you and the children more will be fantastic."

"I'm pleased for you. Now, how about another drink?" Lindy swivelled her empty glass.

Jack signalled the waiter and ordered two more drinks.

Lindy's phone rang. She looked at the caller ID and sighed, "It's Ralph."

"Take it if you want," Jack said.

"Hi Ralph."

"Lindy, sorry to bother you but I just stopped by to check on Cameron, but he's not home. Would you know where he is?"

"Actually, I do. He and Sophie are up here with Jack and I for the weekend."

"Oh, thank goodness."

"Why didn't you ring him directly?"

"He and Sophie want nothing to do with me. And I get it, I do. But I check up on them a couple of times a week to make sure they're okay. When I couldn't see Cameron's car I got worried."

"That's good of you," Lindy was grateful that as their father the children's safety was important to him. Albeit a little late, it was still comforting to know he was trying.

"Well, at least they're okay. I'll let you go."

"Ralph," Lindy said before he could hang up, "I think after Christmas we should all get together and try to heal this rift," The division the children were creating wasn't healthy for any of them.

"I'm not sure they will be open to it, but thanks for wanting to try," Ralph sounded disheartened and Lindy wasn't comfortable with his suffering.

"How about I get in touch in late January and we'll organise something?"

"If you think it would help that'd be great."

"I must go. Take care."

"Thanks, stay safe."

JACK

Jack watched Lindy as she talked to Ralph, and a part of him wished she hadn't taken the call. "Everything okay?" He tried for upbeat, when Lindy put down her phone.

"Ralph was checking up on Cameron and when there weren't any lights on at home, I think he panicked."

"Wow, he really has come a long way," Jack forced himself not to swallow or bite down on his lip.

"Apparently neither Sophie nor Cameron wants anything to do with him," Lindy said.

"But he still checks up on them?"

"Looks that way," Lindy put her phone away and took Jack's hand in hers again. "I hope you don't mind me playing mediator?"

"Why would I mind?" but he stared through her not able to meet her eyes.

"Because he's my ex," he sensed the weight of her assessing eyes.

"I'll admit at first I wished you hadn't taken the call but I'll be in the same position with Elsa if she cleans herself up. Supporting each other will be much easier than pulling away when it comes to our past. Anyway, come on, let's not spoil our night," Jack's eyes locked on Lindy's, he could see she wasn't buying any of his lies.

Back in their room, Jack went into the bathroom and ran Lindy a bath. He was adding the bubble bath when Lindy came in.

"Everything all right?"

"Fine," he leant over and kissed her, "Get yourself ready for your bath, I'll give you some peace," he took her phone and set up some of her classical music and then left her to it. Though there was an ulterior motive, Jack was fully aware he wasn't projecting any good vibes at the moment.

LINDY

Lindy cupped the bubbles in her hand and watched as they cascaded back into the bath. She may have been watching the water and the bubbles, but her mind was picturing Jack. Why had he been so reserved about her talking to Ralph? Surely, he believed her when she told him he was the only man in her life. They would always have their past presenting itself in their present and they'd have to deal with it.

The tension in her body built. Lindy couldn't relax. This was a futile effort. In fact, she wanted to throw something, that wasn't normally her way. The moment a groan escaped her, Lindy had to get out. Sitting pondering something that was Jack's doing wasn't going to be solved in here. Instead of finishing her bath as Jack instructed, she blew out the candles, pulled the plug and got out. The idea of Jack giving her time to soak and relax in a bath had backfired. Something was wrong. Something needed to be dealt with.

Jack sat in a single chair in the corner of the room. He was leaning forward with his elbows on his knees and hands clasped together. And though his jeans hugged his legs tightly, revealing the firm muscles on his thighs, Lindy only noticed his clenched hands and unreadable expression.

Her hair was wet, as she'd bundled herself up in the bathrobe.

"Are you okay?"

He mustn't have heard her leave the bathroom.

At first, he said nothing. Lindy tilted her head to the side.

He shook his head, "Not really."

Lindy walked over to the bed and sat down. There was a small void developing between them and Lindy wasn't comfortable with that. She needed to find out what was wrong.

"Are you going to tell me?"

"I was trying not to," Jack admitted. He stood up and walked over to the window and looked out into the pitch black of the night.

The cloudy sky hid the millions of stars and the moon, and in that moment, Lindy sensed a change for them.

"I'm sorry but I won't pander to you and beg to know. You and I have always been open with each other, so if you can't maintain the ease of communication as we move forward together, I'm not sure this will work."

Still, he didn't speak.

Lindy turned her back to him and got dressed. She wouldn't stay here while he battled with his inner demons. They'd made a promise to each other, and here he was shutting down on her.

JACK

The door slammed. Jack spun around. She was gone. Too caught up in his own jealousy. He wasn't keeping things from her, but he never agreed to Ralph being part of their lives. The intense connection with Lindy was so deep he didn't know his head from his tail some days. With Elsa having other men in her life, Jack didn't care because their life together by then was over. With Lindy, it was a different story.

Picking up the room key, Jack followed her out and watched as she headed for a seating area under a pergola and settled herself down. Jack didn't miss her wipe away tears.

Oh, what the hell had he done?

His insecurities caused her pain. What a fool! Their first night away, just the two of them, and he'd allowed a phone call from Ralph to spoil the evening.

"May I?" Jack asked as he stepped up onto the raised platform.

"Only if you have an explanation," she didn't look at him, instead her eyes sort the blackness of the distant range.

After repositioning a chair so they were facing one another he reached out for her hands but she pulled them away.

"We were having a wonderful dinner, I take a phone call from Ralph and everything changes. You tense up, the conversation peters out and now you won't talk," Lindy looked away from him. But he didn't miss her wide eyes and furrowed brows, or the sharpness in her tone.

Jack gritted his teeth at his foolishness. This needed to be fixed.

"I'm sorry. I was jealous, I suppose I still am and probably always will be with Ralph." Jack admitted.

"You're jealous of Ralph? Why?"

"I want to be the one who helps you with the kids. You're always there for me and mine. I wished it would be the same with Liam, Cameron and Sophie," Jack paused, "I'm sorry but I never pictured Ralph being part of our life," Jack tapped his chest, "It hurt right here. I want to be the support, the love of your life, I want to be your best friend."

"You are my best friend," Lindy broke eye contact and let out a grunt. When she looked back at him she asked, "Who do my children talk to most days? You or their father?"

"Me," Jack's head hung low.

"Tell me something, if Elsa cleaned herself up and came back, would you just deliver the children for visitation and share nothing about their lives with her? Would she become nothing to you?"

"No. She's the mother of my children," Jack answered, knowing he was looking like a fool the more this conversation continued.

"Just as Ralph is to mine. Now we either become the extra parent to each other's kids and accept the connection with their biological parent or we end this," then Lindy whispered, "Because I'm certain it won't work the other way."

This time when Jack took her hands, she didn't pull back.

"It's because I love you so much it hurts."

"Even though I will be in touch with Ralph, it doesn't mean I love you any less. In fact, the more you're around for my children, the more I love you. It was your dream to have us all around the one table, Jack.

But that won't work if we don't reserve a seat for both Elsa and Ralph."

He dropped his head onto her shoulder. "I think I was embarrassed to say I'm jealous."

Lindy lifted his head to look into his eyes, "Elsa hasn't come back to the children yet but when she does, I won't be the only important woman in their lives. I'll have to share them with their mother and I know there's an element of rejection attached to that. But with you by my side, we'll get through it."

"So, you're saying I'm worried about feeling rejected?"

"Yes. My three need to understand that their father made a mistake."

"A bloody colossal mistake," Jack emphasised.

"Yeah, it was. But they have to move on. Holding a grudge won't help anyone in the long run. You're a better man than that, or at least I believed you were. You stood by my side and supported me when I confronted Ralph. That released all the inner demons I'd been carrying. Don't go changing your mind about me being open to sorting things out with him," Lindy squeezed his hand, "God forbid should something happen to one of the children, we'd have to ring either Elsa or Ralph to tell them, wouldn't it be easier if we were all on better terms?"

"Much," Jack nodded.

"I'm not saying you can't be jealous, actually you show me how much you love me when you are but we can't allow that to come between us," Lindy stressed words.

"But we're not always going to agree on things."

"No, but we have to talk about it. All I ask is we are open, understanding, and transparent. No secrets."

"I can't promise to be perfect at this, but I'll try."

"I won't be perfect either, but I won't go down that rabbit hole again. I won't watch the insignificant things snowball or go unattended. I promised myself I wouldn't be kept in the dark about anything again. Sorry, but this is important to me."

Jack leant forward and kissed her. He pulled back, "I'm sorry. I spoilt our evening. I wanted our time away to be so special." He understood the effort it would take to win back her trust. The plans he had for this weekend were officially on hold. The engagement ring he'd hidden in his luggage wasn't going anywhere. He'd wanted this weekend away to be so special for both of them. But he would have to prove himself. From now on, he'd make it his mission.

"These are the turning points that will make it all special. The ones we'll look back on and remember the struggles that shaped us. Not as individuals, but as a couple. I love you," Lindy cupped his cheek, "And I promise to do everything in my power to support you and your children and that's all I ask of you for me and mine."

Jack took her by the hand and led her back inside, "You know that's not the issue. What I'm struggling with is learning to have Ralph around as we go through this."

Lindy patted his chest a few times and smiled up at him.

"If anyone can do this, it'll be you. Now let's make the most of our time away."

CHRISTMAS SURPRISES

JACK

*W*ith Christmas only two weeks away, Jack, Lindy, Tessa, and Harry pooled ideas to make Christmas what it would have been in the past for Darla and Tony. Resulting in the grandkids having the most memorable Christmas. Why not, after the year they'd lived?

"Should we have one last Christmas on the farm?" Lindy asked.

Jack understood this place didn't feel like home to Lindy, she was only suggesting Christmas here for his family's sake. A chance for the Saunders family to say goodbye.

Tessa walked to the window looking out over the vast backyard, bungalow and scattered sheds with the paddocks that surrounded them. "I don't think so. This is the first Christmas together in a few years, I don't want to remember the hard times."

Jack joined her, and saw her face pinched with pain.

"I agree. How about we go to Mum and Dad's but we provide all the food?"

"You don't mind that, do you?" Tessa rested her head on her brother's shoulder.

"Nah, this place lost its shine. What's the saying? Home is where the heart is. What's more important is we're all together."

Tessa spun around and asked Lindy, "Will your family come up?"

"We're doing Christmas the day after we arrive in Melbourne. And besides, the kids were up last weekend. They'll spend Christmas day with my family."

Jack walked back over towards the table and kissed Lindy before taking his seat again. "Are you happy to help us cook?"

"Of course. The children and I will do whatever you need us to."

After a lengthy discussion they itemised the Christmas menus, they wanted the first Christmas together in a while to be what their parents remembered of Christmases past.

"Just an idea," Lindy took Jack's hand, "Should we leave the children at your parents' place on Christmas eve? So they can all wake up together."

Tessa's head snapped up with an enormous grin. "Why don't we all stay there? Mum and Dad would love it."

Jack tipped his head towards Lindy, "How about it?"

She sat lost in thought, her mind whirling with propriety. She and Jack never shared a bed with the children around. Somehow it seemed wrong. Sucking in her bottom lip, Lindy pondered the consequences and released it and answer, "If your parents agree to it, why not?"

From across the table Tessa hollered, picked up her phone and dialled her mother. Jack could see she wasn't giving anyone a chance to change their mind.

The conversation with Darla and Tony lasted an age. Voices grew louder trying to be heard over each other with suggestions. The occasional pause, and a debate when Tony and Darla wanted to take care of the food. And of course, Tony insisted Ivy be included.

"That goes without saying, Dad," Tessa said, "We'll phone her next."

The plans for food, sleeping arrangements and presents were discussed and sorted.

"You don't know how much it means to us," Darla said, "We can all attend the children's mass together on Christmas Eve."

When Jack suggested his family would stay till Boxing Day, Harry and Tessa agreed to do the same.

"Oh, that's wonderful," Darla cooed.

Harry's folks were away visiting his sister on the New South Wales coast, so they'd really make the most of Christmas celebrations together.

As promised, they rang Ivy, her screech of delight had them all laughing. One thing about their cousin, she was still a big kid at heart. Watching other children so happy and fully engrossed in family life, she told Lindy and Jack one Sunday at lunch, did funny things to her insides.

Now it was full steam ahead to make this a memorable Christmas.

JACK

Christmas Morning arrived.

Jack and Lindy were woken by hopeless attempts at whispering, followed by an explosion of squeals, giggles and then high-pitched shrieks. "Three, two," he counted down to Lindy before their bedroom door flung open.

"He's here. No, he's been. Come see the presents," Caleb shouted as he leapt onto the bed between his father and Lindy.

Jack sighed, "Oh Caleb, look at the time. Why are you up and about this early?" Jack checked the clock beside his bed, reciting a prayer of thanks that the children made it till five thirty-seven. Not only was it a modern miracle, but today was going to be a huge day for all of them.

"Santa, Dad, Santa's been. Come on, don't just lie there," Caleb grabbed his father's arm, trying to pull him up into a sitting position.

"What about Lindy, does she get to sleep in?" Jack asked, knowing full well no one would sleep in this morning. He donned his tracksuit pants and T-shirt that were lying on the end of his bed for just this reason and laughed as Lindy received the same treatment.

In the doorway heads looked in and then raced off hollering to the others further up the hallway.

"Go get Nanna and Pa," Nobody would want to miss this morning's fun.

After they dressed, Lindy and Jack followed the children out to the lounge and ran into Ivy in the hallway. Her hair stood on end and she was yawning.

"It sounded like a superb idea at the time," Ivy yawned.

Lindy laughed, "It always does."

They headed straight for the kitchen to put the kettle on and found Harry and Tessa had the same idea.

"Merry Christmas," they all chorused.

"Look Lindy," Evie pointed at all the Christmas presents.

"Oh my! The adults must have been well behaved this year," Lindy hugged the children and watched on as they searched for their names on the Santa sacks.

"They're not for you," Joanna chuckled.

"No? Who are they for?"

But before Joanna could answer, Tony was calling them all to attention.

They were all laughing for a different reason now, their grandpa stood in the lounge wearing his pyjamas, Santa pyjamas that drawn the children even more into the moment.

"Sana," Bradley yelled.

"Well, shall we get this show on the road?" Tony rubbed his hands together.

Harry turned on the video, and Lindy had her camera sitting on her knee, ready to catch the precious moments from today. Well, she was in for a treat.

Tony picked up the first sack, "Wow this is heavy, who does this belong to?"

"Bradley," the children squealed, hollered, and hooted. Jack watched as his baby stood and tottered over to his pa. The little face displaying a toothy grin warming Jack's heart.

Jack settled Bradley on the floor between his legs and together they ripped the paper from the largest box in the sack.

Jack purchased a Tonka truck to replace the one both Nate and Caleb played with for hours as toddlers. That was before Elsa pawned it.

"Mine, mine, mine," Bradley chirped to a roar of laughter.

Tony handed out the rest of the sacks, and the ripping paper sounded like a concerto. There were squeals followed by, 'that's exactly what I asked Santa for'.

The scene was the most marvellous chaos. Pulling Lindy into his arms, he kissed her.

"Thank you."

Her smile continued to steal his heart daily.

"This is what Christmas is all about—family."

Jack drew in a deep breath when he noticed the momentary dullness in her eyes. She missed her family. But after that thought passed, her spark returned, dazzling him yet again. "We'll be there with them in two days doing this all over again," Jack reassured her.

Her grin grew. Jack understood how much she'd missed the kids, hell her entire family. Gritting his teeth against saying too much, Jack bent down to kiss her. It was safer than saying anything he'd kick himself for later.

By the time all the wrapping paper was stuffed into a large black rubbish bag and the children had studied each gift with Ivy and then each other, it was quarter to seven. Time to send Lindy for her shower while he set his plan into action.

"Hey Lin," Jack went in search of her, "How about you take first shower in the main bathroom?"

"Oh bugger," Tessa cursed as she entered the lounge with her toiletries bag in her left hand and her clothes draped over her right arm.

"You can use our bathroom Tessa, help yourself," Tony called out.

With the two women occupied, Jack summoned the rest of the family and worded them up, letting them into a secret only Darla and Tony were privileged to. The children exchanged looks of surprise as everyone listened to their allocated jobs, they ran off to complete them.

Jack and Harry changed quickly and joined Ivy to help the kids get ready. Time was against them.

LINDY

Lindy stepped out of the bathroom feeling refreshed in her Christmas green summer dress and sandals. Her life had been jeans or pants since arriving in Chester's Run. It was nice to dress up for this occasion. Heading down the hall, she could smell the coffee and something else. The smell was familiar, but she couldn't quite place the scent. It smelt like fresh bread but with a sweet aroma. Lindy drew in a lung full of the tantalising smell, walked into the bedroom she and Jack shared and hung her towel on the rail. Next, she folded her nightie and smiled, noticing Jack had taken the time to make the bed.

The gnawing growl of hunger rumbling in her stomach, reminded Lindy she was ready for breakfast. The kitchen was empty. Chatter came from the back veranda, so she headed through the dining room to the back door and stopped dead in her tracks when the long table was now longer and every chair was taken. When two handsome young men and a younger image of herself stood up, she clamped a hand over her mouth fighting hard to suck back determined tears.

"Merry Christmas, Mum," the three of them greeted in unison.

Searching for Jack, she noticed it was the entire Chapman clan, her parents, brothers, and their families. This was all too much. Emotion spiralled from the depths of her toes, up through her body.

"Lindy, we got more presents. We can have Christmas all over again," Caleb's rich voice sang out and a roar of laughter followed. She considered maybe they'd gone completely overboard, but what the hell, these children deserved one day of being totally spoilt.

The backyard erupted into Christmas greetings. Ivy slipped out and with Tessa and Harry in tow, they returned, each carrying trays of croissants back to the table. Next the women went back for trays of fresh fruit.

Accusingly, Lindy mouthed to Tessa, "Just family, huh."

"Don't blame me, only Mum, Dad and Jack were in on this. Harry rushed me through my shower, I'm rather displeased with my brother," Tessa didn't bother to lower her voice.

Lindy leant over to the man sitting beside her and kissed his cheek. "Thank you," she whispered.

Taking her hand in his, Jack whispered for her ears only. "You couldn't believe I'd not want everyone to be together. These people are family Lindy, yours and mine," his smile reflected in his eyes, and in that moment a message of truth passed between them. Only the call of her name enticed her to break the connection.

"Yes," she answered, looking down the table, uncertain who'd called her.

"Please lead the family in prayer?" Tony asked.

"Sure," Lindy clasped her hands and cleared her throat. This blessing on the meal and family deserved something special, so she ad-libbed something from the heart.

"Dear Lord, for family and friends, we thank you. For love and support, we thank you. For hope, happiness, and a wonderful future we ask you to bless us all. Amen."

"Amen," came enthusiastic replies. Followed by a full-on assault of the food they surrounded.

JACK

The second round of present giving only managed to hype the children up more, especially Caleb. So they were sent out into the backyard to play and run off some of the excess energy from the excitement of the day. The adult children joined them for a game of cricket while they waited for lunch. Laughter, cheers, and an occasional argument drifted into the house as the women busied themselves in the kitchen, while the men attended to the large cuts of roast meat in the kettle barbecue.

After hearing his son's sleepy cry, Jack went down the hall and lifted Bradley from his cot. "Hey Buddy, how was your sleep?" Laying him on the change table, Jack kept up the conversation until they were called for lunch.

Jack patted his pocket for the tenth time in as many minutes and scooped Bradley up, "Come on little man, are you ready for more fun?" Bradley clapped his little hands and gave his father a toothy grin.

Once everyone settled around the table, Jack stood and pushed his chair back. Collecting the delicate ring from his jeans pocket between two work-roughened fingers, he dropped to one knee. He could hear whispers close by, but his focus was on Lindy as her blue eyes widened and locked on his.

She swallowed hard, licked her slightly parted lips and tucked a strand of her shoulder length hair behind her ear. The world and its surroundings fell away. He could watch this sight all day, looking at this beautiful woman who changed his world and that of his children so completely.

"Lindy you have turned our lives upside down and inside out. You pulled us all out of a void which we'd been forced into. You rekindled the true meaning of family to so many of us all while you coped with your own struggles. You selflessly reached out with love and compassion and in doing so you stole my heart," Jack drew a breath. He had so much to say but wasn't sure he'd get it all out.

Taking Lindy's hand in his, he continued, "I promise you my love, respect, care and openness. I'll be beside you every step of the way as we watch our children grow and discover the world. I kneel before you not only to ask for your hand in marriage, when we can marry, but also for a lifelong commitment to honesty, loyalty, happiness and forever love."

Lindy bit down on her lip as her trembling hand gripped his.

"Jack," Lindy's soft voice muttered. She faltered, paused, and then spoke again. Her voice held more strength this time. "Jack you have always had my loyalty and commitment from the first meal we shared, even though your sister tried to sabotage us."

Jack threw his head back and laughed. He remembered their first meal as if it was yesterday.

"I gave you my heart, and I found my soul mate," Lindy shifted her clasped hand from around his and cupped his cheek, "I love you Jack Saunders and yes, I'll marry you, when we can."

Jack leant in to meet her approaching lips as the table broke out in cheers, whistles, and applause. Shouts of congratulations echoed around them, Jack placed the ring on Lindy's finger. Staring at the ring, she took in the unique setting.

"The solitaire represents our love and around the outside are eight round accents one for each of our children. We are a united family now." Jack told her before kissing her again. Lindy stood up to be enfolded into hugs of congratulations from the family, the great big family they now shared.

"Well, all this gift giving has made me hungry," Jack joked as he accepted the plate of pork from his mother and dished up some for Lindy, Bradley and then himself. Down the table, people who were strangers this morning laughed and talked as they helped the young children fill their plates with yummy food smothered in gravy. His smile broadened as he caught Lindy's eye. She too watched on, the children were fine.

When Tony began with a prayer of thanks, Lindy took Jack's offered hand and smiled as he squeezed hers a little. The connection to her was deeper than what he'd ever experienced for the mother of his children. Now was his chance to be the man he should have been, funny, happy-go-lucky and a spur-of-the-moment type guy. His woman and his family would be the recipient of his attention, love, and dedication. Looking down at his plate, Jack couldn't see the array of colour and wonderful food before him. All he pictured was Lindy's smiling face and her sweet voice saying, "I love you."

LINDY

Jack and Lindy stood side by side with arms wrapped around each other, waving good night to her family.

"See you in the morning."

"Bye." Her family called back.

As the last of the taillights disappeared around the corner, Lindy said, "You were full of surprises today, Mr Saunders."

He led her towards the house, "After everything you've done for us, having your family with us today was important. I think they all got along famously," Jack observed. "Oh, by the way, Liam asked if there were any architects up here, I wasn't sure if he was joking or not."

"I know our life is here but if they need..."

"We'll both be there in a flash. And I've reiterated as much to them all today," Jack hastened to add.

"Thank you, for today with my family and for how much you love me."

Jack pulled her to a stop just before they reached the front door, "I'm the one who should thank you. What you have done for all of us has been amazing. I still can't believe Bradley handpicked you," Jack teased.

"How could I resist those beautiful big, light brown, pleading eyes? Just like his father's," they stole a kiss before heading inside.

The only sound was Tessa and Darla chatting in the lounge while both Harry and Tony sat contentedly beside their wives.

"Well, little brother, you were full of surprises today," Tessa praised. "Congratulations again both of you. When will the wedding be?"

"We have each other, our kids and families, we're engaged and have purchased a house so the actual wedding will be a formality," Lindy shrugged, "So when we can. What's important now is the children."

"Speaking of which," Tony began, "Those three of yours Lindy, are lovely. But young Cameron seems a bit lost."

Lindy sighed as she settled next to Jack on the two-seater couch, "He's always been content in his own company. I worry about him the most."

"If I'm not speaking out of turn," Tony continued, "Let him know he can stay here, we have a spare room and I honestly believe he'll be here at the drop of a hat."

"You know," Darla turned to Lindy, "I overheard Ivy and Sophie talking about the bakery. Ivy implied she'd employ Sophie if she made the move to Chester's Run."

Lindy's mouth dropped opened as her hand hurried to her chest, "Truly?"

"Cross my heart," Darla traced the sign of the cross on her chest, "I would ask her, but she was as exhausted as the children and went to bed."

Jack picked up his mobile and began typing. He studied the screen for a minute before putting it back down on the arm of the couch. Moments later it pinged, repeatedly.

"Who was that?" Lindy asked.

Jack picked up the phone.

"Cameron, '*if you and Mum are sure. Could we discuss it tomorrow?*'"

"Sophie, '*Ivy said she could do with a pastry chef. Are you being serious?*'"

"Liam, '*Unlike the other two, I have my job in Melbourne. Cameron and Sophie are jumping around. It's rather amusing.*'"

"What offer?" Lindy swallowed hard, she could only imagine what Jack was up to.

"I think Cameron and Sophie are moving into the bungalow. Yet again, Missus, you're right. The bungalow is a necessity," Jack's eyebrows danced, making them all laugh.

Tessa handed over the box of tissues as Lindy fought to control more tears. Had their lives really been so topsy turvy? Lindy had never been such a sook before moving to Chester's Run.

"Oh my, I'm such a baby. I can just imagine the children in the morning when they find out," Lindy smiled through her tears, "But I should wait and see how things pan out tomorrow. We shouldn't put the cart before the horse."

They all laughed. Tomorrow was another day with endless possibilities.

LINDY

All the kids, except Bradley, were still asleep when Lindy's family arrived the following morning. Tony opened the front door with Bradley in his arms, chatting away to no one in particular. He'd slept soundly after his last bottle. Tessa got the final cuddle before putting him to bed, totally exhausted. Lindy stuck her head out of the kitchen to see her family. She couldn't suppress her delight.

"Good morning," Tony greeted, "Come on in, the coffee's hot and breakfast is ready."

Bradley happily landed in Barbara's arms for a cuddle. He was comfortable with Lindy's family.

"Morning Tony. Thanks for this," Charlotte said when she kissed him.

"Oh, don't be silly. This really has been a wonderful Christmas," Tony's broad smile from the previous day hadn't diminished one iota.

It was all hands-on deck in the kitchen. The croissants were in the oven, the kettle was boiling, platters of scrambled eggs and fruit were being plated up as the Chapman's walked in.

"What can I do?" Sophie asked after giving them all a kiss.

"Could you get the jugs of water and juice from the fridge and put them on the table outside," Ivy asked as she finished transferring the fried bacon into a serving bowl.

"Sure thing." Sophie handed some to Cameron and Liam and followed them outside.

Within minutes everyone was seated, apart from the sleepy heads.

Jack broke the tension. The text conversation the night before had Lindy tossing most of the night.

"So, have you guys considered more about our offer?" Jack looked at Sophie and Cameron.

"I think we were up half the night discussing it," Sophie explained. "Pop, Uncle Mal and Uncle Danny sat with us for at least an hour and none of us can see a reason why we wouldn't give it a go, other than leaving Liam by himself. But he's promised to come up often to see us all."

"I'd have to make a few minor changes to the kitchen for the extra equipment you'll need but you can start as soon as you're ready," Ivy repeated the offer to Sophie again.

"Really? You're serious?" an excited Sophie squealed.

"There's so many extra things we can implement, and besides with the two of us we could take it in turns to do mornings and maybe even look at taking a weekend off here and there. It's a win-win," Ivy smiled. Turning to Lindy she added, "You've seen my books, I can definitely afford a person of her calibre."

"Yes, you can, but I don't want you doing this just for my sake," Lindy clarified.

"Don't worry I wouldn't be, Sophie has your insight into business, she'll earn her keep soon enough."

With that settled, all eyes turned to Cameron.

"How about you, love?" Lindy asked.

"Mum, you know I'm able to work from anywhere. And if Sophie and I could rent out this so-called bungalow then the decision's made." Cameron's quiet disposition lacked the gleam Lindy always saw in Liam and Sophie's eyes. He was always so matter-of-fact. Lindy understood the effort he was making by accepting the offer and in turn moving out of his comfort zone to be with her.

"Liam?" Lindy turned to her eldest son. "How do you feel about all this?"

"Honestly, I'll miss you guys but these two should definitely move. Cameron needs you, and as for Sophie, she's been getting the run-around from those guys since they took her on as an apprentice. A change will do her good and after meeting Ivy, I'm confident they'll work well together."

Lindy nodded at his observation of the situation. Like his father, Liam had the ability to recognise an excellent opportunity when it presented itself.

"Anyway, I still have these guys," Liam pointed down the table, "Pa's been such a great sounding board with so much lately, I won't be alone," Liam added totally at ease with the upcoming changes.

"Well, if this is happening," Jack chimed in, "How about we move your stuff when we come for your mother's things?"

Sophie and Cameron exchanged glances, both nodding their approval. Sophie unable to hide her pleasure at the prospect. Cameron shared a grin as a flush of colour invaded his face when everyone looked at him. He hated being centre of attention, which was unlike Sophie.

"Excellent. We'll work out where to put you guys until we move," Jack added. The bungalow was full of already packed boxes. Lindy could barely make it to her bed. And besides she and Jack agreed, since they were engaged, she'd move into the house once they returned home.

"I've got two spare rooms with me above the shop," Ivy leant forward looking at Jack and Lindy.

Lindy bit her lip while nodding her head. Something she'd been doing a lot lately.

"Sorted. Okay, well we'll be down on the 28th with the truck and I'm hoping it will only take two days to pack everything up. Could you be ready by then?" Jack questioned with a raised brow.

"We're really doing this?" Sophie asked, practically bouncing in her seat.

"Looks like it," Duncan said from beside her even though his eyes were on Lindy.

"Well, in that case we'll both be ready. Won't we Cameron?"

His smile and nod said it all. And Lindy was sure she saw a tiny glint in his eye.

ELSA'S DEMANDS

LINDY

*W*atching Jack and Bernie loading boxes from the bungalow onto the truck, Lindy couldn't contain her smile. They were on the home straight.

"We're almost finished," Lindy told the children, "So, let's get moving."

Taking Bradley by the hand, Lindy led him across the yard as the children bounded ahead of her towards the truck.

"Here guys," Jack called to the gaggle of children, "Can you pick up those boxes, the light things," they joined in with gusto, while both Jack and Bernie loaded up trolleys with the heavier family belongings.

"Hey love, we're nearly done here," Jack called as she approached. He wiped the sweat from his brow on the sleeve of his T-shirt.

Lindy stepped right up and planted a kiss on his cheek. He pulled her in closer as she leant against him. "I can't believe how this is all coming together."

Jack grinned, "And now we have the rest of our lives."

The last few weeks had been so busy, they couldn't wait until they finally settled into the homestead.

"I love you Jack Saunders, so very much."

"Likewise, my girl," he replied and leant in for another kiss.

"When you two are finished, we have a house to move," Bernie joked.

With Jack still resting his arm around Lindy and partaking in humorous banter, the scrunch of tyres on the gravel announced an arrival. Harry and Tessa were here to help.

Harry called out to Lindy, "Ivy just got those boys of yours out of bed. Lazy buggers. They'll be here in half an hour."

Lindy laughed, not even the boy's laziness would dampen her mood today. They were so close, nothing could dishearten her.

The children ran to greet their cousins while the women headed inside to finish the final clean-up.

"Excited?" Tessa asked, walking into the kitchen behind Lindy.

"Immensely. The children were up at the crack of dawn." She laughed as she shared the story of the children running into Jack's room and trying to back out when they remembered Lindy now shared their father's bed.

Tessa snorted with laughter.

"Nate backed up slowly and when I smiled, they all stopped, except Nate. He stood on Evie's toes causing tears. All the commotion woke Jack up and that was that, we were awake and the children were asking for brekkie."

She paused thinking about the farmhouse. "I'll never forget this place, so many memories." She didn't elaborate because the memories were good and bad, with some amazing ones thrown into the mix.

By the time the bungalow was empty, Tessa and Lindy had already cleaned the back half of the house as the children carried what they could to the veranda, making it easier to load the truck. Lindy checked her watch, they would be out of here before lunch.

Jack promised lunch at Ivy's, and as always, the children never forgot a promise. Particularly one that involved food from the bakery.

"Wow, you guys are nearly finished," Jack admired as he came down the hall to see how much more furniture was left to load into the truck.

"Well, don't natter, your woman's hot on your heels," Tessa teased.

Lindy heard a car coming up the driveway and stepped out onto the veranda to see Cameron park behind the van. She shook her head as Liam struggled to put his shoes on. Nothing had changed.

"Morning," Cameron laughed as Liam practically fell out of the car.

"I'd offer you coffee but everything's packed," Lindy told them, not that she had any intention of stopping to make coffee for this lazy lot.

"All good," Cameron held up a takeaway cup. "Thank God for Ivy."

With the additional help, the truck was loaded ahead of time, "Where did these muscles come from?" Lindy asked.

Liam flexed his arms as he walked past.

"See, I told you hard work wouldn't kill you," Cameron laughed at his mother's banter.

She turned the vacuum cleaner on again to finish the last of the bedrooms. "Just this and the lounge and we're done," she yelled at Jack over the noise.

"Good. We've finished. Everything's in the truck."

With the vacuum cleaner trekking over the last square meter of the carpet, the end was near. With a sigh and a smile, she turned off the vacuum as Jack pulled the plug out from the wall. He collected the cumbersome appliance, and walked out the front door.

Once Lindy joined everyone on the veranda, Jack pulled her into his arms again. Just getting to this point had been an interminable journey. "Shall we take the kids and you come with Tessa?" mumbled Jack as he pulled her in close, never squandering a chance for an embrace.

"You promised them lunch at the bakery."

"Oh bugger. Do you think they'll take a rain check?"

"Doubt it," she was desperate for a sit down and a fresh pot of tea herself. "You guys head off, we'll lock up." Lindy kissed him goodbye and watched as he walked down the front steps towards his

Ute. "We'll call when we get to the bakery to see what you guys want."

"Perfect," Jack answered, ruffling Nate and Caleb's hair as he walked past. "See you all at our new home."

"Bye," the children waved as the truck and a line of cars headed up the driveway for the last time.

When Lindy locked the front door, she was exhausted. She sighed, knowing full well the job was only half done. At least Sophie was unpacking at the homestead, but one person on their own wouldn't go close to putting a dent into this job. Mustering up the energy, Lindy stepped one foot in front of the other.

Since the lead up to Christmas, it had been non-stop for both of them. And now she was feeling the effects. Just getting to the house and unloading would be a start. Lindy continuously told herself, not everything had to be finished today. Sophie was charged with the responsibility of setting up Bradley's room and having his cot ready for when they arrived. That was vital.

It didn't surprise her that Jack's children were more than happy to move on. She still struggled, contemplating the things they tolerated living here at the hands of their own mother. Shaking her head and closing her eyes, Lindy was grateful Elsa wasn't in the picture at the moment.

LINDY

Lindy swept the front veranda till it almost shone and looked back at the house.

"Done," she puffed out.

"Lindy, watch me," Joanna jumped off the front steps. The children cheered when she cleared Nate's last jump.

"Way to go," Tessa called as they loaded the last of the cleaning products into the car. Bradley toddled around with the others, tiring himself out. Once he settled into his car seat, he'd not have the energy to challenge a snooze, although it'd be earlier today. Lindy scooped up her little man and cuddled him close. He giggled as she tickled his big belly, his thumb sought his mouth and he snuggled into her. She kissed him and was about to settle him into his car seat when the familiar sound of tyres heading towards the house drew everyone's attention.

Looking over the heads of the children, Lindy noticed Nate's body stiffen as the car came to a stop. He protectively pushed Caleb behind him.

Before either Tessa or Lindy registered what was happening, Nate stepped around the van and approached the newcomers.

"You need to go Mum, you're not allowed here."

Lindy noted Tessa's furrowed brow. Her dislike for this woman was clear. A cold chill of shiver ran up Lindy's spine. Fully conscious that Nate, always the protector, would never allow Elsa to harm any of his siblings again, Lindy handed Bradley to Evie.

"Buckle him into his car seat, Evie."

Stepping around the others to join Nate, Lindy's hand instinctively reached out for Joanna as she ran past but she was too late. Joanna threw herself at her mother.

"Mum, you've come back, I knew you would."

Lindy's heart broke for Joanna as Elsa just pushed her away. The woman appeared to be on a mission. Tears gathered in Joanna's eyes. Not that her mother paid her any attention.

Tessa took over before Lindy could say anything, "Nate's right. Please leave Elsa."

"Not till I've got what I came for."

Lindy stepped up to comfort Joanna and whispered in her ear, "Hop in the car please, we'll sort this out," With all the children scrambling to the car, Lindy spurred herself into action. Focusing on Nate, her voice level and matter of fact.

"Join the other children."

Where she would normally use an endearment while talking to him or any of the children Lindy kept everything formal. She waited till he turned back towards the van.

Hearing Nate giving the children orders, she focused on the couple ahead of her.

"Can I help you with anything?" Lindy asked.

"Where's Jack, he owes me money," Elsa's voice began low and calm but built as she spoke.

Tessa gasped but before she followed it with words, Lindy stepped forward putting herself between the two strangers and Tessa.

"He's out working on the property. Would you like me to take you to him?"

Watching the strangers communicate with their eyes, Lindy sensed something wasn't right. This man wasn't here for a friendly bonding session with Elsa's family.

With Elsa distracted trying to decide what to do. Tessa and Lindy exchanged glances and Tessa raised a questioning brow. Lindy's reaction was to look at the car crammed with the most precious treasures, all the children. Although she sensed Tessa understood her reasoning, her frown spoke of her disapproval of the unsaid plan.

"Yeah, take us to him," Elsa agreed.

Lindy stepped towards the vehicle Elsa arrived in, there was no time to waste. "Can you drive, my daughter dropped me off this morning so I don't have a car." Lindy slid into the backseat. There was an urgency to protect the children by getting their mother and this man far away. Not to mention the fact that Harry and Tessa's children would also be caught up in this if something transpired.

Lindy diligently buckled up in the back seat as the car took off back up the driveway. She resisted the urge to look back towards the carload of children she loved dearly. The image of Nate, protective and responsible, would be forever tattooed into her brain. She'd never seen a child's entire demeanour alter so significantly in a matter of seconds.

Sending up a silent prayer, Lindy settled into the back seat and forced herself to chatter, not allowing the others a chance to think.

"At the end of the drive, turn right," She told the driver, "Sorry we haven't met yet, I'm Lindy, the housekeeper."

Elsa spoke, "I'm Elsa, and this is Dylan."

"Nice to meet you both," Lindy forced herself to remain confident, looking straight ahead. She plastered on a smile, all the while noticing Dylan looking at her through the rear-view mirror.

LINDY

Lindy directed Elsa and Dylan down to the paddock where she and the children met Jack for a picnic dinner under a scattering of peppercorn trees. Her memories of the place helped keep a smile on her face.

Dragging her mind back to her current predicament, Lindy had nothing planned beyond getting Elsa and the stranger away from the children. The injuries this woman inflicted on Bradley were unforgivable, and she'd been the one to step in and pick up the pieces. Approaching the back of the large paddock realisation set in, she was on her own. Her phone and purse were on the dashboard of the van.

It struck Lindy she didn't explain to Tessa where they were going. Would anyone guess where she was taking Jack's ex? There were several paddocks Jack previously owned. With that realisation there was a tightening in her chest. Her ambition had gone from saving the children to her coming out of this unscathed. Limp hands rested in her lap and she looked down not sure what to do now.

Would Jack understand what she had done and why?

Dropping her head back onto the head rest, she pondered the possibility of never seeing any of them again?

Snapping out of her deliberation, Lindy caught the tail end of a question, "Sorry, what did you say?"

"Where is he? I can't see the tractor," Elsa's crude voice pierced through Lindy.

"Oh, he's just fixing a pump, he might have gone into town for parts," Internally Lindy sighed, where had that come from. "Oh, blast, I haven't got my mobile to ring him."

"That's bullshit Elsa, she's played us," Dylan thundered as he stopped the car in a cloud of dust and turned to face Lindy.

Lindy reached for the door handle just as Dylan's clenched fist connected with her face. Her head ricocheted onto the back of the seat. Everything spun before darkness settled around her.

JACK

Jack hefted a single couch off the truck when his phone rang. On a sigh he lowered the awkward, heavy chair back down onto the truck and reached for his phone. Noting the caller ID, he answered his sister with his usual comedic tone, "Your timing was always bloody poor woman."

When her quivering voice hit his ears, his stomach lurched. Something that hadn't happened in a while. Well, not since Elsa took off after hurting Bradley.

"Elsa's back in town. She's looking for you saying you owe her money." The strain in Tessa's voice caused Jack to flinch from the pain of a previous life. One he'd fought so hard to leave behind.

"Where is she now?"

"That's the thing. She showed up here and when Nate told her to go, she made her demand not even acknowledging the children. Lindy told her and this male muscle man, you were working out on the farm. Jack, Lindy didn't bat an eyelid and went with them. I could see it in her eyes, she was getting Elsa as far away from the children as possible."

"Shit!" Jack cursed into the phone.

"Harry!" he yelled with no consideration for Tessa's eardrum. Jack's hollering had Sophie, Liam, Cameron, and Bernie following Harry out the front door curious to see what had him so riled up.

Everyone stood around as Jack explained what Tessa shared. "Apparently she's taken them out onto the property looking for me."

"What?" Liam's now gruff voice bellowed.

"Ring Lindy," Harry instructed. "Let's get her take on this."

Jack put the phone on loud speaker as Tessa explained, "She didn't take her phone. It's here on the dash."

Thinking on his feet, Harry suggested, "Try Elsa's phone, Jack. Downplay it."

Jack hung up from his sister and dialled the last woman in the world he wanted to speak to. Ever.

He and Elsa were meant to be finished. What the hell was she thinking when she told Tessa he still owed her money? Jack cracked his neck and fingers, Elsa's latest antics flabbergasted him. He'd invested the money on her behalf and she agreed to being paid an income. The money was hers, but he'd protected it so she couldn't spend it all on drugs. He waited while the phone rang. His mind raced, what was his ex playing at?

"Hi Elsa, Tessa said you were looking for me," Jack reined in his tone. The lengthening silence was the second most painful experience he ever endured. That and the first were both at the hands of his ex-wife.

"You need to give me more money," there was a tremor in her voice.

Jack paused as he forced his body to relax. Allowing Elsa to get under his skin now may cause undue harm to Lindy.

So instead, Jack played along.

"I'm in town at the moment. Tessa said Lindy was with you. Could I speak with her, please?"

"No Jack. Your housekeeper has nothing to do with this. This is between you and me, give me the money!" Elsa's voice rose with every word.

"Please put Lindy on the phone," Jack begged, hoping she'd cave in and allow him to speak with Lindy. If he could hang up and be able to tell Liam, Cameron, and Sophie their mother was safe he'd agree to whatever Elsa wanted.

"You can speak to her when we get the money," the shout that burst down the phone told Jack all he needed to know, Elsa was coming down off a high and had no control of the situation. He could only imagine this was how she was when Bradley had been hurt.

"Okay, meet me at the bank. I'll give you a cheque."

"How stupid do you think I am? You'll have Harry onto me."

A curse sounded. It was no longer Elsa on the phone, Jack heard a harsh male voice. "Your wife owes us money, big money and you'll pay. Now listen and listen good."

By now they were all listening. Jack held his phone, as a tightness invaded his chest.

The voice continued, "Get me cash, and ring me when you have it. And do it quick." The phone changed hands a second time and then Elsa spoke.

Her now frightened voice was barely audible. "I need the money."

Before Jack could lose his temper, Harry's hand landed on his shoulder. His brother-in-law nodded. Jack fixed his eyes on Harry's and followed his cues.

"Okay Elsa. I'll need time. But please put Lindy on so I can speak with her. You and I both know she's innocent in all of this."

"I wish I could Jack but I can't right now," Her shaky voice had Jack's mind reeling to the worst-case scenario. "I'm terrified. They won't give me my fix until I get the money and I can't think straight without it," her whining voice droned on.

There it was again, always about her and what she wanted. Jack drew in a sharp breath, he had to keep it together for Lindy's sake.

"Just tell me if she's okay," Jack begged while still watching Harry.

"Not really."

As the words echoed out of the speaker, Sophie covered her mouth but not in time to halt a loud gasp. Liam held his sister, listening while whispered calming words in her ear. Jack focused on Elsa's voice again.

"You have to get me the money. And quickly. I promise I'll get help for my addiction, but right now I have to pay them."

Ignoring the signals from Harry, Jack let rip, "You want me to pay for your addiction with the money I need to raise our children?" before Jack could continue his tirade, Harry wrenched the phone from his grip and hung up.

"They have her hostage. Just one wrong move..." Harry was in Jack's face as he ground out the words.

"He was more reasonable than I would have been," Liam hissed in Jack's defence.

"Okay, let's get one thing straight. All of you," Harry spoke loud and slow, "This is not some kid mucking around. Whoever he is, he means business."

SEARCHING THE FARM

JACK

*A*fter a heated discussion, Jack's eyes followed Harry's four-wheel drive as it sped out of his driveway. His lights flashing a warning, announcing the unthinkable situation they were now facing. This wasn't how their first day at the homestead was meant to look like.

"Jack, come on," Liam urged.

He glimpsed the house, their place to call home. The place to start their lives together.

"I'll lock up, you get going," called Bernie.

"Thanks mate," Jack ran to his ute, "We'll be following Harry to the station, see what we can do to help."

"Cameron, you come with me, Sophie you go with Liam. Bernie…"

"I'm right behind you."

Jack turned his car towards town. The echoing silence stung, but Jack couldn't think of a damn thing to say. He focused on what the hell possessed Lindy to use herself as live bait.

He understood why she'd done what she did, especially after promising Elsa would never cause pain to the kids again. So, she'd used herself as a distraction just long enough for Tessa to get the children to safety. Jack slammed his fist on the steering wheel and let out a tortured groan.

"What's your ex-wife capable of?" Cameron asked.

"I'm not worried about my ex, it's the guy she's with that unnerves me. There was nothing reassuring in his tone."

Jack pulled the car to a stop outside the police station as Bernie and Liam parked either side of him. Jack looked over at his buddy, he must have broken every speed limit and Jack was relieved to have his support. They all got out in time to see Tessa arrive. Her red eyes matched Sophie's.

"What are you doing here?" Jack asked, "Where are the kids?"

"Mum and Dad are with Nola. I have to look over mug shots to see if I recognised the guy with Elsa," Tessa led the way into the station.

"How was Mum when they left?" Sophie asked.

"Smiling. I can honestly say I've never seen such a selfless act in my life," Tessa pulled Sophie into a hug, "Between Nate and Lindy, Elsa touched none of the children. Well except Joanna, when she pushed her away."

Tessa's distaste for Elsa rang out. Right now, Jack wanted to scream at the mother of his children. She didn't even have the sense to greet her own flesh and blood.

Poor Joanna, after she'd made the effort to write her mother letters, the woman didn't even spare her a second glance. Some people were never meant to be parents and his ex was one of them. His fiancée, on the other hand, was the total opposite. She couldn't do enough for anybody, child, or adult.

Jack dropped his arm around Sophie's shoulder, hugging her close as they followed the others through the door. "She'll be back with us before we know it."

Sophie leant into him, "I hope so Jack. Hell, I hope so."

"Here Tessa," Harry said, "Take a seat." He set her to work looking at images of known criminals.

Next, he called Jack and Lindy's children in and explained the situation.

"I've sent out patrol vehicles with instructions to search all of Jack's old paddocks while three other vehicles, which were heading in from neighbouring towns, were on the lookout for the car Lindy left in. They are systematically checking all the roads into and out of town."

"What if we head out to the property? No one knows it like I do," Jack asked in desperation.

Harry stared him down, "Okay, but don't approach them, you guys are just checking out the paddocks. Do you hear me?" he pointed a finger at Jack.

"Clear. Crystal bloody clear," Jack hissed, "The plan is to check the property well. We'll call in if we find anything."

Harry nodded, but if he did anything else Jack missed it. They'd already turned and were heading for the cars.

"Right, Liam, we'll ring you and tell you where to go. Got it?" Jack didn't wait for a reply, "Bernie, go down to the back paddocks on the left and start from there. If you find anything ring Harry then me, in that order."

As he headed to his car, Jack glanced at the ominous clouds rolling in. "Get in the Ute, I'll be back in a minute," Jack threw the keys to Cameron and ran back into the station.

"Harry, the weather's turned," Jack didn't wait for an answer. He was on a mission. In this part of the country, dark clouds turned a warm sunny day into a torrential downpour within minutes. Turning dry riverbeds into torrents and dusty paddocks into a quagmire. No one in their right mind would be out if they didn't have to.

"Let's go. Have you rung Liam?" Jack asked as he slammed his door.

LINDY

Lindy moaned into the dirt, the pain radiating from her face was unbearable and her head throbbed. Lindy squinted into the wind gathering strength around her. With all the energy she could muster, Lindy pushed herself up into a sitting position, crying out from the pain and her effort while spitting dirt from her mouth.

Her eyes watered and vision blurred. Looking around, Lindy tried to recall where she was. Rubbing her eyes as she focused, Lindy surveyed the area. What happened and why was she here? Gently touching her aching face, Lindy retraced her movements.

Clarity dawned.

Elsa came to the house looking for Jack. Oh, that's right, she remembered offering to take them to find him, trying to get Elsa away from the children. What happened to Elsa and the guy she was with? Lindy spun around to see if they were behind her. The sharp pain from her sudden movement had her crying out once again. As the pain eased to a dull throb Lindy focused on her predicament and saw she was alone. Something told her that her safety wasn't guaranteed until she was back with Jack and the children. Resolute in her decision not to be found by Elsa and Dylan, she struggled to her feet, ignoring every excruciating shooting pain.

The nearby tree trunk supported her weight while she waited for her head to stop spinning. Once the earth greeted her at a normal angle, Lindy studied her surroundings again. Mentally assessing her options. To her left was the highway, a long way off, to her right was the dry riverbed. As she stood deciding her best path a flashback rolled through her mind of the days riding on Bernie's property. She and Nola spent one afternoon walking with the horses, Nola pointed out all the landmarks. One of the notable tracks led from the river up to the back of Bernie and Nola's place and continued to the homestead, their new home.

Pressing her lips together, Lindy reached down, selected a solid branch as a walking stick, gritting her teeth through the head spins and churning stomach to eventually stand. She decided her best option was through the riverbed and along the path. Pushing away from the tree trunk, she gingerly dragged her aching body over to the embankment.

The slope to the river was steep, but Lindy forced herself to manoeuvre her aching body down slowly. Each step was arduous as she focused on her end goal. There was a determination to get away from here. Lindy persisted, step by painful step. Getting to the path on the other side became her first clear goal. Setting small targets would help her reach her ultimate destination.

Entering the river, the rocks were another challenge, but luck was on her side; she focused on each potential step ahead of her.

JACK

"Where do we start?" Liam asked.

"The farmhouse, maybe she's back there." After a minute's silence Jack dug into his pocket for his phone, pressed a few buttons and waited for his neighbour to answer.

"Troy."

"Hey Jack, how's the moving?"

"Not good, mate. Listen, I need some help. Elsa's shown up and causing trouble. Lindy got her and some thug away from the kids, but we can't find Lindy."

"What the hell does that bloody woman want?"

"More money to pay off another drug debt," Jack spat out.

"Bloody hell. That bitch! What do you want, just name it?" Jack heard him gather up keys as he spoke.

"Can you start down the back of the property on the right? We'll start at the farmhouse and work our way towards you. If you see anything ring Harry and then me, in that order." Jack described the car they were looking for while turning up the farmhouse driveway, "Thanks Troy, we really appreciate this."

Five minutes later Jack turned back onto the highway with Liam following. "Liam, you take the left paddocks and I'll take the right. Keep your eyes peeled everyone."

Deafening silence invaded the cars. They systematically drove in and out of gates, up and down paddocks with no luck. Wasting valuable time when at each gate they had to stop to open them.

"Don't worry about closing the gates," Jack said as Cameron hopped back into the car. They bumped down the home paddock as his phone rang, "Hey Nate, how are you buddy?" Jack asked, thinking to himself this was the exact reason he'd given his son a mobile phone, though he couldn't imagine they'd ever need to use it for anything like this.

"Found Lindy yet?"

"We're looking in all the paddocks trying to work out which one she would have taken them to."

"Lindy only knows one paddock, remember the one we had the picnic in?"

"Oh hell. That's right, I forgot about that. You bloody legend. Thanks buddy, I'll ring back when we have news."

"Please find her, Dad" the sniffling down the phone tore at Jack's heart. They all loved this woman.

"We'll find her."

Leaving a cloud of dust in his wake as he spun the car around, he said, "We're in the wrong paddock. Liam, did you hear that?"

"Turning around now," Liam answered.

Something stirred inside Jack. Maybe they were waiting under the trees for his call. Turning to Cameron, Jack said, "Ring Troy and Bernie," Jack explained to both men what Nate told him.

A few minutes down the highway, large raindrops fell.

"Shit," Jack screeched. "You're gonna need a four-wheel-drive Liam. With this rain your car's useless," Jack could have done with the extra help, "Ring Harry with the information," he told Cameron, to Liam he added, "Stop at the top of the paddock but stay on the line."

COMING UP EMPTY

JACK

"What's that?" Cameron asked, pointing to what resembled a splotch of colour ahead.

Jack leaned closer to the windscreen, trying to get a better look through the pelting rain. "Not sure what it is, but it's something. Call it in!" Jack instructed. As predicted the dirt had turned to mud and Jack concentrated on the track ahead. After successfully navigating through the boggy surface, Jack veered to the right where the path was covered with course rock, making the going easier.

"Whoever it is up ahead seems to be out of the car," Cameron said, keeping Harry up to date as to their whereabouts.

The high beams shone, lighting their way, the darkened skies gave poor visibility. The car jerked and careened off to the left. As Jack recovered control of the vehicle, he saw a large pothole in his rear-view mirror, Jack cursed, "Bloody hell. You okay?" He asked Cameron turning to check on him once he'd righted the car.

"Yep," Cameron answered, his eyes still focused on the path ahead.

With the Ute under control again, they crawled towards the car with its high beams shining like a beacon. Jack slowed down as the peppercorn trees came into view. "Bingo. That kid's a bloody legend," Jack made out movement near the other vehicle, they were now close enough to make out two people walking around.

"Your lights!" Cameron yelled over the heavy downpour. But it was too late.

"Hell, they've seen us," Jack ground out.

They watched on as Elsa and her muscle man returned to the car.

Taking off, the driver lurched the vehicle into motion but headed in the wrong direction.

"What the bloody hell is he doing?" Jack screamed.

Watching the show before them, everything appeared to happen in slow motion. The car lurched forward so hard it dropped off the edge of the embankment. The only thing visible were the taillights, and even those were at such an angle they weren't easy to make out.

Jack eased off the accelerator.

"We're right behind you and Bernie's with us," Liam told Jack. "Can you see anything?"

Jack checked his rear-view mirror, and saw his backup. Troy and Ray must have been speeding to have caught up.

"Yeah," Jack groaned, "We've found them, they've driven into the river." Once the cars stopped everyone jumped out and ran towards the plunged vehicle.

The driver's side door opened slightly, Jack ran towards it. He heard a grunt as the door was pushed opened. Jack stood legs half deep in water, but none of that registered to him, his eyes were on the guy about to jump down from the vehicle. As the stranger dropped to the floor of the now flowing riverbed, Jack was on him before he landed.

It was a strain to hear sirens or see flashing lights amid the heavy rain.

Jack unceremoniously grabbed the driver and pushed him back onto the car.

"Where the hell is Lindy?" he yelled, but that didn't stop the stranger. Arms flew until a gunshot sounded around them. Jack tightened his grip on the man's jacket, as he looked around to see where the sound came from.

Troy stood at the top of the embankment, the gun aimed directly at the stranger's upper body. Knowing he was covered Jack tried again through gritted teeth, "Where the bloody hell is Lindy?"

Four police officers scrambled down the embankment with Harry giving orders. Two of them cuffed the man and hauled him up to the flats.

A drenched Sophie hugged herself, frozen to the spot as she asked, "Where's Mum?"

Everyone rushed towards the car. Jack deduced, if she was in the car and safe, she'd have got out by now.

Harry yelled out. "Jack, it's Elsa, she's unconscious."

Jack rounded the vehicle and noticed for the first time a slumped body resting against the windscreen, a smearing of blood slowly coursing its way down the glass.

Jack screamed to the heavens with his clenched fists raised, "Where the hell's Lindy?"

DISTRESSING DISCOVERY

LINDY

*E*very muscle ached. The throbbing in her face was relentless. This must have been the fourth time the unbearable pain delayed her progress. Trying to get her bearings proved harder than she ever believed, but she persisted, unsure of her destination. If only someone would come down the path to her aid, but who would be stupid enough to be out horse riding or exercising in weather like this.

Pushing on, planting one foot in front of the other, she progressed, albeit slowly.

How much time passed Lindy didn't know, but her aching body hinted at hours. Her slow stagger brought her to a familiar bend. Lindy hesitated. Her inner compass had evaporated. Should she go on home or turn up the sandy path to Nola's? Logic racing around in her head told her Nola's was not far off, probably her best bet.

With the aid of her walking stick, she headed slowly and painfully onto the vaguely familiar trail. Recognition dawned, she saw the family's horses on the other side of the long paddock. They were moving them to the homestead tomorrow.

If it was possible, she would have smiled thinking about how happy she was to see them again.

"Not long now," she told herself. Leaning on the fence, Lindy took a breath, her face stinging whenever she breathed in. The dizziness of earlier returned again. She focused on the first sign of hope. Through the dancing branches of the gum trees, she noticed lights shining out of Nola's kitchen window. Steadying herself through another wave of dizziness and pain, Lindy waited for it to pass.

Pushing on for the last leg of her long quest, Lindy could feel her warm tears combining with the still heavy drops of rain. She stumbled back a step before righting herself and continued her unsteady gait. The rain managed to drench her outer layers, but that didn't matter, her destination was in sight. Pushing herself beyond her limits to reach Nola's, the world spun about her. Gritting her teeth and dragging one foot ahead of the other, her vision slowly faded to black. No matter what she tried to do, Lindy couldn't stop her body sinking to the flooded track beneath. The makeshift walking stick became her anchor as she made a graceful descent. With her head facing the skies, Lindy lay as if she enjoyed a peaceful sleep.

JACK

"Sorry Sophie," her sobs tore at his heart. They were so hopeful when Cameron spotted the vehicle up ahead, they had no clue where Lindy was. "Let's head to your place, Bernie," his dejected voice muttered. Being positive might be the order of the day, but Jack couldn't put on a front anymore.

He turned towards Harry's raging voice, "Dylan Taylor you're up for attempted murder, so now is an excellent chance to tell me everything I ought to know. We know you were attempting to extort money from Elsa's estranged husband," Harry yelled above the heavy rain. If Harry knew his name, this bloke had a past. That wasn't comforting.

Dylan dropped his head, "I can't, they've got my wife and two kids' hostage. If I don't turn up by tomorrow with the money, he's threatened to murder them."

"Who Dylan? Who's heading this operation? Let's flush him out." Harry's fists still gripped Dylan's sleeveless denim jacket, "Just so you know, the woman in your car earlier is the sister of a Senior Detective in Melbourne, so you can either talk now or I'll hand you over to him."

Dylan flinched.

The group stood about waiting for his response, oblivious to the heavy rain falling. His head dropped, and he conceded, "Okay, but when we left her, she was still alive."

"What happened to her?" Liam pushed closer, shouting his demand.

"I punched her, I didn't mean to. She played us and I fell for it. I got mad." He attempted to shake the rain from his face. "I dumped her unconscious body under the trees over there," he gestured to the peppercorn scattering. "We came back to get her so I could hand her over when Jack had the money. But she was gone, I swear."

Jack and Cameron exchanged glances.

"Sounds feasible. They were looking for something," Cameron clarified.

Jack nodded in agreement.

"Take him to the station," Harry said, pushing Dylan into the van. "I want a search party out," he called to his partner.

Harry headed back to Jack, "Would she have cut through the paddocks back to the farmhouse?"

"I don't know. Surely, she wouldn't have tried to cross the river," Jack turned at the rapidly flowing, muddy slush.

"Hang on a minute," Bernie called, "Depending on how long ago, there might not have been any water flowing. She could have crossed safely."

Jack wanted to roar. Where was she, looking from Harry to Bernie, Troy and Ray, if anyone was versed in the weather and its changes it was the old timer, "What do you think, Ray?"

Ray leant past Troy as he spoke, "We'll head out of town and come in from the west. You guys go to Bernie's and head in from the east."

Jack didn't see the police car leave. He was too busy planning.

"Harry, I need an escort," Jack yelled as they ran back to the cars.

Sophie and Liam jumped in with Bernie as Harry yelled back, "I'm with you, mate."

JACK

As Jack brought his Ute to a stop behind Bernie's they jumped out of the car where Nola and Nate held the reigns of the horses. Bernie hefted himself into the saddle. Nate sat on a restless Bandy, while holding the reins of his father's horse, Dakota.

"Hurry Dad," Nate screamed as Jack and Cameron jumped out of the car.

Cameron stood with Harry, Liam and Sophie as Jack grabbed Dakota's reigns and hoisted himself up.

Nate took off the moment Jack gathered the reigns and was about twenty paces ahead, cantering down the long path.

"Slow down, Nate!" Jack yelled.

"Let him have his head. That boy's not stupid," Bernie told him.

They kept Nate in their sights as they worked their horses to catch him. Jack cursed again when Nate pulled to a reckless stop. He was about to yell out when his eyes landed on a figure lying on the ground.

Motionless.

Bernie immediately pulled on the reins turning his horse back towards the house, "I'll get Harry."

But Jack's attention was on his son as he dropped beside the still figure.

His hands gripping her shoulders as Nate shook her and screamed, "Lindy, Lindy. Wake up Lindy," Nate's agonising wail was drowned out by the still heavy rain.

Jack jumped off his horse and dropped to Lindy's other side, picking her up in his arms and cradling her body to his. He pushed the sodden hair back off her face, placed his chilly hand in front of her mouth and gasped as a trickle of warm breath passed her blue lips.

"Uncle Harry's here, Dad," Nate shouted shaking his father's shoulder as he watched a car approach.

LINDY

The chaos unfolding was exhausting. She sensed the family's presence, and the medicos attending her. But right now, she desperately wanted to close her eyes and enter a world of peace and silence. A world where her face didn't ache with the pain of wild horses trampling her.

The echo of someone sobbing broke her concentration. If only the noise would stop! Lindy tried to focus.

Sophie whispered, "Let it all out Mum, you're safe now. Have a good cry. It's all over."

Sophie's tearful voice encouraged her to focus. Void of any control, she did as Sophie said, a sharp prick penetrated her arm, and she drifted towards a deep sleep.

Descending into the void, the faces of all the children one by one came into her vision. Each one stole a special place in her heart. Jack's image hovered for the longest time, his powerful arms holding her close. Internally, she smiled as warmth radiated from the depths of her soul. A truth struck her. There, was her wonderful family, an exceptional, extended family.

AFTERMATH

JACK

For Jack the next few hours were filled with a mix of joy at having Lindy back and, bitterness at the cause of her misadventure. He covered his face with his hands. Jack blamed Elsa for all his family suffered. Though that suffering delivered Lindy into their lives and his heart, now it tried to take her away.

He stayed awake for hours trying to comprehend Lindy's misfortune. Imagining the worst kinds of torture and pain, his blood boiled to think how she endangered her life but it also occurred to him she'd endured all this for his children. The depth of what she meant to him bored deeper and deeper into his soul. He'd never excavate her from his life, if the pain in his heart was anything to go by.

With her lying before him and knowing she was safe should have been enough comfort.

"Hey, how's she doing?" The doctor asked as he picked up her chart.

Jack only shrugged.

"Jack, Elsa's regained consciousness."

He sat motionless not having the energy to deal with her right now.

He mentally shook himself, Lindy was safe, he needed to focus.

He bent down to kiss her warm slender hand, afraid to kiss those beautiful lips, all too conscious of the facial pain she must be suffering. He rested his forehead on her leg, closed his eyes. And that's how he was found when all the children arrived after eight o'clock the following morning. Jack's hand in Lindy's and his head resting on her leg.

Inseparable.

LINDY

Bradley's voice echoed around the room, "Mumma, Mumma, Mumma!" his indignant cries rang out.

"Where's Bradley?" Lindy asked, trying to open her eyes to study her surroundings.

Sophie stepped up to the bed with her future step-brother wriggling recklessly in her arms. The other children followed, spreading themselves around the foot of the bed.

Jack stood up, "Morning love. How's everything?"

The dull throbbing worsened when she tried to move. She winced and gave up on that idea. Slowly, her eyes focused on everyone. A small smile settled on her lips, only because she was incapable of giving the wide smile she was renowned for, "Worth it, to see you're all safe. Pass Bradley here, Sophie." Lindy feebly patted the space next to her.

Sophie sent Jack a questioning look as she struggled with a wriggling Bradley. On Jack's nod Bradley landed on the bed and without hesitation he snuggled in next to Lindy.

Nate unzipped the nappy bag, "Here Bradley. You ready for your bottle now?"

Bradley took the bottle in both hands and fed himself, "Mumma," the little fellow sighed as he snuggled in happily. Lindy and Bradley dozed off next to each other.

JACK

With the sound of footsteps, they all turned to the door to see the doctor walk in quietly greeting the throng.

"Morning everyone, has she woken yet?" he asked Jack.

"Yeah, just for a few minutes."

"When can we take her home, Doc?" Caleb asked.

"I'd say tomorrow," he grinned at Caleb, "You missing Lindy already?" he flicked through the pages on her chart.

"Yes, we have to look after her," Caleb answered, watching as both Lindy and Bradley lay sleeping peacefully.

"Well then. If you're there to take care of her, you can take her tomorrow."

The doctor surveyed her bruising and checked her pulse. "Yep, definitely tomorrow."

"Tomorrow, huh? Well, we've got work to do." Jack stood and ran his fingers through his hair that stood on end. He walked out into the hallway, took out his phone and dialled.

"Hi Ivy."

"Oh, how is she?"

"Better." He rubbed tired eyes, "We can take her home tomorrow. Listen, I need your help."

"Anything. Just name it."

"Bush telegraph," Jack trusted Ivy to get the show on the road.

"Leave it with me."

EPILOGUE

LINDY

*L*indy sat in the driveway, the car full to overflowing with flowers. Bunches of them from well-wishers, some from people she'd never even met. The fragrance was wasted on her in her current state, but the visual was a delight. The front door opened and tears welled as the family lined themselves up on the veranda and waited. She waved and smiled through tears of absolute pleasure, then it hit her, those children were her life. What would have happened if harm came to any of them? She forced herself to stop that line of thinking. She slowly climbed out of the car with Jack's help.

"Get moving guys, the flowers need to be unloaded." Jack said, but the humour in his voice put everyone at ease. They all rushed down the stairs to help unpack. Words 'welcome home' were uttered as Lindy leaned her weight on Jack and together, they slowly made their way to the veranda. Not that walking was an issue. It was more every step reverberated through her face sending pain. Bouquets of flowers raced in ahead of them. By the time Lindy reached the veranda, the car was empty.

Jack and Liam guided her inside, careful not to push her too fast.

After the screen door closed for the last time everyone lined up before her again. The behaviour was odd, but Lindy didn't have the energy to question it. Not right now.

"How about you sit in here?" Sophie suggested as Lindy swayed slightly.

"Thanks love, that's a wonderful idea." Lindy mumbled.

They headed towards the front lounge and Lindy carefully took the three steps down into the large room she'd fallen in love with.

"Oh, my," she sighed looking about, "This looks beautiful."

"If you don't like it. We're happy to move whatever you want," Liam told her.

"You all did this?"

"We did the entire house," Jack laughed.

"How? When did you have time?" Lindy couldn't believe what she was seeing.

"Ivy and the bush telegraph," Cameron told his mother, "Yesterday the locals took over this place."

"Oh, wow!" Lindy slowly examined the room and then the smiling faces of the children. "Thank you, every one of you. I wish I had the energy to see the rest of the house," Lindy groaned as she settled into the dusty pink, Queen Anne couch from her house in Melbourne. It reminded her of insignificant memories of her and the children over the years, ones she'd treasure for an eternity. Her plan was to make more memories with Jack and their children in the future.

They all settled round the room, some on chairs and others sitting on the floor. Nate jumped up when they heard the crunch of tyres on the driveway.

"It's Ivy," he hollered as he ran for the door.

"Hi Ivy," Lindy heard him call.

"Morning Buddy, is she home?"

"You betcha," everyone laughed as his voice rose.

Nate walked outside, then walked back in a minute later with his hands full.

"Ivy bought slice for everyone," he said, looking into the lounge.

"Come in Ivy," Jack gestured to a spare spot on the couch.

She stopped and took in Lindy's face, "I want to hug you but you look like you might break," she fought back tears.

Looking around the room, it dawned on Lindy, they all wanted the same thing. A hug. "I won't break," she insisted, pulling Evie in close, "I'm just sore."

To Ivy she said, "I hear you're to thank for all this," Lindy pointed to the furniture.

Ivy stepped up and hugged her, "No, I just made a call. And by the way you were amazing."

"Thanks love," Lindy whispered, "And I'd do it all again in a heartbeat."

"Careful," Jack said as the children crawled all over Lindy as they often did, Joanna's sniffles caught everyone's attention. Lindy cupped her sweet face and carefully kissed her. "I'll be fine love, I promise."

"But it's not fair," Joanna sobbed, "This happened to you because of my mum. I hate her."

Lindy and Jack exchanged glances as the silence grew heavy around them.

What did you say to children too young to understand the reasoning of an addict?

"Your mother didn't do this. It was the man she was with," Lindy pointed to her bruised face, "Remember your dad saying that your mother is unwell?"

Joanna nodded, and the others murmured, "Yes."

"But she didn't even say hello," Joanna cried.

Lindy couldn't imagine the pain Joanna spoke of, but then she looked at Cameron and Sophie. Oh yes, it was the pain her two youngest grew up experiencing from their own father; she remembered that pain now.

"Drinks are ready," Sophie carefully placed an overloaded tray on the coffee table.

"Thanks love," Lindy accepted a cup of tea from Cameron.

"Want some caramel slice?" he asked.

The ringing of Jack's phone distracted her. She watched as he checked the screen and then took the call.

"Baz, how are you?"

Lindy gave a gentle wave of her hand. Biting into a Carmel slice was beyond her at the moment.

"The horses," Nate said excitedly. His face flushed and eyes grew with excitement as he listened to his father on the phone.

"Right," Jack replied to something Baz said.

"Excellent, not that I expected anything less from Bernie."

Jack checked his watch, "Here in half an hour?"

"Well, I'd better get this lot working on the stalls then," Jack looked at Lindy and she could see he was trying to tone down his own excitement.

A cheer went up around the room from the younger children.

"The horses are coming," Caleb said, jumping up and down.

"We need to check the stables," Nate took the last gulp of chocolate milkshake before using the straw to slurp up the dregs.

"That we do. How about you get Liam and Cameron to help."

"We're right behind you," Ivy called, "You'll need our help too."

Jack laughed, "You're more than welcome to stay, Ivy. I just didn't want to presume."

"Start presuming, I have a family again and it feels wonderful," Ivy told him, swallowing back her emotion.

"Good," smiled Lindy before adding to both women, "Don't let the boys' boss you around."

"No chance," they laughed at their responses and gathered up the leftover cups and plates and followed the others from the room.

Jack and Lindy stayed together, her head resting against his shoulder, "I can't believe you got all this done," she whispered.

"Well, not all of it," Jack admitted. "The little things are still in boxes. As for the stables and sheds, everything's been dumped but Dad and I will sort all that lot out later."

"I'm worried about Joanna, she's holding onto a lot of pain and rejection."

"I think we need to look at counselling for all the children," Jack said and Lindy felt the drop of his shoulders. "I'll ring the doctor and have a chat."

"Good, I can see what happened between Ralph and Cameron has caused lasting pain. If we can prevent that for these guys, then we have to do something."

But before they could continue, the sound of yelling preceded an angry Caleb with Cameron hot on his heels.

"What's wrong?" Lindy held her hand out to the red, tear stained faced boy.

"Liam said," Caleb sucked air deep into his lungs, "Pirate isn't allowed in the stables. He said he was naughty at Bernie's!"

"Do you think Liam was teasing you?" Jack asked.

"He's not allowed to tease me!"

"Didn't you say the other night he's your brother?" Lindy's soothing voice had Caleb's sobs ease.

"Yes."

"Well, brothers tease each other. That's what you're meant to do," Lindy explained.

"So, can I tease him?" Caleb hopped from one foot to the other, his face still streaked with tears but there was a smile.

"Guess what Cameron used to do to Liam when they were your age."

"What?"

Lindy turned to Cameron, "Time to short-sheet someone's bed, I think."

Cameron let out a laugh and got down on one knee, "How about we play a trick on Liam?"

"Can we?" Caleb's face brightened.

"Come on, quick before he figures out we're up to something," Cameron said heading towards the bungalow with an excited Caleb in tow.

"I think war is imminent, and it's your fault," Jack shook his head.

"Let them be kids again. They deserve to have some fun," Lindy's genuine request had him nodding.

"You're right, they've grown up way too fast," Shrugging his shoulders, he added, "And to hell with the consequences," hinting at the inevitable chaos.

The laugh escaping her lips had Jack smiling. Lindy tapped his chest and whispered, "It's wonderful to be home with our family, Jack. So special to have each other and enough unconditional love for our large, loud hoard."

"What's wonderful is you're here and safe. Life's never been this good for me before."

"We'll devote our lives to each other and our children," Lindy trusted this man like she trusted her parents. She reached out for help and Jack replied the only way he could. Having the children, all eight of them as the centre of their lives.

They smiled at each other before Jack stole another soft kiss.

"Devotion! That's our word, Lindy. You have mine, you and all our wonderful, noisy, happy family."

The End

ABOUT THE AUTHOR

Cheryl lives in a picturesque town just out of Melbourne, Australia with her husband, two adult children, two Border Collie babies, a small pond of gold fish, newly acquired chickens, the local birdlife and one rather cantankerous cat. When she's not at her desk writing or at work you'll find her walking, reading, doing a jigsaw puzzle or two, on the ride-on mower or occasionally weeding the garden. She loves getting up early and taking photos of the sunrise.

This was a trek of discovery. Pushing herself beyond the norm and out of her comfort zone. Never in Cheryl's wildest dreams would she have considered achieving this goal a reality. But instead found a determination hidden among the fears and hurdles of life. By following her dream, Cheryl unearthed a love of story and self-development which now feeds her curiosity daily.

www.cherylrosariowriter.com

ACKNOWLEDGEMENT

To Matt Woods, your time and patience in getting the cover out into the world has resulted in something I'm so proud of. I can't thank you enough for your expertise and support.

To Nas Dean, thank you for all you have taught me on this journey. Your patience and care have given me the confidence to pursue my dream of publishing Lindy and Jack's story. I know there's still more to grasp and I look forward to doing it all again.

Thanks to fellow authors Sandy Spencer, Alli Sinclair, Joanne Dannon, Sandy Vaile, and Nicki Edwards for showing me the way and answering my questions as I struggled along.

A special thanks to Anna Jacobs for her wonderful books that inspired me. For her messages of encouragement all those years ago, which helped me overcome my challenges, open my imagination, and write.

To my friends, Susan Campelj, Christine Everingham, Aimee Woods, Sue Parsons, Donna Caon, Belinda Razinovski, Deb Lambert for being in my corner. Friends like you are hard to find.

To my husband Alois, and children, Emma, and Matthew, thank you for encouraging and believing in me.

Betrayed Expectations

Chester's Run - Book 2

A past shrouded in mystery. A life of rejection, fear and pain. Will their circumstances finally bring these two together? Or will misunderstanding come between them forever?

Ivy senses Cameron is building a barrier between them. When she comes across a letter from her mother, she seeks answers to a lifetime of questions. Only a trip to England will uncover the harsh truth. Is she strong enough to hear it?

Cameron grew up surrounded by his mother's love and his father's hatred under the same roof. Now starting his new life in Chester's Run, he connects with the outside world. When he discovers his brother and Ivy together, he plans to leave for a while to pursue an overseas client.

Chaos ensues when they separately announce they are heading to England. Despite Cameron's reluctance, the two travel together for Ivy's safety. Sharing accommodation has its hurdles and makes them both face their complicated realities.

COMING SOON

Betrayed Reality

Chester's Run - Book 3

Concealing an old identity to survive. Falling in love with a woman behind a mask. Can they overcome the past or will the truth destroy them?

Though Reuben's love for Maggie grows, he struggles to find meaning in his work and is holding onto unanswered questions about her past.

The anonymity of living in a big city is comforting to Maggie. When Reuben accepts his dream job in Chester's Run, she wants him to be happy but worries for her safety in a small country town. Despite her fears, she lands a great job, develops wonderful friendships and watches Reuben flourish.

Settling in and slowly discovering her old self, their connection only strengthens. They find a place of peace and a lifestyle to fight for. But when her past catches up to her, can she keep Reuben safe and still survive?